WILLIA...

Declared ...
by the Interna... Horror Guild!

RAVES FOR *DARK UNIVERSE*!
Finalist for the International Horror Guild
and World Fantasy Awards

"An expert in the art and science of scaring the hell out of people."

—Stephen King

"I am terrified, delighted and truly moved by William F. Nolan's work."

—Ray Bradbury

"One of horror's best storytellers. No one has ever done it better."

—Peter Straub

"Highly recommended!"

—*Cemetery Dance*

"I admire William F. Nolan, whom I've been reading since I was a nipper."

—Dean Koontz

"A masterfully written and memorable collection of dark fiction."

—*Midwest Book Review*

MORE RAVES
FOR WILLIAM F. NOLAN!

William F. Nolan's stories are "skillful renderings of the twisted psyche that blur the boundary between psychological and supernatural horror."

—Publishers Weekly

"Bright and individual. Mr. Nolan has considerable skills."
—The New York Times

"Nolan writes with dazzling dexterity."
—The Vancouver Express

"Nolan is a master of horror fantasy."

—Charles L. Grant

Nolan's work is "frighteningly alive and compelling."
—School Library Journal

"This collection proves Nolan's talents are equal to Charles Beaumont, Richard Matheson and Ray Bradbury."
—Hellnotes

WILLIAM F. NOLAN

NIGHTWORLDS

LEISURE BOOKS NEW YORK CITY

LEISURE BOOKS ®

December 2004

Published by

Dorchester Publishing Co., Inc.
200 Madison Avenue
New York, NY 10016

ISBN 0-8439-5191-5

To my good friends who inspired many of these stories:
Ray Bradbury
Richard Matheson
Charles Beaumont

NIGHTWORLDS

TABLE OF CONTENTS

Preface

by William F. Nolan

Over the past half century, beginning in 1951, I have written one hundred and seventy-five short stories. The best are in this book. What I wrote before the 1950s doesn't matter because I really didn't know what I was doing. I was blundering along, attempting to balance narrative and dialogue, trying to find a style, getting rid of all the bad stuff in the hope of reaching the good stuff.

I started writing fiction in school at the age of ten in lined nickel notebooks. Tales of intrepid air aces, quick-shooting cowboys, daring G-men, and brave soldiers of the French Foreign Legion (about which I knew nothing). All hopeless efforts, displaying nothing beyond raw energy and shallow imagination. Embarrassing to read today. I recall one particularly silly tale about a hero who could turn himself into a crime-fighting snake. Another lurid creation was known as "The Flaming Schrab" (because I couldn't spell "scarab").

It's not surprising that my earliest stories were

wildly melodramatic. I am a shameless product of 20th-century pop culture. I grew up in the Midwest (in Kansas City, Missouri), feeding on cliff-hanging serials at Saturday matinees, Big-Little Books, super-hero comics, radio drama (*Lights Out . . . Escape . . . I Love a Mystery*), sagas of heroic dogs in the Yukon, and juvenile adventure novels about Bomba the Jungle Boy. The corner movie theater was my shrine and I absorbed motion pictures the way skin absorbs sunlight. My idols were Gary Cooper and Errol Flynn, along with a gaggle of western stars from Buck Jones to John Wayne. Not to forget Karloff and Lugosi.

Action! Fantasy! Melodrama! Chills and Thrills!

No wonder I wrote what I did in those nickel notebooks.

At sixteen, I produced what can be considered my first "mature" short story, "Broken Spurs," and began a never-completed western novel, "The Trail to Adventure" (heavily indebted to Max Brand). Writing had me by the throat in its bulldog grip—and I've never been able to shake free.

That's how it happens, people. You don't choose writing, it chooses you. Writers are *compelled* to keep churning out words on paper, and I've certainly churned out my share. A dozen novels, eleven biographies, twenty-five anthologies, fifteen collections, forty-one scripts for films and TV, half-a-hundred poems, forty reviews, and five hundred fifty articles and profiles.

Plus, of course, my one hundred seventy-five short stories. In recent years, observing the collected fiction of my peers—Phil Dick, Bob Bloch, Richard Matheson, Ted Sturgeon, and Charles Beaumont—I had been thinking about a retrospective collection of my own best fiction. Thus, the task was not difficult. My stories shouted: "Over here! I'm good! Pick me!" All I had to do was listen. (Oh, yes, my stories are alive. They tell me things.)

So here they are, with a special preface for each in which I supply the story's origin, the background events that inspired it, and just how it ties in with my life and career.

I owe thanks to many, most particularly to my wife and collaborator, Cameron Nolan, who is not only a talented professional author on her own, but who has helped me immeasurably with my work through her expert editing, research, plot ideas, and writing. We are a team, Cam and I. Without her, I am convinced that I would never have achieved ultimate depth and maturity in my career.

I also owe thanks to Chris Conlon, to my friends Ray Bradbury, Richard Matheson, and the late Charles Beaumont for their guidance and loyal support, and to all the editors who originally printed the stories in this collection in their magazines, text-books, and anthologies.

Each story I've finished has helped me become a better writer, a better person, and a more complete human being. Together, they form my personal cosmos.

Welcome to my universe.

W. F. N.

West Hills, California

This is a very personal story. Almost all of it is auto-biographical, relating to my growing-up years in Kansas City. My mother's maiden name was Kelly. My father was Michael Nolan and he died of cancer in the hospital, just as I describe it here. I read Mickey Mouse . . . sledded in winter . . . watched Gary Cooper movies . . . rode with the Lone Ranger at Saturday matinees . . . collected Big-Little Books . . . rowed for my Dad as he fished the Lake of the Ozarks . . . laughed at Charlie Chaplin . . . and savored the heroic dog stories of James Oliver Curwood.

Of course, I've never been aboard a space rocket. That's where my imagination kicked in. Here is a meld of fact and fiction, of very real yesterdays and an imagined tomorrow.

A very personal story.

Kelly, Fredric Michael

(Written: April 1972)

MONITORED THOUGHT PATTERNS CONTINUE:

. . . wrong, twisted . . . and I'm being . . . being . . . Steen is already . . . they want me to free form again . . . goddam it, I don't understand just what this . . .

We had a coal-burning furnace in the basement with a slotted iron door, and you broke up the clinkers inside with a poker, lifting the door latch with the heat sweating you . . .

And Mickey left Minnie standing at the little white picket fence. She was blushing. "Love ya," he said. "Gee," she said. "Gotta fly the mail for Uncle Sam," he said. "Golly, you're so brave!" she said. His plane was a cute single-seater with a smiling face and rubbery wings . . .

The Moon! They'd made it after all, by Christ, and Armstrong was walking, jiggling, kind of floating sometimes with sixty million or more of us watching.

He could still be a part of it. He was only 41 and that wasn't old, not too old if he really . . .

. . . kept shooting, but the bullets bounced right off his chest. "Time someone taught you fellows a lesson in manners!" He tucked a thug under each arm, pin-striped suits with their hats still on, and leaped through the window of the skyscraper with him in the air now and them yelling and him smiling, squarejawed, with that little black curl over his forehead and the red cape flaring out behind . . . soaring above the poorly-drawn city with the two . . .

. . . in the back of the car, not watching the movie (a comedy with Hope in drag and Benny pretending to be his daughter), not giving a damn about the movie and him with his hand there inside her elastic white silk panties . . . "Don't, Freddie. I can't let you." Sure she could. He'd taken her out often enough for her to let him. He wouldn't hurt her, ever. He was sure he loved her, or if he didn't he *would*—if she'd just . . . He had her blouse all the way open and God those tits! ". . . never have come here with you if I thought you'd . . ." Seat slippery under him but he got her legs open enough to do it, but all he did was rub her down there. He'd lost his erection and his penis was soft; it flopped against her white stomach and she was . . .

Tight against the rocks with the Arabs coming. The legion guy next to Coop was plenty nervous. "Think we can hold 'em off?" And Coop smiled that slow easy boy-smile that meant nothing could touch him; we all knew nothing could touch Coop. "Sure, sure we can. They won't attack at night. We'll slip out after dark." He fired twice and two fanatic Arabs fell in closeup. A hidden ground wire tripped their horses, but we were too young to know about hidden ground wires . . .

". . . so I'm going to tell Dawson he can go fuck himself!" "They'll bounce your ass right out," I told Bob. "So what, so who needs a Ph.D. from this lousy . . . Look, man, college is shit. Dawson is a phony little prick and he knows it and so do his students, but they just sit there listening to him spout out his . . ."

. . . planet wants me to . . . no, no . . . it isn't the planet itself. It isn't alive, doesn't tell me anything . . . dead planet out here on the fringe of the System . . . but it has . . . a kind of influence—in conjunction with the rest of this System . . . the whole thing is a form of . . . new force, or goddam it I wish they'd let me . . . just wouldn't . . .

Mother wanted to know what I was doing in my bedroom all alone for so long and I said reading a Big-

Little Book and she came in to see. I had a pretty fair collection and the best were the ones set on the planet Mongo. "You read too much. It'll ruin your eyes." But she looked relieved. I didn't know why. She was smiling and roughing my hair, which I hated but I didn't hate her. I loved her very, very much. ". . . to sleep now. You can read more tomorrow." The room was small and comfort-making and I could smell the special soap she used and I liked the way she smelled, always, and she was always . . .

. . . close to the shore, along the rocks, while Dad fed line into the quiet lake. "This is where the fat ones like to come in," he said. The sky was so blue it hurt my eyes so I kept my head down. A mosquito bit me. That was the only trouble with lakes, the mosquitoes. They loved water the way Dad did. I liked rowing, feeling the long wooden boat slide through the water with Dad at one end, feeding out his line, and the lake blackgreen with no motorboats on it, quiet and hot and . . .

She twisted under me, doing a thing with her pelvis, and I came. Hard, fiery. First time inside . . . She groaned and kept her eyes squeezed shut and she looked tortured and I kept thinking what her father would say if he knew I had her doing this. He always worried about her. "You two kids take care, ya hear?"

And then he'd say, "I trust you, Fred, because you're a Catholic." And I told him that I . . .

. . . more . . . keep wanting more . . . I'm being . . . forced to spill out all the . . .

"Hey, Kelly, the old man wants to see you." Sure he did, and I knew why. Because I was late three mornings in a row this week. I had reasons. The lousy freeways were jammed so I took surface streets but Old Cooney would never listen to reason, which is why he's such a prick to work for. "Tell him I won't be late anymore." I was going to the Moon. To work there. To train for space. And someday, with luck, maybe I could . . .

Whap! Pow! Pie right in the kisser. The little tramp wipes it off, sucks his thumbs, does a kind of ballet step back and falls down three flights of stairs. Terrific! Up he bounces, dusts the seat of his baggy pants, tips his hat, spins his cane, and walks into a cop! *Whomp!* Cop is furious. Jumps up and down, shaking his stick. Tramp does a polite little bow, tips his hat again and ducks between the cop's legs. Zing—right down the middle of the street. Cars missing them by inches. Two more cops join the first cop. Three more. A dozen. Falling and yelling. Tramp is up a fire escape, over a roof, through a fat lady's apartment—she's in the tub!—out a door, down an alley, and . . .

. . . when the snow came I'd rush for the basement to dig out my old sled. Rust had coated the runners with a thin red film and I had to get them shiny again with sandpaper, doing it fast, wanting to get out on the hill and cut loose. School closed, the hill waiting, Tommy Griffith yelling at me to get a move on and then the long whooshing slide down from Troost with snowdust in my nose and steering to miss Tommy's sled and picking up speed coming onto Forest, mittens and yellow snow goggles and warm under the coat Uncle Frank bought me for Christmas . . .

The sons of bitches were worried about the fucking score while his father was *dying*. Okay, okay—pull back, cool down, all the way down—because if he wasn't dying he'd want to know the score too. It was the Series and he'd want to know the score like the others did. The hall smelled of white paint and starch and, faintly, of urine. Hospital smells. The young priest had been emotionless about it, kept smiling at him and saying "a passel of years" when he told him how old his father was. He was glad to be out of Holy Mother Church, because she didn't really

give a damn about him or his father. Maybe God did,
somewhere, but not Holy Mother Church. What did
it matter how old his father was? So what? He was
still dying of cancer and you never want to go that
way no matter how fucking old you are, even if . . .

"My country tis of thee, Sweet land of liberty . . ."

Sing it boy, sing it loud and let the world know that
you're an American. Sure, he was too young to fight,
but he was proud. And scared, too. They were giving
us hell on those beaches. Giving us bloody hell . . .

*born in 1928 . . . into space when I was sixty . . . Moon
first, then Mars . . . If I could just tell them straight and
they didn't . . . keep trying to force all the . . . said I was
too old, but nobody listened. Experience. We need you out
there, Fred. Help chart the new Systems. Warps did it,
make it all possible . . . one jump and into another
galaxy. Fact. Cold reality. All right then, I
volunteered . . . but not for this . . . didn't know I'd ever
be . . . goddam sick of being sucked dry this way . . .
without my having any choice in how I . . .*

"That's it, oh, that's fine! Keep coming, honey!"
Mom, with her arms out. Wobble. Almost into the
lamp. "C'mon, son, you can do it. *Walk* to me!"
Daddy there, kneeling next to her, looking excited.

The room swaying. Terror. Falling. Rug in my face. Sneezing with them laughing and pulling me up and me trying again, with it better this time. Steady now, and Daddy was . . .

Feeding her power, letting her drift out, then snapping her back. "You're great, Fred," Anne told me. "Nope. Car's great," I said. "Handles, doesn't she? Richie did the suspension. Short throw on the shift. Four downdraft carbs. She'll do 200 easy. And a road like this, she eats it up." Life was good. Power under my foot and power in my mind and the future waiting.

". . . when the sniper got him." "What?" "Sniper. In Dealy Plaza." "Where's that?" "Texas." "What was he doing there?" "Wife was with him. They were—" "She dead too?" "No, just him. Blood all over her dress, but she's fine, she's fine . . ."

"Let's see what he looks like under that mask?" Oh, oh, they *had* him now. Guns on him, his hands tied, no chance to get away. "Yeah, Jake, let's us have a good look at him." Spaaaaang! "What the—" Oh, boy, just in time. Neat! "It's the durn Injun! Near killed me. Looks like he's got us boxed in." What are they going to do? "Better untie me, Jake, and I'll see to it that you both get a fair trial in Carson City." Deep voice. "You have my word on it." They won't. Or will they? Not much choice. Spaaaang! "His next shot won't miss, Jake." Oh, they're scared now, all right. Look at them sweat. "We'd best do as the masked man says," the big one growls. Spaaaang! Boy, if they don't . . .

"But, Fred, the job's on Mars. We can't go to Mars!" I wanted to know why not. "Because, for one thing, our place is *here,* our friends, everything is here. The Moon is our *home.*" I told her I was going, that it was a chance I couldn't afford to miss. But she kept up the argument, kept . . .

. . . on his stomach under the porch with the James Oliver Curwood book, the one about the dog who runs away and falls in love with a wolf and they have a son who's half dog and half wolf. Jack gave it to him for his fourteenth birthday. It was his favorite James Oliver Curwood. Rain outside, making cat-paw sounds on the porch, but him dry and secret underneath with all the good reading ahead of him. He pushed a jaw-breaker, one of the red ones, into his mouth and . . .

"Christ, Fred, let her go! She doesn't want to hear from you. She's never going to answer. She wants to forget you." That was all right. Sue was still his wife and maybe he could put it all back together. Maybe he could . . .

The stars . . . the *stars* . . . a massed hive of space-fire, a swarm of constellations . . . the diamonds of God . . . It was worth it. Worth everything to be out here, a part of *this.* Everything else was . . .

Enough! . . . I've given enough . . . sick . . . exhausted . . . hollow inside, drained . . . They were lucky, the others were lucky and didn't know it, dying with the ship . . . but they took us down here, two of us . . . and Steen's insane. They got . . . He free formed until they . . . know now . . . know what they still want from me, what they have to experience along with all the rest of it . . . before they're satisfied. They want to taste that too—the final thing . . . Well, give it to them. Why not? There's no way back to anywhere . . . Your friends are gone . . . Steen's a raving fool . . . so give them the final thing they want, goddam them . . . whoever they are . . . whatever they are. Just give them

THOUGHT TRANSCRIPT ENDS.

This one is based directly on an actual night in New York when my agent took me on a "sleaze tour" of Manhattan's Forty-second Street. We ended up watching young ladies dancing nude on a circular stage, exactly as described in my story. It was a strange experience, dreamlike and somehow ominous.

Back in California, I kept thinking about that night. New York can be a sinister place after dark.

My trip there supplied the plot.

My imagination supplied the maggots.

On 42nd St.

(Written: June 1988)

He hadn't been to New York since he was a kid, not since his last year of high school. That had been his graduation present: a trip to the Big Apple. He'd bugged his parents for years about New York, how it was the center of everything and how not to see it was like never seeing God. As a kid, he used to think of New York as the god of the U.S. He read every book he could find about it at his local library in Atkin.

His parents were quite content to stay in Ohio, in this little town they'd met and married in, where he'd been born and where his father had his tool business. His parents never traveled anywhere, and neither had he until he took the train to New York that summer when he was eighteen.

The city was hot and humid, but the weather hadn't bothered him. He'd been too enchanted, too dazzled by the high-thrusting towers of Manhattan, the jungle roar of midtown traffic, the glitter of Fifth Avenue, the pulse of night life on Broadway—and by the green vastness of Central Park, plunked like a chunk of Ohio into the center of this awesome steel-and-concrete giant.

And by the people. Especially on the subways; he'd never seen so many people jammed together in a single place. Jostling each other, shouting, laughing, cursing. Big and small, rich and poor, young and old, black and brown and yellow and white. An assault on the senses, so many of them.

"The subways are no good anymore," his friends now told him. "You can get mugged real easy on a subway. Cabs are your best bet. Once inside a taxi, you're safe . . . at least until you get out!"

And they had also warned him, all these years later, to stay away from 42nd Street. "Forty-second's like a blight," they declared. "New York's changed since you were a kid. It can get ugly, *real* ugly."

And they'd talked about the billions of cock-roaches and rats that lived under the city and in it, how even in the swankiest apartment on Fifth Avenue they have cockroaches late at night, crawling the walls . . .

So here he was, Ben Sutton, thirty-eight, balding and unmarried, on a plane to Kennedy—returning to the Apple after twenty years to represent the Sutton Tool Manufacturing Company of Atkin, Ohio. His father, Ed Sutton, who had founded the company, was long dead. Now Ben owned the business, because his mother had died within a year of his father. Over the past decade, he'd been sending other company employees to the National Tool Convention each year in New York, but this time, on a sudden impulse, he'd decided to go himself.

His friends backed the decision. "'Bout time for you to stir your stumps, Ben," they told him. "Take the trip. Get some *excitement* into your life."

They were right. Ben's life had settled into a series of dull routine days, one following another like a row of black dominos. By now the business practically ran itself, and Ben was feeling more and more like a figurehead. A trip such as this would revitalize him; he'd be plugged into the mainstream of life again. Indeed, it *was* time to "stir his stumps."

Kennedy was a madhouse. Ben lost his baggage claim check and had a difficult time proving that his two bags really belonged to him. Then the airport bus he took from Kennedy to Grand Central suffered some kind of mechanical malfunction and he had to wait by the side of the highway with a dozen angry passengers until another bus arrived a full hour later.

At Grand Central a gaunt-bodied teenager, with the words "The Dead Live!" stitched across the back of his red poplin jacket, ran off with one of Ben's suitcases while he was phoning the hotel to ask for an extension on his room reservation. A beefy station cop grabbed the kid and got the suitcase back.

The cop asked if he wanted to press charges, but Ben shook his head. "Let somebody else press charges when he steals another suitcase. I can't get involved."

The cop scowled. "That's a piss-poor attitude, mister." He glared at the teenager. "This little dickhead ought to be put away."

When the cop finally let him go, the kid gave them both the finger before vanishing in the crowd.

"You see that?" asked the cop, flushed with anger. "You see what that little shit did? I oughta run him down and pound him good. An' I got half a mind to do it!"

"That's your choice, Officer," Ben declared. "But I have to get a cab to my hotel before I lose my room."

"Sure, go ahead," said the cop. "It's no sweat off my balls what the hell you do."

Well, thought Ben, they warned me things could get ugly.

The convention hotel was quite nice and his room was pleasant. His window faced Central Park and there was a wonderful view of the spreading greenery.

The bellhop nodded when Ben told him how much he liked the view. "Yeah—maybe you'll get to watch an o' lady being mugged down there." He chuckled, then asked if Ben was "with the convention."

"Yes, I'm here from Ohio."

"Well, a lot of the convention people are boozin' it up at the bar. Maybe you'll make some new friends."

The bellhop's words were prophetic.

After he had showered and changed into fresh clothes, Ben took the elevator down to the bar (called The Haven), and he had not been there for more than five minutes when two men sat down on stools, one to either side of him.

"So, you're a tool man, huh?" asked the fellow to Ben's left. Bearded, with large, very dark eyes and a lot of teeth in his smile.

"Correct," said Ben. "How did you know?"

"Lapel," said the other man, the one on the right. He was thin and extremely pale with washed-out blue eyes behind thick glasses.

Ben looked confused. "I don't—"

"That pin in the lapel of your coat," the bearded man said. "Dead giveaway."

Ben smiled, touching the bright metal lapel pin which featured a hammer, wrench, and pliers in an embossed design above the logo: "Sutton's—Tools You Can Trust."

"Are you two gentlemen also here for the convention?" Ben asked.

"You got it," said the man in glasses. "I'm Jock Kirby, and this bearded character is Billy Dennis."

"Ben Sutton."

They shook hands.

"Us, we're local boys, from the core of the Apple," said Billy Dennis. "Where you hail from?"

"Atkin, Ohio."

"Akron?" asked Jock. "I know a tire man from Akron."

"No, *Atkin*," Ben corrected him. "We're a few hundred miles from Akron. People tend to get the names mixed."

"Never heard of it," said Billy.

"It's a small town," Ben told them. "Nothing much to hear about."

"What you drinking?" Jock asked.

"Scotch and water," said Ben.

"Great. Same for us." Kirby gestured to the bartender, raising Ben's glass. "Three more of these, okay?"

"Okay," nodded the barman.

"Well," said Billy Dennis, running a slow hand along his bearded cheek, "So you're an Ohio man. Not much pizzazz back there, huh?"

"Pizzazz?" Ben blinked at him.

"He means," added Kirby, "you must get bored out of your gourd with nothing much shaking in Akins."

"Atkin. It's Atkin."

"Well, whatever," Kirby grunted.

Their drinks arrived and Dennis shoved a twenty-dollar bill toward the barman.

"What do you do for kicks back in Ohio?" asked Kirby.

"I watch television," Ben said, sipping his Scotch. "Listen to music. Eat out on occasion. Go to a movie where there's one I really want to see." He shrugged. "But frankly, I'm not much of a moviegoer."

"Boy," sighed Billy Dennis. "Sounds like you have yourself a blast."

"Fun time," said Jock Kirby.

Ben shifted on the barstool. "I don't require a whole lot out of life. I guess I'm what you'd call 'laid back.'"

Billy Dennis chuckled, showing his teeth. "Take my word, Bennie, it's better gettin' laid than bein' laid back!"

"Fuckin' A," said Jock.

Ben flushed and hastily finished his drink. He wasn't accustomed to rough language and he didn't appreciate it.

Dennis gestured to the barman, making a circle in the air. "Another round," he said.

"No, no, I've really had enough," Ben protested. He was already feeling light-headed. He'd never been a drinker.

"Aw, c'mon, Bennie boy," urged Jock Kirby. "*Live* a little. Take a bite out of the Big Apple."

"Yeah," nodded Billy Dennis, his dark eyes fixed on the Ohio man. "Have another shot on us."

And each of them put an arm around Ben Sutton.

The walk down Broadway was like a dream. Ben couldn't remember leaving the bar. Had they taken a cab here? His head seemed full of rosy smoke.

"I think I drank too much," he said. The words were blurred. His tongue was thick and rebellious.

"Can't ever drink too much at a party," said Billy Dennis. "An' that's what we got goin' here tonight!"

"Fuckin' A," Jock said. "It's party time."

"I've got to get back to the hotel," Ben told them. "The convention opens at ten tomorrow morning. I need sleep."

"Sleep?" Dennis gave Ben a toothy smile. "Hell, you can sleep when you're dead. We're gonna show you a fun time, Bennie."

"Sure are," agreed Jock Kirby. "Make you forget all about Ohio."

"Where are we going?" asked Ben. He found it difficult to keep pace with them, and the lights along the street seemed to be buried in mist.

"Forty-second is where," nodded Kirby. "Jump street."

Ben stopped. He raised a protesting hand. "That's a dangerous area," he said thickly. "My friends warned me to avoid it."

"*We're* your friends now," said Billy Dennis. "An' *we* say it's where all the action is. Right, Jocko?"

"Fuckin' A," Kirby said.

A street bum approached them, his clawed right hand extended. Ben dug out a quarter, dropping it into the scabbed palm. "Bless you," said the bum.

"Butt off," said Kirby.

The bum ignored him. He gestured to the sacks of garbage stacked along the curb, black-plastic bags swollen with waste. Roaches and insects burrowed among them. He nodded toward Ben. "Don't step on the maggots," he said.

And moved on up Broadway.

"I'm not so sure about this," Ben told them. "I still think I should take a taxi back to the hotel."

"The friggin' hotel can wait," said Kirby. His pale skin seemed to glow in the darkness. "Hotel's not goin' anywhere."

"Right," agreed Billy Dennis. "Stuck in that hotel, you might as well be back in Elkins."

"Atkin," corrected Ben. His head felt detached from his body, which floated below it.

"Hey, we're here," grinned Jock Kirby. "Welcome to sin street!"

They had reached Forty-second and Broadway. The intersection traffic throbbed around them in swirls of moving light and sound. Neons blazed and sizzled. The air smelled of ash.

Ben blinked rapidly, trying to sharpen his focus.

"I think I'm drunk," he said.

"No, man," Jock assured him. "You've just got a little *glow* on is all. Go with it. Enjoy."

Billy Dennis held Ben's left elbow, propelling him along Forty-second. Ben felt weightless, as if his body were made of tissue paper.

"Where . . . are you taking me?"

"To a special place," said Billy. "You'll really dig it. Right, Jocko?"

"Fuckin' A," said Kirby.

Ben struggled to get a clear visual fix on the area. His senses recorded a kaleidoscope of color and noise. The walk swarmed with pimps and prostitutes, beggars and barkers, tourists and heavy trippers. Movie marquees bloomed with light, a fireworks of neon. Souvenir shops and porno peep shows gaudily competed for attention. A sea of disembodied voices poured over Ben as he walked; faces drifted past him like a gallery of ghosts.

"I'm dizzy," he said. "I've got to sit down."

"You can sit down when we get inside," Kirby told him.

"Inside where?"

"You'll see," said Billy. "We're almost there."

They stopped at a building of bright-flashing lights with a twenty-foot female nude outlined on its facade in twisting snakes of color. GIRLS . . . NUDE . . . GIRLS . . . NUDE . . . flashed the lights.

A feral-faced barker in a soiled white shirt and worn Levi's gestured at them. His eyes were blood-shot.

"Step right in, gents, the show's ready to start. The girls are all absolutely naked and *un*adorned. They'll tease and titillate, delight and dazzle you."

Ben's new friends marched him inside the building, one to each elbow, up a flight of wide, red-painted stairs to a landing illumined by bands of blue fluorescent tubing, and down a hallway to a room in which a series of plastic stools formed a large circle. All very surreal, dreamlike. And, somehow, threatening.

Each stool faced a window, shuttered in gleaming red metal, with a coin slot at the bottom. The other stools were unoccupied, which Ben found odd.

"Have a seat, brother," said a tall beanstalk of a man with badly pitted skin. "Ten minutes for a quarter. And the feels are free."

"Open your fingers, Ben," said Jock Kirby—and he put several silver quarters into Ben's hand. "Just pop one in at the bottom," he said. Then he grinned. "Nothin' like this back in Ohio!"

Ben Sutton obeyed, numbly slotting in the first coin.

Now he waited as, slowly, the metal shutter rolled up to reveal a large circular platform bathed in a powdery blaze of overhead spots.

A thick-faced, sullen-eyed woman stepped from an inner door. She wore a dress of red sequins and a cheap red wig. She looked at Ben.

"Welcome to the Hellhole," she said. Her smile was ugly.

Ben kept expecting to see other windows opening, but he remained the only customer. Not much profit in this show, he thought dully.

"We herewith present, for your special entertainment, the Flame of Araby."

The thick-faced woman pressed a button by the side of the platform and, to a burst of prerecorded drum music, a long-limbed blonde stepped through the doorway.

She was wearing several gauzy veils which she

quickly began discarding. Young and full-figured, she was attractive in a vulgar sense as she whirled and twisted to the beating drums. Her glittery eyes were locked on Ben, who sat numb and transfixed at the window. Kirby was right; he had seen nothing like this in Ohio.

Now the final veil whispered from her hips and she was, as the barker had promised, "absolutely naked and unadorned."

In all of his thirty-eight years, Ben Sutton had never seen a totally nude woman. Linda Mae Lewis had allowed him to see her left breast under the dim illumination of the dash lights in Ben's old Pontiac convertible when he was in college, and a waitress at the Quick-Cup coffee shop on the outskirts of Atkin had once let him place his hand under her uniform—and he'd been able to view her upper thigh—but that was the full extent of Ben's sexual experience with females.

Thus, he was truly dazzled by the curved, shimmering white body writhing just inches in front of him.

"Go ahead, sweetie, touch one," the girl said in a husky voice, aiming her naked buttocks at Ben. "Go for it!"

Trembling, Ben reached out to touch the naked slope of mooned buttock; the flesh was marble-smooth and seemed to vibrate under his fingers.

Then, at that moment, the red-metal shutter began sliding down. Ben jerked his hand back with a groan of frustration. His ten minutes had expired.

Frantically, spilling several coins to the floor, Ben slotted in another quarter—and the shutter rolled slowly up again.

But the platform was empty.

The girl was gone.

The music had stopped.

Ben spun around on his stool to ask his two friends why the show had ended, but the room was deserted.

Ben stood up. "Hello! Anybody here?"

No reply. Just the muted sounds of street traffic, punctuated by the thin wail of a distant police siren.

Ben walked into the hall.

"Kirby? . . . Dennis? . . . You out here?"

No reply.

He moved toward the stairs. Or that was the direction he intended to take. Obviously, he had gone the wrong way because the hallway twisted, leading him deeper into the building.

The passage seemed dimmer, narrower.

Ben heard laughter ahead of him. A door opened along the hall, flooding the area with light.

He walked to the open door, looked in. The thick-faced woman and the blond dancing girl were there, with Jock Kirby and Billy Dennis. They were all laughing together, with drinks in their . . . in their . . . their . . .

Not hands. Dear God, not hands!

"Hi, Ben," said the Billy-thing. "We're celebrating."

"Because of you, chum," said the Jock-thing. "Meat on the hoof!"

"Yeah," nodded the blonde, running a pink tongue over her lips, "even maggots hafta eat."

Ben stared at them. His stomach was churning; a sudden rush of nausea made him stagger back, vomiting into the hall.

Inside the room, the four of them were discarding body parts . . . limbs . . . ears . . . noses . . . their flesh dropping away like chunks of rotten cheese.

Ben allowed himself one last, horror-struck backward glance into the room as he turned to run.

The things he saw were like the maggots and roaches in the swollen bags of trash along Broadway, but much larger, much more . . . advanced.

Ben Sutton ran.

He couldn't find the stairs. The hall kept twisting back on itself—but if he kept running he'd find a way out.

He was *sure* he would find a way out.

One of my earliest creative endeavors was a poem about Halloween, written when I was twelve. I've always looked forward to this holiday, with its ghosts-and-goblins tradition and its celebration of Dark and Terrible Things. And what could be more terrible than a demon-creature on the hunt—each Halloween night—for children's souls?

When I finished this one (selected, in England, for Dark Voices 2: The Best in Modern Horror), I realized that the Halloween Man might exist only in the mind of my character; maybe he was no more than a projection of Katie's inflamed fears. But then again, maybe not. He might be as real and terrible as she believes him to be. Thus, the story can be read on two levels: Does he exist, or doesn't he?

Read "The Halloween Man" and decide for yourself.

The Halloween Man

(Written: December 1984)

Oh, Katie believed in him for sure, the Halloween Man. Him with his long skinny-spindly arms and sharp-toothed mouth and eyes sunk deep in skull sockets like softly glowing embers, charcoal red. Him with his long coat of tatters, smelling of tombstones and grave dirt. All spider-hairy he was, the Halloween Man.

"You made him up!" said Jan the first time Katie told her about him. Jan was nine, a year younger than Katie, but she could run faster and jump higher. "He isn't real."

"Is so," said Katie.

"Is not."

"Is."

"*Isn't!*"

Jan slapped Katie. Hard. Hard enough to make her eyes sting.

"You're just mean," Jan declared. "Going around telling lies and scaring people."

"It's true," said Katie, trying not to cry. "He's real

and he could be coming here on Halloween night—
right to this town. This could be the year he comes
here."

The town was Center City, a small farming com-
munity in the Missouri heartland, brightened by fire-
colored October trees, with a high courthouse clock
(Little Ben) to chime the hour, with plowed fields to
the east and a sweep of sun-glittered lake to the west.

A neat little jewel of a town by day. By night, when
the big oaks and maples bulked dark and the oozy
lakewater was tar-black and brooding, Center City
could be scary for a ten-year-old who believed in
demons.

Especially on Halloween night.

All month at school, all through October, Katie had
been thinking about the Halloween Man, about what
Todd Pepper had told her about him. Todd was very
mature and very wise. And a lot older, too. Todd was
thirteen. He came from a really big city, Cleveland,
and knew a lot of things that only big-city kids know.
He was visiting his grandparents for the summer (old
Mr. and Mrs. Willard) and Katie met him in the town
library late in August when he was looking through a
book on demons.

They got to talking, and Katie asked him if he'd

ever seen a demon. He had narrow features with squinty eyes and a crooked grin that tucked up the left side of his face.

"Sure, I seen one," said Todd Pepper. "The old Halloween Man, I seen him. Wears a big pissy-smelling hat and carries a bag over one shoulder, like Santa. But he's got no toys in it, nosir. Not in *that* bag!"

"What's he got in it?"

"Souls. That's what he collects. Human souls."

Katie swallowed. "Where . . . where does he get them from?"

"From kids. Little kids. On Halloween night."

They were sitting at one of the big wooden library tables, and now he leaned across it, getting his narrow face closer to hers. "That's the only time you'll see him. It's the only night he's got *power*." And he gave her his crooked grin. "He comes slidin' along, in his rotty tattered coat, like a big scarecrow come alive, with those glowy red eyes of his, and the bag all ready. Steppin' along the sidewalk in the dark easy as you please, the old Halloween Man."

"How does he do it?" Katie wanted to know. "How does he get a kid's soul?"

"Puts his big hairy hands on both sides of the kid's head and gives it a terrible shake. Out pops the soul, like a cork out of a bottle. Bingo! And into the sack it goes."

Katie felt hot and excited. And shaky-scared. But she couldn't stop asking questions. "What does he do with all the kids' souls after he's collected them?"

Another crooked grin. *"Eats 'em,"* said Todd. "They're his food for the year. Then, come Halloween, he gets hungry again and slinks out to collect a new batch—like a squirrel collecting nuts for the winter."

"And you—you saw him? Really *saw* him?"

"Sure did. The old Halloween Man, he chased me once when I was your age. In Havershim, Texas. Little bitty town, like this one. He *likes* small towns."

"How come?"

"Nowhere for kids to hide in a small town. Everything out in the open. He stays clear of the big cities."

Katie shifted on her chair. She bit her lower lip. "Did he catch you—that time in Texas?"

"Nosir, not me." Todd squinched his eyes. "If he had of, I'd be dead—with my soul in his bag."

"How'd you get away?"

"Outran him. He was pretty quick, ran like a big lizard he did, but I was quicker. Once I got shut of him, I hid out. Till after midnight. That's when he loses his power. After midnight he's just *gone*—like a puff of smoke."

"Well, *I've* never seen him, I know," said Katie softly. "I'd remember if I'd seen him."

"You bet," said Todd Pepper, nodding vigorously. "But then, he isn't always so easy to spot."

"What'da mean?"

"Magical, that old Halloween Man is. Can take over people. Big people, I mean. Just climbs right inside 'em, like steppin' into another room. One step, and he's inside lookin' out."

"Then how can you tell if it's *him*?" Katie asked.

"Can't," said Todd Pepper. "Not till he jumps at you. But if you're lookin' sharp for him, and you *know* he's around, then you can kind of spot him by instinct."

"What's that?"

"It's like an animal's got in the jungle when a hunter is after him. The animal gets an instinct about the hunter and knows when to run. It's that way with the ole Halloween Man—you can sort of sniff him out when you're sharp enough. He can't fool you then. Not if you're really concentrating. Then your instinct takes over."

"Is there a picture of him in that book?"

Todd riffled the pages casually. "Nope. No kid's ever lived long enough to take a picture of the Halloween Man. But I've described him to you—and unless he climbs inside somebody you'll be able to spot him easy."

"Thanks," said Katie. "I appreciate that." She

looked pensive. "But maybe he'll never come to Center City."

"Maybe not." Todd shut the book of demons with a snap. "Then again, you never know. Like I said, he favors small towns. If you want my opinion, I'd say he's overdue in this one."

And that was the only talk she'd had with Todd Pepper. At summer's end he went back to Cleveland to school, and Katie was left in Center City with a head full of new thoughts. About the Halloween Man.

And then it was October, with the leaves blowing orange and yellow and red-gold over her shoes when she walked to school, and the lake getting colder and darker off beyond the trees, and the gusting wind tugging at her coat and fingering her hair. Sometimes it rained, a chill October drizzle that gave the streets a wet-cat shine and made the sodden leaves stick to her clothes like dead skin.

Katie had never liked October, but *this* year was the worst, knowing about the Halloween Man, knowing that he could be walking through her town come Halloween night, with his grimy soul-bag over one shoulder and his red-coal eyes penetrating the dark.

Through the whole past week at school that was all Katie could think about and Miss Prentiss, her teacher, finally sent Katie home. With a note to her father that read:

Katie is not her normal self. She is listless and inattentive in class. She does not respond to lessons, nor will she answer questions related to them. She has not been completing her homework. Since Katie is one of our brightest children, I suggest you have her examined for possible illness.

"Are you sick, sugar?" her father had asked her. Her mother was dead and had been for as long as Katie could remember.

"I don't think so," Katie had replied. "But I feel kind of funny. I'll be all right after Halloween. I want to stay home from school till after Halloween."

Her father had been puzzled by this attitude. Katie had always loved Halloween. It had been her favorite holiday. Out Trick-or-Treating soon as it got dark with her best friend Jan. Now Jan never called the house anymore. Katie's father wondered why.

"I don't like her," Katie declared firmly. "She slapped me."

"Hey, that's not nice," said Katie's father. "Why did she do that?"

"She said I lied to her."

"About what?"

"I can't tell you." Katie looked down at her hands.

"Why not, sugar?"

"Cuz."

"Cuz why?"

"Cuz it's something too scary to talk about."

"Are you sure you can't tell your ole Daddy?"

She looked up at him. "Maybe after Halloween. *Then* I'll tell you."

"Okay, it's a deal. Halloween's just a few days off. So I guess I won't have long to wait."

And he smiled, ruffling her hair.

And now it was Halloween day and when it got dark it would be Halloween night.

Katie had a sure feeling that *this* year he'd show up in Center City. Somehow, she knew this would be the year.

That afternoon Katie moved through the town square in a kind of dazed fever. Her father had sent her downtown for some groceries and she had taken a long time getting them. It was so hard to remember what he wanted her to bring home. She had to keep checking the list in her purse. She just couldn't keep her mind on shopping.

Jan was on the street outside when Katie left Mr. Hakin's grocery store. They glared at each other.

"Do you take back what you said?" asked Jan, sullen and pouting. "About that awful, smelly man."

"No, I don't," said Katie. Her lips were tight.

"You lied!"

"I told the *truth*," declared Katie. "But you're just scared to believe it. And if you try to slap me again I'll kick your shins!"

Jan stepped back. "You're the *meanest* person I know!"

"Listen, you'd better stay home tonight," warned Katie. "That is, if you don't want the Halloween Man to pop out your soul and eat it."

Jan blinked at this, frowning.

"I figure he'll be out tonight," nodded Katie. "He's *due*."

"You're crazy! I'm going Trick-or-Treating, like always."

"Well, don't say I didn't warn you," Katie told her. "When he grabs you just remember what I said."

"I *hate* you!" Jan cried, and turned away.

Katie started home.

It was later than she thought. Katie had spent so much time shopping she'd lost track of the day. It had just slipped past.

Now it was almost dark.

God!

Almost dark.

The brightness had drained from the sky, and the westering sun was buried in thick-massed clouds. A thin rain was beginning to dampen the streets.

Katie shifted the heavy bag of groceries and began to walk faster. Only two miles and she'd be home. Just twenty blocks.

A rising wind had joined the rain, driving wet leaves against her face, whipping her coat.

Not many kids will be going out tonight, Katie thought. Not in this kind of weather. Which meant lean pickings for the Halloween Man. If he shows up there won't be many souls to bag. Meaning he'll grab any kid he finds on the street. No pick and choose for him.

I'm all right, Katie told herself. I've still got time to make it home before it gets really dark . . .

But the clouds were thickening rapidly, drawing a heavy gray blanket across the sky.

It *was* getting dark.

Katie hurried. An orange fell from the top of the rain-damp sack, plopped to the walk. Katie stopped to pick it up.

And saw him.

Coming along the walk under the blowing trees,

tall and skeleton-gaunt, with his rotted coat flapping in tatters around his stick-thin legs, and with his sack slung over one bony shoulder. The red of his deep-sunk eyes burned under a big wide-brimmed slouch hat.

He saw Katie.

The Halloween Man smiled.

She whirled around with an insucked cry, the soggy paper sack ripping, slipping from her fingers, the groceries tumbling to the sidewalk, cans rolling, spilt milk cartons spitting white foam across the dark concrete.

Katie ran.

Not looking back, heart hammer-thumping her chest, she flung her body forward in strangled panic.

Where? Where to go? He was between her and home; she'd have to go back into the heart of town, run across the square and try to reach her house by another route.

But could she run that far? Jan was the runner; *she* could do it, she was faster and stronger. Already Katie felt a rising weakness in her legs. Terror was constricting her muscles, numbing her reflexes.

He could run like a lizard. That's what Todd had said, and lizards are fast. She didn't want to look back, didn't want to turn to see him, but she had to know how much distance she'd put between them. *Where was he?*

With a low moan, Katie swung her head around. And suddenly stopped running.

He was gone.

The long wet street stretched empty behind her, char black at its far end—just the wind-lashed trees, the gusting leaves, the blowing curtain of rain silvering the dark pavement. There was no sign of the Halloween Man.

He'd outfoxed her. He'd guessed her intention about doubling back and had cut across the square ahead of her. And he'd done the final demon-clever thing to trap her. He'd climbed inside.

But inside *who*? And *where*?

Concentrate, she told herself. Remember what Todd Pepper said about trusting your instinct. Oh, I'll know him when I see him!

Now Katie was in the middle of the town square. No matter which route she took home she had to pass several stores and shops—and he could be waiting in any doorway, ready to pounce.

She drew a long, shuddering breath, steeling herself for survival. Her head ached; she felt dizzy, but she was prepared to run.

Then, suddenly, horribly, a hand tugged at her shoulder!

Katie flinched like a dog under the whip, looked

up in dry-mouthed terror—into the calm, smiling face of Dr. Peter Osgood.

"Your father tells me you've been ill, young lady," he said in his smooth doctor's voice. "Just step into my office and we'll find out what's wrong."

Step into my parlor said the spider to the fly.

Katie backed away from him. "No . . . No. Nothing's wrong. I'm fine."

"Your face looks flushed. You may have a touch of fever, Katie. Now I really think we should—"

"Get away from me!" she screamed. "I'm not going anywhere with you. I know who you are—you're *him!*"

And she broke into a pounding run.

Past Mr. Thurtle's candy shop: *Him,* waving from the window at her, with his red eyes shining . . .

Past the drug store: *Him,* standing at the door inside Mr. Joergens, smiling with his shark's teeth. "In a big rush today, Katie?"

Yes, away from *you!* A big rush.

Across the street on the red light. *Him,* in a dirty Ford pickup, jamming on the brakes, poking his head out the window: "Watch where you're running, you stupid little bitch!"

Oh, she knew the Halloween Man.

* * *

When Katie reached her house, on Oakvale, she fell to her knees on the cold wooden porch, gasping, eyes full of tears, ears ringing. Her head felt like a balloon about to burst, and she was hot and woozy and sick to her stomach.

But she was safe. She'd made it; he hadn't caught her.

Katie stood up shakily, got the door open and crossed the living room to the big rose sofa, dropped into it with a heavy, exhausted sigh.

Outside, a car pulled to the curb. She could see it through the window. A dark blue Chevy! *Dr. Osgood's car!*

"No!" screamed Katie, running back to the front door and throwing the bolt.

Her father came downstairs, looking confused. "What's wrong, sugar?"

Katie faced him, panting, her back tight against the bolted door. "We can't let him in. He's gonna steal my soul!"

"It's just Dr. Osgood, Katie. I asked him to drop by and see you."

"No, it *isn't*, Daddy. He's not Dr. Osgood. He's *him!*"

"Him?"

"The Halloween Man. He can get into big people's bodies. And he's inside Dr. Osgood right now."

Her father smiled gently, then moved to unlock the door. "I think you've been watching too many movies. You don't have to be afraid of—"

But Katie didn't wait for him to finish. She rushed up the stairs, ran to her room at the end of the hall, hurried inside, and slammed the door.

Panic. There was no lock on her door, no way to keep him out. She ran to the bed, jumping under the covers the way she used to do when she was little and things frightened her in the dark.

Below, muted sounds of greeting. Male voices. Daddy talking to *him*.

Then footsteps.

Coming up the stairs.

Katie leaped from the bed in a sudden frenzy, tipped over the tall wooden bookcase near her closet, dragged it against the door. *It probably wouldn't hold him, but . . .*

A rapping at the door. Rap-rap-rap. Rap-rap-rap.

"Katie!"

"Go way!" she yelled.

"Katie, open the door." It was Daddy's voice.

"No. You've got him with you. I know he's right there with you."

"Go to the window," her father told her. "See for yourself."

She ran across the room, stumbling over spilled

books, and looked out. Dr. Osgood was just driving away through the misting rain in his blue Chevy.

Which meant that her *father* could now be—

He pushed the door open.

Katie swung around to face him. "Oh, no!" She was trembling. "It's true! Now *you're* him!"

Katie's father reached out, put a big hand on each side of her face. "Happy Halloween, sugar!" he said.

And gave her head a terrible shake.

Written for Dennis Etchison's state-of-the-art horror anthology, Cutting Edge, this one formed the basis for my 1985 Movie of the Week from NBC, Terror at London Bridge.

The seeds were planted during a cross-country trip when my wife insisted on stopping in Lake Havasu, Arizona, to see London Bridge. The bridge had been taken apart in England, stone by stone, and then boated across the Atlantic to be reconstructed in Arizona over a diverted section of the Colorado River.

We'd been driving all day. I was tired and grumpy. The last thing I wanted to do was waste time and energy gawking at some old stone bridge. But my wife prevailed.

A mock-English village had been built in the area for atmosphere. By the time we arrived (very late), all of the other tourists were gone. We were alone in the darkness. My wife and I sauntered through the village to the foot of the wide, historic bridge steps leading up to the structure. I said: "You know, Jack the Ripper may have crossed this bridge a hundred years ago, after his murders at Whitechapel. His ghost could be standing up there right now, looking down at us."

"That's a scary thought," my wife said.

And . . . bingo . . . a TV movie!

Back in Los Angeles, I developed this idea into a story about the discovery, at the bottom of the Thames River, of one final stone from London Bridge (missing since the night Jack the Ripper disappeared). The stone had crushed the Ripper's body and absorbed his essence during its long years in the river. When the stone is found, it's shipped to America to be fitted back into its proper place in the bridge.

In my TV version (the prose version is somewhat different), a tourist accidentally cuts her hand while walking over the bridge in Lake Havasu. Her blood, seeping into the ancient stone, allows the Ripper to be reborn. A black mist rises from the stone and forms itself into the body of the infamous killer, after which the century-old pattern of murders begins anew in modern-day Arizona.

I sold the story to Charles Fries Entertainment and, subsequently, to NBC. The entire movie was filmed at the bridge and the surrounding area. (I even found a cobbled street in Lake Havasu that doubled beautifully for Old London in our opening sequence.) When telecast, Terror at London Bridge earned the highest ratings of any Fries production (and turned out to be the highest-grossing film in the history of Fries Entertainment).

Through television, Jack the Ripper was again alive and well, now surrounded by Saguaro cactus in the midst of the arid desert of the American Southwest.

A Final Stone

(Written: July 1984)

They were from Indianapolis. Newly married. Dave and *stirring, flexing muscle, feeling power now . . . a sudden driving thirst for* Alice Williamson, both in their late twenties, both excited about their trip to the West Coast. This would be their last night in Arizona. Tomorrow they planned to be in Palm Springs. To visit Dave's sister. But only one of them would make it to California. Dave, not Alice. *with the scalpel glittering*

Alice would die before midnight, her throat slashed cleanly across. *glittering, raised against the moon*

"Wait till you see what's here," Dave told her. "Gonna just be fantastic."

They were pulling their used Camaro into the parking lot at a tourist site in Lake Havasu, Arizona. He wouldn't tell her where they were. It was late. The lot was wide and dark, with only two other cars parked there, one a service vehicle.

"What *is* this place?" Alice was tired and hungry. *hungry*

"You'll find out. Once you see it, you'll never forget it. That's what they say."

"I just want to eat," she said. *the blade eating flesh, drinking*

"First we'll have a look at it, then we'll eat," said Dave, *them getting out of the car, walking toward the gate* smiling at her, giving her a hug.

The tall gate, black pebbled iron, led into a picture-perfect Tudor village. A bit of Olde England rising up from raw Arizona desert. A winged dragon looked down at them from the top of the gate.

"That's ugly," said Alice.

"It's historic," Dave told her. "That's the official Heraldic Dragon for the City of London."

"Is *that* what all this is—some sort of replica of London?"

"Much more than that. Heck, Ally, this was all built *around* it, to give it the proper atmosphere."

"I'm in no mood for atmosphere," she said. "We've been driving all day and I don't feel like playing games. I want to know what you—"

Dave cut into the flow of her words: "There it is!"

They both stared at it. Ten thousand tons of fitted stone. Over nine hundred feet of arched granite spanning the dark waters of the Colorado River. Tall and massive and magnificent.

"Christ!" murmured Dave. "Doesn't it just knock

you out? Imagine—all the way from England, from the Thames River . . . the by-God-for-real London Bridge!"

"It *is* amazing," Alice admitted. She smiled, kissed him on the cheek. "And I'm glad you didn't tell me . . . that you kept it for a surprise."

glittering cold steel

They moved along the concrete walkway beneath the Bridge, staring upward at the giant gray-black structure. Dave said: "When the British tore it down they numbered all the stones so our people would know where each one went. Thousands of stones. Like a jigsaw puzzle. Took three years to build it all over again here in Arizona." He gestured around them. "All this was just open desert when they started. After the Bridge was finished they diverted a section of the Colorado River to run under it. And built the Village."

"Why did the British give us their bridge?"

"They were putting up a better one," said Dave. "But, hey, they didn't *give* this one to us. The guy that had it built here paid nearly two and a half million for it. Plus the cost of shipping all the stones over. Some rich guy named McCulloch. Died since then, I think."

dead death dead dead death

"Well, we've seen it," said Alice. "Let's eat now. C'mon, I'm really starving."

"You don't want to *walk* on it?"

"Maybe after we eat," said Alice. *going inside the restaurant now . . . will wait . . . she's perfect . . . white throat, blue vein pulsing under the chin . . . long graceful neck . . .*

They ate at the City of London Arms in the Village. Late. Last couple in for dinner that evening. Last meal served.

"You folks should have come earlier," the waitress told them. "Lots of excitement here today, putting in the final stone. I mean, with the Bridge dedication and all."

"I thought it was dedicated in 1971," said Dave.

"Oh, it was. But there was this *one* stone missing. Everyone figured it had been lost on the trip over. But they found it last month in London. Had fallen into the water when they were taking the Bridge apart. Today, it got fitted back where it belonged." She smiled brightly. "So London Bridge is *really* complete now!"

Alice set her empty wineglass on the tablecloth. "All this Bridge talk is beginning to *bore* me," she said. "I need another drink."

"You've had enough," said Dave.

"Hell I have!" To the waitress: "Bring us another bottle of wine."

"Sorry, but we're closing. I'm not allowed to—"

"I *said* bring another!"

"And she said they're closing," snapped Dave. "Let's go."

They paid the check, left. The doors were locked behind them.

The City of London Arms sign blinked off as they moved down the restaurant steps. *to me to me*

"You'll feel better when we get back to the motel," Dave said.

"I feel fine. Let's go walk on London Bridge. That's what you wanted, isn't it?"

"Not now, Ally," he said. "We can do that tomorrow, before we leave. Drive over from the motel."

"*You* go to the damn motel," she said tightly. "*I'm* walking on the damn Bridge!"

He stared at her. "You're *drunk*!"

She giggled. "So what? Can't drunk people walk on the damn Bridge?"

"Come on," said Dave, taking her arm. "We're going to the car."

"You go to the car," she snapped, pulling away. "I'm gonna walk on the damn Bridge."

"Fine," said Dave. "Then you can get a *taxi* to the motel."

And, dark-faced with anger, he walked away from her, back to their car. Got in. Drove off.

alone now for me . . . just for me

Alice Williamson walked toward London Bridge through the massed tree shadows along the dark river pathway. She reached the foot of the wide gray-granite Bridge steps, looked up.

At a tall figure in black. Slouch hat, dark cloak, boots.

She was looking at death.

She stumbled back, turned, poised to run—but the figure moved, glided, flowed *mine now* down the granite steps with horrific speed.

And the scalpel glitter-danced against the moon.

Two days later.

Evening, with the tour boat empty, heading for its home dock, Angie Shepherd at the wheel. Angie was the boat's owner. She lived beside the river, had all her life. Knew its currents, its moods, under moon and sun, knew it intimately. Thompson Bay . . . Copper Canyon . . . Cattail Cove . . . Red Rock . . . Black Meadow . . . Topock Gorge. Knew its eagles and hawks and mallards, its mud turtles and great horned owls. Knew the sound of its waters in calm and in storm.

Her home was a tall, weathered-wood building that once served as a general store. She lived alone here. Made a living with her boat, running scenic tours along the Colorado. Age twenty-eight. Never married, and no plans in that area.

Angie docked the boat, secured it, entered the tall wooden building she called Riverhouse. She fussed in the small kitchen, taking some wine, bread, and cheese out to the dock. It was late; the night was ripe with river sounds and the heart-pulse of crickets.

She sat at the dock's edge, legs dangling in the cool water. Nibbled cheese. Listened to a night bird crying over the river.

Something bumped her foot in the dark water. Something heavy, sodden. Drifting in the slow night current.

Something called Alice Williamson.

Dan Gregory had no clues to the murder. The husband was a logical suspect (most murders are family-connected), but Gregory knew that Dave Williamson was not guilty. You develop an instinct about people, and he knew Williamson was no wife-killer. For one thing, the man's grief was deep and genuine; he seemed totally shattered by the murder—blamed himself, bitterly, for deserting Alice in the Village.

Gregory was tipped back in his desk chair, an unlit Marlboro in his mouth. (He was trying to give up smoking.) Williamson slouched in the office chair in front of him, looking broken and defeated. "Your wife was drunk, you had an argument. You got pissed and drove off. Happens to people all the time. Don't blame yourself for this."

"But if I'd stayed there, been there when—"

"Then you'd probably *both* be dead," said Gregory. "You go back to the motel, take those pills the doc gave you and get some sleep. Then head for Palm Springs. We'll contact you at your sister's if we come up with anything."

Williamson left the office. Gregory talked to Angie Shepherd next, about finding the body. She was shaken, but cooperative.

"I've never seen anyone dead before," she told him.

"No family funerals?"

"Sure. A couple. But I'd never walk past the open caskets. I didn't want to see people I loved . . . *that* way." She shrugged. "In your business I guess you see a lot of death."

"Not actually," said Gregory. "Your average Highway Patrol officer sees more of it in a month than I have in ten years. You don't get many murders in a town this size."

"That how long you've been chief of Police here, ten years?"

"Nope. Just over a year. Used to be a police lieutenant in Phoenix. Moved up to this job." He raised an eyebrow at her. "How come, you being a local, you don't know how long I've been Chief?"

"I never follow politics—*especially* small-town politics. Sorry about that." And she smiled.

Gregory was a square-faced man in his thirties with hard, iced-blue eyes, offset by a quick, warm way of grinning. Had never married; most women bored him. But he liked Angie. And the attraction was mutual.

Alice Williamson's death had launched a relationship.

In August, four months after the first murder, there were two more. Both women. Both with their throats cut. Both found along the banks of the Colorado. One at Pilot Rock, the other near Whipple Bay.

Dan Gregory had no reason to believe the two August "River Killings" (as the local paper had dubbed them) had been committed near London Bridge. He told a reporter that the killer might be a transient, passing through the area, killing at random. The murders lacked motive; the three victims had nothing in common beyond being female. Maybe the murderer, suggested Gregory, was just someone who hates women.

The press had a field day. "Madman on Loose" . . . "Woman-Hating Killer Haunts Area" . . . "Chief of Police Admits No Clues to River Killings."

Reading the stories, Gregory muttered softly: "Assholes!"

Early September. A classroom at Lake Havasu City High School. Senior English. Lyn Esterly was finishing a lecture on William Faulkner's *Light in August*.

". . . therefore, Joe Christmas became the victim of his own twisted personality. He truly believed he was cursed by an outlaw strain of blood, a white man branded black by a racially bigoted society. Your assignment is to write a five-hundred word essay on his inner conflicts."

After she'd dismissed the class, Lyn phoned her best friend, Angie Shepherd, for lunch. They had met when Lyn had almost drowned swimming near Castle Rock. Angie had saved her life.

"You're not running the boat today, and I need to talk to you, okay?"

"Sure . . . okay," agreed Angie. "Meet you in town. Tom's all right?"

"Tom's it is."

Trader Tom's was a seafood restaurant, specializing in fresh shrimp, an improbable business establishment in the middle of the Arizona desert. Angie, "the primitive," adored fresh shrimp, which had been introduced to her by Lyn, the "city animal," their joke names for one another.

Over broiled shrimp and sole almondine they relaxed into a familiar discussion: "I'll never be able to understand how you can live out there all alone on the river," said Lyn. "It's positively eerie—especially with a killer running loose. Aren't you afraid?"

"No. I keep a gun with me in the house, and I know how to use it."

"*I'd* be terrified."

"That's because you're a victim of your own imagination," said Angie, dipping a huge shrimp into Tom's special Cajun sauce. "You and your fascination with murder."

"Lots of people are true-crime buffs," said Lyn. "In fact that's why I wanted to talk to you today. It's about the River Killings."

"You've got a theory about 'em, right?"

"This one's pretty wild."

"Aren't they all?" Angie smiled, peeling another shrimp. "I'm listening."

"The first murder, the Williamson woman, that one took place on the third of April."

"So?"

"The second murder was on the seventh of August, the third on the thirty-first. All three dates are a perfect match."

"For what?"

"For a series of killings, seven in all, committed in 1888 by Jack the Ripper. His first three were on exact matching dates."

Angie paused, a shrimp halfway to her mouth. "Wow! Okay . . . you *did* say wild."

"And there's more. Alice Williamson, we know, was attacked near London Bridge—which is where the Ripper finally disappeared in 1888. They had him trapped there but the fog was really thick that night and when they closed in on him from both ends of the Bridge he just . . . vanished. And he was never seen or heard of again."

"Are you telling me that some nut is out there in the dark near London Bridge trying to duplicate the original Ripper murders? Is that your theory?"

"That's it."

"But why *now*? What triggered the pattern?"

"I'm working on that angle." Lyn's eyes were intense. "I'm telling you this today for a vitally important reason."

"I'm still listening."

"You've become very friendly with Chief Gregory. He'll listen to you. He must be told that the fourth murder will take place *tonight,* the eighth of September, before midnight."

"But I . . ."

"You've got to warn him to post extra men near the Bridge tonight. And he should be there himself."

"Because of your theory?"

"Of course! Because of my theory."

Angie slowly shook her head. "Dan would think I was around the bend. He's a realist. He'd laugh at me."

"Isn't it *worth* being laughed at to save a life?" Lyn's eyes burned at her. "Honest, Angie, if you don't convince Gregory that I'm making sense, that I'm onto a real pattern here, then another woman is going to get her throat slashed near London Bridge tonight."

Angie pushed her plate away. "You sure do know how to spoil a terrific lunch."

That afternoon, back at Riverhouse, Angie tried to make sense of Lyn's theory. The fact that these murders had fallen on the same dates as three murders a century earlier was interesting and curious, but not enough to set a hard-minded man like Gregory in motion.

It was crazy, but still Lyn *might* be onto something.

At least she could phone Dan and suggest dinner in the Village. She could tell him what Lyn said—and then he *would* be there in the area, just in case something happened.

Dan said yes, they'd meet at the City of London Arms.

When Angie left for the Village that night she carried a pearl-handled .32-caliber automatic in her purse.

If. Just if.

Dan was late. On the phone he'd mentioned a meeting with the City Council, so maybe that was it. The Village was quiet, nearly empty of tourists.

Angie waited, seated on a park bench near the restaurant, nervous in spite of herself, thinking that *alone, her back to the trees, thick shadow trees, vulnerable* maybe she should wait inside, at the bar.

A tall figure, moving toward her. Behind her.

A thick-fingered hand reaching out for her. She flinched back, eyes wide, fingers closing on the automatic inside her open purse.

"Didn't mean to scare you."

It was Dan. His grin made her relax. "I've . . . been a little nervous today."

"Over what?"

"Something Lyn Esterly told me." She took his arm. "I'll tell you all about it at dinner."

lost her . . . can't with him

And they went inside.

* * *

". . . so what do you think?" Angie asked. They were having an after-dinner drink. The booths around them were silent, unoccupied.

"I think your friend's imagination is working over-time."

Angie frowned. "I knew you'd say something like that."

Dan leaned forward, taking her hand. "You don't really believe there's going to be another murder in this area tonight just because *she* says so, do you?"

"No, I guess I don't really believe that."

And she guessed she didn't.

But . . .

There! Walking idly on the Bridge, looking down at the water, alone, young woman alone . . . her throat naked, skin naked and long-necked . . . open to me . . . blade sharp sharp . . . soft throat.

A dark pulsing glide onto the Bridge, a swift reaching out, a small choked cry of shocked horror, a sudden drawn-across half-moon of bright crimson—and the body falling . . . falling into deep Colorado waters.

* * *

Although Dan Gregory was a skeptic, he was not a fool. He ordered the entire Village area closed to tourists and began a thorough search.

Which proved rewarding.

An object was found on the Bridge, wedged into an aperture between two stones below one of the main arches: a surgeon's scalpel with fresh blood on it. And with blackened stains on the handle and blade.

It was confirmed that the fresh blood matched that of the latest victim. The dark stains proved to be dried blood. But they did not match the blood types of the other three murder victims. It was old blood. Very old.

Lab tests revealed that the bloodstains had remained on the scalpel for approximately one hundred years.

Dating back to the 1880s.

"Are you Angela Shepherd?"

A quiet Sunday morning along the river. Angie was repairing a water-damaged section of dock, briskly hammering in fresh nails, and had not heard the woman walk up behind her. She put down the claw hammer, stood, pushing back her hair. "Yes, I'm Angie Shepherd. Who are you?"

"Lenore Harper. I'm a journalist."

"What paper?"

"Freelance. Could we talk?"

Angie gestured toward the house. Lenore was tall, trim-bodied, with penetrating green eyes.

"Want a Coke?" asked Angie. "Afraid it's all I've got. I wasn't expecting company."

"No, I'm fine," said Lenore, seating herself on the living-room couch and removing a small notepad from her purse.

"You're doing a story on the River Killings, right?"

Lenore nodded. "But I'm going after something different. That's why I came to you."

"Why me?"

"Well . . . you discovered the first body."

Angie sat down in a chair opposite the couch, ran a hand through her hair. "I didn't *discover* anything. When the body drifted downriver against the dock I happened to be there. That's all there is to it."

"Were you shocked . . . frightened?"

"Sickened is a better word. I don't enjoy seeing people with their throats cut."

"Of course. I understand, but . . ."

Angie stood up. "Look, there's really nothing more I can tell you. If you want facts on the case, talk to Chief Gregory at the police department."

"I'm more interested in ideas, emotions—in personal reactions to these killings. I'd like to know *your* ideas. *Your* theories."

"If you want to talk theory, go see Lyn Esterly. She's got some original ideas on the case. Lyn's a true-crime buff. She'll probably be anxious to help you."

"Sounds like a good lead. Where can I find her?"

"Lake Havasu High. She teaches English there."

"Great." Lenore put away her notepad, then shook Angie's hand. "You've been very kind. Appreciate you talking to me."

"No problem."

Angie looked deeply into Lenore Harper's green eyes. Something about her I like, she thought. Maybe I've made a new friend. Well . . . "Good luck with your story," she said.

Lenore's talk with Lyn Esterly bore colorful results. The following day's paper carried "an exclusive feature interview" by Lenore Harper:

"Is River Killer Another Jack the Ripper?" the headline asked. Then, below it, a subheading: "Havasu High Teacher Traces Century-Old Murder Pattern."

According to the story, if the killer continued to follow the original Ripper's pattern, he would strike again on the thirtieth of September. And not once, but twice. On the night of September 30, 1888, Jack the Ripper butchered *two* women in London's Whitechapel district—victims #5 and #6. Would these gruesome double murders be repeated here in Lake Havasu?

The story ended with a large question mark.

Angie, on the phone to Lyn: "Maybe I did the wrong thing, sending her to see you."

"Why? I like her. She really *listened* to me."

"I just get the feeling that her story makes you . . . well, a kind of target."

"I doubt that."

"The killer knows all about you now. Even your picture was there in the paper. He knows that you're doing all this special research, that you worked out the whole copycat-Ripper idea . . ."

"So what? I can't catch him. That's up to the police. He's not going to bother with me. Getting my theory into print was important. Now that his sick little game has been exposed, maybe he'll quit. Might not be fun for him anymore. These weirdos are like that. Angie, it could all be over."

"So you're not sore at me for sending her to you?"

"Are you kidding? For once, someone has taken a theory of mine seriously enough to print it. Makes all this work mean something. Hell, I'm a celebrity now."

"That's what worries me."

And their conversation ended.

* * *

Angie had been correct in her hunch regarding Lenore Harper: the two women *did* become friends. As a freelance journalist, Lenore had roved the world, while Angie had spent her entire life in Arizona. Europe seemed, to her, exotic and impossibly far away. She was fascinated with Lenore's tales of global travel and of her childhood and early schooling in London.

On the night of September 30, Lyn Esterly turned down Angie's invitation to spend the evening at Riverhouse.

"I'm into something *new,* something really exciting on this Ripper thing," Lyn told her. "But I need to do more research. If what I think is true, then a lot of people are going to be surprised."

"God," sighed Angie, "how you love being mysterious!"

"Guilty as charged," admitted Lyn. "Anyhow, I'll feel a lot safer working at the library in the middle of town than being out there on that desolate river with you."

"Dan's taking your ideas seriously," Angie told her. "He's still got the Village closed to tourists—and he's bringing in extra men tonight in case you're right about the possibility of a double murder."

"I *want* to be wrong, Angie, honest to God I do. Maybe this creep has been scared off by all the publicity. Maybe tonight will prove that—but to be on the safe side, if I were you, I'd spend the night in town . . . not alone out there in that damn haunted castle of yours!"

"Okay, you've made your point. I'll take in a movie, then meet Dan later. Ought to be safe enough with the Chief of Police, eh?"

"Absolutely. And by tomorrow I may have a big surprise for you. This is like a puzzle that's finally coming together. It's exciting!"

"Call me in the morning?"

"That's a promise."

And they rang off.

Ten P.M. Lyn working alone in the reference room on the second floor of the city library. The building had been closed to the public for two hours. Even the staff had gone. But, as a teacher, Lyn had special privileges. And her own key.

A heavy night silence. Just the shuffling sound of her books, the faint scratch of her ballpoint pen, her own soft breathing.

When the outside door to the parking lot clicked open on the floor below her, Lyn didn't hear it.

The Ripper glided upward, a dark spider-shape on the stairs, *and she's there waiting to meet me, heart pumping blood for the blade* reached the second floor, moved down the silent hallway to the reference room, *pumping crimson* pushed open the door. *pumping*

To her. Behind her. Soundless.

Lyn's head was jerked violently back.

Death in her eyes—and the blade at her throat.

A single, swift movement.

pumping

And after this one, another before midnight.

Sherry, twenty-three, a graduate student from Chicago on vacation. Staying with a girlfriend. Out for a six-pack of Heineken, a quart of nonfat, and a Hershey's Big Bar.

She left the 7-Eleven with her bag of groceries, walked to her car parked behind the building. Somebody was in the back seat, but Sherry didn't know that.

She got in, fished for the ignition key in her purse, and heard a sliding, rustling sound behind her. Twisted in sudden, breathless panic.

Ripper.

* * *

Angie did not attend Lyn Esterly's funeral. She refused to see Dan or Lenore, canceled her tours, stocked her boat with food, and took it far upriver, living like a wounded animal. She allowed the river itself to soothe and comfort her, not speaking to anyone, drifting into tiny coves and inlets . . .

Until the wounds began to heal. Until she had regained sufficient emotional strength to return to Lake Havasu City.

She phoned Dan: "I'm back."

"I've been trying to trace you. Even ran a copter upriver, but I guess you didn't want to be found."

"I was all right."

"I *know* that, Angie. I wasn't worried about you. Especially after we caught him. That was what I wanted to find you for, to tell you the news. We *got* the bastard!"

"The River Killer?"

"Yeah. Calls himself 'Bloody Jack.' Says that he's the ghost of the Ripper."

"But how did you . . . ?"

"We spotted this guy prowling near the Bridge. 'Bout a week ago. He'd been living in a shack by the river, up near Mesquite Campground. One of my men followed him there. Walked right in and made the arrest."

"And he admitted he was the killer?"

"Bragged about it! Couldn't wait to get his picture in the papers."

"Dan . . . are you *sure* he's the right man?"

"Hell, we've got a ton of evidence. We found several weapons in the shack, including surgical knives. *Three* scalpels. And he had the newspaper stories on each of his murders tacked to the wall. He'd slashed the faces of all the women, their pictures, I mean. Deep knife cuts in each news photo."

"That's . . . *sick*," said Angie.

"And we have a witness who saw him go into that 7-Eleven on the night of the double murder—where the college girl was killed. He's the one, all right. A real psycho."

"Can I see you tonight? I *need* to be with you, Dan."

"I need you just as much. Meet you soon as I've finished here at the office. And, hey . . ."

"Yes?"

"I've *missed* you."

That night they made love in the moonlight, with the silken whisper of the river as erotic accompaniment. Lying naked in bed, side by side, they listened to the night crickets and touched each other gently, as if to make certain all of this was real for both of them.

"Murder is an awful way to meet somebody," said Angie, leaning close to him, her eyes shining in the darkness. "But I'm glad I met you. I never thought I could."

"Could what?"

"Find someone to love. To *really* love."

"Well, you've found me," he said quietly. "And *I've* found you."

She giggled. "You're . . ."

"I know." He grinned. "You do that to me."

And they made love again.

And the Colorado rippled its languorous night waters.

And from the dark woods a tall figure watched them.

It wasn't over.

Another month passed.

With the self-confessed killer in jail, the English Village and Bridge site were once again open to tourists.

Angie had not seen Lenore for several weeks and was anxious to tell her about the marriage plans she and Dan had made. She wanted Lenore to be her maid of honor at the wedding.

They met for a celebration dinner at the City of London Arms in the Village. But the mood was all wrong.

Angie noticed that Lenore's responses were brief, muted. She ate slowly, picking at her food.

"You don't seem all that thrilled to see me getting married," said Angie.

"Oh, but I *am*. Truly. And I know I've been a wet blanket. I'm sorry."

"What's wrong?"

"I just . . . don't think it's over."

"What are you talking about?"

"The Ripper thing. The killings."

Angie stared at her. "But they've got him. He's in jail right now. Dan is convinced that he . . ."

"He's not the one." Lenore said it flatly, softly. "I just *know* he's not the one."

"You're nuts. All the evidence . . ."

". . . is circumstantial. Oh, I'm sure this kook *thinks* he's the Ripper—but where is the *real* proof: blood samples . . . fingerprints . . . the actual murder weapons?"

"You're paranoid, Lenore! I had some doubts too, in the beginning, but Dan's a good cop. He's done his job. The killer's locked up."

Lenore's green eyes flashed. "Look, I asked you to meet me down here in the Village tonight for a reason—and it had nothing to do with your wedding." She drew in her breath. "I just didn't want to face this alone."

"Face what?"

"The fear. It's November the ninth. *Tonight* is the ninth!"

"So?"

"The date of the Ripper's seventh murder—back in 1888." Her tone was strained. "If that man in jail really is the Ripper, then nothing will happen here tonight. But . . . if he *isn't* . . ."

"My God, you're really scared!" And she gripped Lenore's hand, pressing it tightly.

"Damn right I'm scared. One of *us* could become his seventh victim."

"Look," said Angie. "It's like they say to pilots after a crash. You've got to go right back up or you'll never fly again. Well, it's time for you to do some flying tonight."

"I don't understand."

"You can't let yourself get spooked by what isn't real. And this fear of yours just isn't *real*, Lenore. There's no killer in the Village tonight. And, to prove it, I'm going to walk you to that damn Bridge."

Lenore grew visibly pale. "No . . . no, that's . . . No, I won't go.

"Yes, you will." Angie nodded. She motioned for the check.

Lenore stared at her numbly.

Outside, in the late night darkness, the Village was once more empty of tourists. The last of them had gone—and the wide parking lot was quiet and deserted beyond the gate.

"We're insane to be doing this," Lenore said. Her mouth was tightly set. "Why should *I* do this?"

"To prove that irrational fear must be faced and overcome. You're my friend now—my best friend—and I won't let you give in to irrationality."

"Okay, okay . . . if I agree to walk to the Bridge, then can we get the hell out of here?"

"Agreed."

And they began to walk.

moving toward the Bridge . . . mine now, mine

"I've been poking through Lyn's research papers," Lenore said, "and I think I know what her big surprise would have been."

"Tell me."

"Most scholars now agree on the true identity of the Ripper."

"Yes. A London doctor, a surgeon, Jonathan Bascum."

"Well, Lyn Esterly didn't believe he was the Ripper. And after what I've seen of her research, neither do I."

"Then who *was* he?" asked Angie.

"Jonathan had a twin sister, Jessica. She helped the poor in that area. They practically sainted her—called her 'the Angel of Whitechapel.'"

"I've heard of her."

"Did you know she was as medically skilled as her brother? . . . That Jonathan allowed her to use his medical books? Taught her. Jessica turned out to be a better surgeon than he was. And she *used* her medical knowledge in Whitechapel."

The stimulation of what she was revealing to Angie seemed to quell much of the fear in Lenore. Her voice was animated.

keep moving . . . closer.

"No *licensed* doctors would practice among the poor in that area. No money to be made. So she doctored these people. All illegal, of course. And, at first, it seemed she *was* a kind of saint, working among the destitute. Until her compulsion asserted itself."

"Compulsion?"

"To kill. Between April third and November ninth, 1888, she butchered seven women—and yet, to this day, historians claim her *brother* was responsible for the murders."

Angie was amazed. "Are you telling me that the Angel of Whitechapel was really Jack the Ripper?"

"That was Lyn's conclusion," said Lenore. "And,

when you think of it, why not? It explains how the Ripper always seemed to *vanish* after a kill. Why was it that no one ever *saw* him leave Whitechapel? Because 'he' was Jessica Bascum. She could move freely through the area without arousing suspicion. No one ever saw the Ripper's face . . . no one who *lived,* that is. To throw off the police, she sent notes to them signed 'Jack.' It was a *woman* they chased onto the Bridge that night in 1888."

Lenore seemed unaware that they were approaching the Bridge now. It loomed ahead of them, a dark, stretched mass of waiting stone.

closer

"Lyn had been tracing the Bascum family history," explained Lenore. "Jessica gave birth to a daughter in 1888, the same year she vanished on the Bridge. The line continued through her granddaughter, born in 1915, and her great-granddaughter, born in 1940. The last Bascum daughter was born in 1960."

"Which means she'd be in her mid-twenties today," said Angie.

"That's right," Lenore nodded. "Like you. *You're* in your midtwenties, Angie."

Angie's eyes flashed. She stopped walking. The line of her jaw tightened.

Bitch!

"Suppose she was drawn here," said Lenore, "to

London Bridge. Where her great-great-grandmother vanished a century ago. And suppose that, with the completion of the Bridge, with the placement of that final missing stone in April, Jessica's spirit entered her great-great-granddaughter. Suppose the six killings in the Lake Havasu area were done by *her*— that it was her cosmic destiny to commit them."

"Are you saying that you think *I* am a Bascum?" Angie asked softly. They continued to walk toward the Bridge.

"I don't *think* anything. I have the facts."

"And just what might those be?" Angie's voice was tense.

"Lyn was very close to solving the Ripper case. When she researched the Bascum family history in England she traced some of the descendants here to America. She *knew*."

"Knew what, Lenore?" Her eyes glittered. "You *do* believe that I'm a Bascum." Harshly: "*Don't* you?"

"No." Lenore shook her head. "I know you're not." She looked intently at Angie. "Because *I* am."

They had reached the steps leading up to the main part of the Bridge. In numb horror, Angie watched Lenore slide back a panel in one of the large granite blocks and remove the Ripper's hat, greatcoat, and cape. And the medical bag.

"This came down to me from the family. It was *her*

surgical bag—the same one she used in Whitechapel. I'd put it away—until April, when they placed the final stone." Her eyes sparked. "When I touched the stone I felt *her* . . . Jessica's soul flowed into *me*, became part of me. And I knew what I had to do."

She removed a glittering scalpel, held it up. The blade flashed in the reflected light of the lamps on the Bridge. Lenore's smile was satanic. "This is for you!"

Angie's heart trip-hammered; she was staring, trancelike, into the eyes of a killer. Suddenly she pivoted, began running.

Down the lonely, shadow-haunted, brick-and-cobblestone streets, under the tall antique lamps, past the clustered Tudor buildings of Old London.

And the Ripper followed. Relentlessly. Confident of a seventh kill.

she'll taste the blade

Angie circled the main square, ran between buildings to find a narrow, dimly lit alleyway that led her to the rear section of the City of London Arms. Phone inside. Call Dan!

Picking up a rock from the alley, she smashed a rear window, climbed inside, began running through the dark interior, searching for a phone. One here somewhere . . . somewhere . . .

The Ripper followed her inside.

Phone! Angie fumbled in her purse, finding change for the call. She also found . . .

The pearl-handled .32 automatic—the weapon she'd been carrying for months, totally forgotten in her panic.

Now she could fight back. She knew how to use a gun.

She inserted the coins, got Dan's number at head-quarters. Ringing . . . ringing . . . "Lake Havasu City Police Department."

"Dan . . . Chief Gregory . . . Emergency!"

"I'll get him on the line."

"Hurry!"

A pause. Angie's heart, hammering.

"This is Gregory. Who's . . . ?"

"Dan!" she broke in. "It's Angie. The Ripper's *here*, trying to kill me!"

"Where are you?"

A dry buzzing. The line was dead.

A clean, down-slicing move with the scalpel had severed the phone cord.

die now . . . time to die

Angie turned to face the killer.

And triggered the automatic.

At close range, a .32-caliber bullet smashed into

Lenore Bascum's flesh. She staggered back, falling to one knee on the polished wood floor of the restaurant, blood flowing from the wound.

Angie ran back to the smashed window, crawled through it, moved quickly down the alley. A rise of ground led up to the parking lot. Her car was there.

She reached it, sobbing to herself, inserted the key.

A shadow flowed across the shining car body. Two bloodspattered hands closed around Angie's throat.

The Ripper's eyes were coals of green fire, burning into Angie. She tore at the clawed fingers, pounded her right fist into the demented face. But the hands tightened. Darkness swept through Angie's brain; she was blacking out.

die, bitch!

She was dying.

Did she hear a siren? Was it real, or in her mind?

A second siren joined the first. Filling the night darkness.

bleeding . . . my blood . . . wrong, all wrong . . .

A dozen police cars roared into the lot, tires sliding on the night-damp tarmac.

Dan!

The Ripper's hands dropped away from Angie's throat. The tall figure turned, ran for the Bridge.

And was trapped there.

Police were closing in from both sides of the vast structure.

Angie and Dan were at the Bridge. "How did you know where to find me?"

"Silent alarm. Feeds right into headquarters. When you broke the window, the alarm was set off. I figured that's where you were."

"She's hit," Angie told him. "I shot her. She's dying."

In the middle of the span the Ripper fell to one knee. Then, a mortally wounded animal, she slipped over the side and plunged into the dark river beneath the Bridge.

Lights blazed on the water, picking out her body. She was sinking, unable to stay afloat. Blood gouted from her open mouth. "Damn you!" she screamed. "Damn all of you!"

She was gone.

The waters rippled over her grave.

Angie was convulsively gripping the automatic, the pearl handle cold against her fingers.

Cold.

Creative writing is often a mysterious process. As writers, we plumb the depths of our subconscious minds, and what emerges on the page is often as startling to us as it is to our readers. When I reached the climax of "My Name is Dolly" I wrote down what my mind dictated, but the end result remains strangely ambiguous.

I'm gratified that this story was chosen for The Year's Best Fantasy, *but I can't guarantee you'll understand it.*

I know I don't.

My Name Is Dolly

(Written: August 1986)

MONDAY—Today I met the witch—which is a good place to start this diary. (I had to look up how to spell it. First I spelled it dairy but that's a place you get milk and from this you're going to get blood so it is plenty different.)

Let me tell you about Meg. She's maybe a thousand years old. (A witch can live forever, right?) She's all gnarly like the bark of an oak tree, her skin I mean, and she has real big eyes. Like looking into deep dark caves and you don't know what's down there. Her nose is hooked and she has sharp teeth like a cat's are. When she smiles some of them are missing. Her hair is all wild and clumpy and she smells bad. Guess she hasn't had a shower for a real long time. Wears a black dress with holes bit in it. By rats most likely. She lives in this old deserted cobwebby boathouse they don't use anymore on the lake—and it's full of fat gray rats. Old Meg doesn't seem to mind.

My name is Dolly. Short for Dorothy like in the Oz books. Only nobody ever calls me Dorothy. I'm still a kid and not very tall and I've got red hair and freckles. (I really *hate* freckles! When I was real little I tried to rub them off but you can't. They stick just like tattoos do.)

Reason I went out to the lake to see old Meg is because of how much I hate my father. Well, he's not really my father, since I'm adopted and I don't know my real father. Maybe he's a nice man and not like Mister Brubaker who adopted me. Mrs. Brubaker died of the flu last winter which is when Mister Brubaker began to molest me. (I looked up the word molest and it's the right one for what he keeps trying to do with me.) When I won't let him he gets really mad and slaps me and I run out of the house until he's all calmed down again. Then he'll get special nice and offer me cookies with chocolate chunks in them which are my very favorite kind. He wants me to like him so he can molest me later.

Last week I heard about the witch who lives by the lake. A friend at school told me. Some of the kids used to go down there to throw rocks at her until she put a spell on Lucy Akins and Lucy ran away and no one's seen her since. Probably she's dead. The kids leave old Meg alone now.

I thought maybe Meg could put a spell on Mister Brubaker for five dollars. (I saved up that much.) Which is why I went to see her. She said she couldn't because she can't put spells on people unless she can see them up close and look in their eyes like she did to Lucy Akins.

The lake was black and smelly with big gas bubbles breaking in it and the boathouse was cold and damp and the rats scared me but old Meg was the only way I knew to get even with Mister Brubaker. She kept my five dollars and told me she was going into town soon and would look around for something to use against Mister Brubaker. I promised to come see her on Friday after school.

We'll have his blood, she said.

FRIDAY NIGHT—I went to see old Meg again and she gave me the doll to take home. A real big one, as tall as I am, with freckles and red hair just like mine. And in a pretty pink dress with little black slippers with red bows on them. The doll's eyes open and close and she has a big metal key in her back where you wind her up. When you do she opens her big dark eyes and says hello, my name is Dolly. Same as mine. I asked Meg where she found Dolly and she said at Mister Carter's toy store. But

I've been in there lots of times and I've never seen a doll like this for five dollars. Take her home, Meg told me, and she'll be your friend. I was real excited and ran off pulling Dolly behind me. She has a box with wheels on it you put her inside and pull along the sidewalk.

She's too big to carry.

MONDAY—Mister Brubaker doesn't like Dolly. He says she's damn strange. That's his words, damn strange. But she's my new friend so I don't care what he says about her. He wouldn't let me take her to school.

SATURDAY—I took some of Mister Brubaker's hair to old Meg today. She asked me to cut some off while he was asleep at night and it was really hard to do without waking him up but I got some and gave it to her. She wanted me to bring Dolly and I did and Meg said that Dolly was going to be her agent. That's the word. Agent. (I try to get all the words right.)

Dolly had opened her deep dark eyes and seen Mister Brubaker and old Meg said that was all she needed. She wrapped two of Mister Brubaker's hairs around the big metal key in Dolly's back and told me not to wind her up again until Sunday afternoon when Mister Brubaker was home watching his sports. He always does that on Sunday.

So I said okay.

SUNDAY NIGHT—This afternoon, like always, Mister Brubaker was watching a sports game on the television when I set Dolly right in front of him and did just what old Meg told me to do. I wound her up with the big key and then took the key out of her back and put it in her right hand. It was long and sharp and Dolly opened her eyes and said hello, my name is Dolly and stuck the metal key in Mister Brubaker's chest. There was a lot of blood. (I told you there would be.)

Mister Brubaker picked Dolly up and threw the front of her into the fire. I mean, that's how she landed, just the front of her at the edge of the fire. (It's winter now, and real cold in the house without a fire.) After he did that he fell down and didn't get up. He was dead so I called Doctor Thompson.

The police came with him and rescued Dolly out of the fire when I told them what happened. Her nice red hair was mostly burnt away and the whole left side of her face was burnt real bad and the paint had all peeled back and blistered. And one of her arms had burnt clear off and her pink dress was all char-colored and with big fire holes in it. The policeman who rescued her said that a toy doll couldn't kill any-body and that I must have stuck the key into Mister Brubaker's chest and blamed it on Dolly. They took me away to a home for bad children.

I didn't tell anybody about old Meg.

TUESDAY—It is a long time later and my hair is real pretty now and my face is almost healed. The lady who runs this house says there will always be big scars on the left side of my face but I was lucky not to lose my eye on that side. It is hard to eat and play with the other kids with just one arm but that's okay because I can still hear Mister Brubaker screaming and see all the blood coming out of his chest and that's nice.

I wish I could tell old Meg thank you. I forgot to—and you should always thank people for doing nice things for you.

In the fall of 1991, when I was deep into a 24,000-word novella for Weird Tales, I received a phone call from a friend. "Seen the latest issue of Newsweek?" he asked. No, I had not. "Well, you're in it."

He was right. On page 60 of the October 28, 1991 issue, I was amazed (and delighted) to find my story, "The Party," listed as one of the seven outstanding terror tales of the century, alongside such all-time greats as "The Monkey's Paw," by W.W. Jacobs, and Saki's "The Open Window." A rare accolade.

This one, which began its life in a 1967 issue of Playboy, has been anthologized in several classic volumes, including Great Tales of Horror and the Supernatural. I adapted it for television in 1981, and printed the TV version in my collection, Things Beyond Midnight.

Here's a party you wouldn't want to attend.

But once you're there . . .

The Party

(Written: February 1966)

Ashland frowned, trying to concentrate in the warm emptiness of the thickly carpeted lobby. Obviously, he had pressed the elevator button, because he was alone here and the elevator was blinking its way down to him, summoned from an upper floor. It arrived with an efficient hiss, the bronze doors clicked open, and he stepped in, thinking blackout. I had a mental blackout.

First the double vision. Now this. It was getting worse. Just where the hell was he? Must be a party, he told himself. Sure. Someone he'd met, whose name was missing along with the rest of it, had invited him to a party. He had an apartment number in his head: 9E. That much he retained. A number—nothing else.

On the way up, in the soundless cage of the elevator, David Ashland reviewed the day. The usual morning routine: work, then lunch with his new secretary. A swinger—but she liked her booze; put away three martinis to his two. Back to the office. More work. A drink in the afternoon with a writer.

("Beefeater. No rocks. Very dry.") Dinner at the new Italian joint on West Forty-Eighth with Linda. Lovely Linda. Expensive girl. Lovely as hell, but expensive. More drinks, then—nothing. Blackout.

The doc had warned him about the hard stuff, but what else can you do in New York? The pressures get to you, so you drink. Everybody drinks. And every night, somewhere in town, there's a party, with contacts (and girls) to be made . . .

The elevator stopped, opened its doors. Ashland stepped out, uncertainly, into the hall. The softly lit passageway was long, empty, silent. No, not silent. Ashland heard the familiar voice of a party: the shifting hive hum of cocktail conversation, dim, high laughter, the sharp chatter of ice against glass, a background wash of modern jazz . . . All quite familiar. And always the same.

He walked to 9E. Featureless apartment door. White. Brass button housing. Gold numbers. No clues here. Sighing, he thumbed the buzzer and waited nervously.

A smiling fat man with bad teeth opened the door. He was holding a half-filled drink in one hand. Ashland didn't know him.

"C'mon in fella," he said. "Join the party."

Ashland squinted into blue-swirled tobacco smoke,

adjusting his eyes to the dim interior. The rising-falling sea tide of voices seemed to envelop him.

"Grab a drink, fella," said the fat man. "Looks like you need one!"

Ashland aimed for the bar in one corner of the crowded apartment. He *did* need a drink. Maybe a drink would clear his head, let him get this all straight. Thus far, he had not recognized any of the faces in the smoke-hazed room.

At the self-service bar a thin, turkey-necked woman wearing paste jewelry was intently mixing a black Russian. "Got to be exceedingly careful with these," she said to Ashland, eyes still on the mixture. "Too much vodka craps them up."

Ashland nodded. "The host arrived?" *I'll know him, I'm sure.*

"Due later—or sooner. Sooner—or later. You know, I once spilled three black Russians on the same man over a thirty-day period. First on the man's sleeve, then on his back, then on his lap. Each time his suit was a sticky, gummy mess. My psychiatrist told me that I did it unconsciously, because of a neurotic hatred of this particular man. He looked like my father."

"The psychiatrist?"

"No, the man I spilled the Russians on." She held

up the tall drink, sipped at it. "Ahhh . . . still too weak."

Ashland probed the room for a face he knew, but these people were all strangers.

He turned to find the turkey-necked woman staring at him. "Nice apartment," he said mechanically.

"Stinks. I detest pseudo-Chinese decor in Manhattan brown-stones." She moved off, not looking back at Ashland.

He mixed himself a straight Scotch, running his gaze around the apartment. The place *was* pretty wild: ivory tables with serpent legs; tall, figured screens with chain-mail warriors cavorting across them; heavy brocade drapes in stitched silver; lamps with jewel-eyed dragons looped at the base. And, at the far end of the room, an immense bronze gong suspended between a pair of demon-faced swordsmen. Ashland studied the gong. A thing to wake the dead, he thought. Great for hangovers in the morning.

"Just get here?" a girl asked him. She was red-haired, full-breasted, in her late twenties. Attractive. Damned attractive. Ashland smiled warmly at her.

"That's right," he said, "I just arrived." He tasted the Scotch; it was flat, watery. "Whose place is this?"

The girl peered at him above her cocktail glass. "Don't you know who invited you?"

Ashland was embarrassed. "Frankly, no. That's why I—"

"My name's Viv. For Vivian. I drink. What do you do? Besides drink?"

"I produce. I'm in television."

"Well, I'm in a dancing mood. Shall we?"

"Nobody's dancing," protested Ashland. "We'd look—foolish."

The jazz suddenly seemed louder. Overhead speakers were sending out a thudding drum solo behind muted strings. The girl's body rippled to the sounds.

"Never be afraid to do anything foolish," she told him. "That's the secret of survival." Her fingers beckoned him. "C'mon . . ."

"No, really—not right now. Maybe later."

"Then I'll dance alone."

She spun into the crowd, her long red dress whirling. The other partygoers ignored her. Ashland emptied the watery Scotch and fixed himself another. He loosened his tie, popping the collar button. *Damn!*

"I train worms."

Ashland turned to a florid-faced little man with bulging, feverish eyes. "I heard you say you were in TV," the little man said. "Ever use any trained worms on your show?"

"No . . . no, I haven't."

"I breed 'em, train 'em. I teach a worm to run a maze. Then I grind him up and feed him to a dumb, untrained worm. Know what happens? The dumb worm can run the maze! But only for twenty-four hours. Then he forgets—unless I keep him on a trained-worm diet. I defy you to tell me that isn't fascinating!"

"It is, indeed." Ashland nodded and moved away from the bar. The feverish little man smiled after him, toasting his departure with a raised glass. Ashland found himself sweating.

Who was his host? Who had invited him? He knew most of the Village crowd, but had spotted none of them here . . .

A dark, doll-like girl asked him for a light. He fumbled out some matches.

"Thanks," she said, exhaling blue smoke into blue smoke. "Saw that worm guy talking to you. What a lousy bore he is! My ex-husband had a pet snake named Baby and he fed it worms. That's all they're good for, unless you fish. Do you fish?"

"I've done some fishing up in Canada."

"My ex-husband hated all sports. Except the indoor variety." She giggled. "Did you hear the one about the indoor hen and the outdoor rooster?"

"Look, miss—"

"Talia. But you can call me Jenny. Get it?" She doubled over, laughing hysterically, then swayed, dropping her cigarette. "Ooops! I'm sick. I better go lie down. My tum-tum feels awful."

She staggered from the party as Ashland crushed out her smoldering cigarette with the heel of his shoe. *Stupid bitch!*

A sharp handclap startled him. In the middle of the room, a tall man in a green satin dinner jacket was demanding his attention. He clapped again. "You," he shouted to Ashland. "Come here."

Ashland walked forward. The tall man asked him to remove his wristwatch. "I'll read your past from it," the man said. "I'm psychic. I'll tell you about yourself."

Reluctantly, Ashland removed his watch, handed it over. He didn't find any of this amusing. The party was annoying him, irritating him.

"I thank you most kindly, sir!" said the tall man, with elaborate stage courtesy. He placed the gold watch against his forehead and closed his eyes, breathing deeply. The crowd noise did not slacken; no one seemed to be paying any attention to the psychic.

"Ah. Your name is David. David Ashland. You are successful, a man of big business . . . a producer . . . and a bachelor. You are twenty-eight . . . young for a successful producer. One has to be something of a bastard to climb that fast. What about that, Mr. Ashland, *are* you something of a bastard?"

Ashland flushed angrily.

"You like women," continued the tall man. "A lot. And you like to drink. A lot. Your doctor told you—"

"I don't have to listen to this," Ashland said tightly, reaching for his watch. The man in green satin handed it over, grinned amiably, and melted back into the shifting crowd.

I ought to get the hell out of here, Ashland told himself. Yet curiosity held him. When the host arrived, Ashland would piece this evening together; he'd know why he was here, at this particular party. He moved to a couch near the closed patio doors and sat down. He'd wait.

A soft-faced man sat down next to him. The man looked pained. "I shouldn't smoke these," he said, holding up a long cigar. "Do you smoke cigars?"

"No."

"I'm a salesman. Dover Insurance. Like the White Cliffs of, ya know. I've studied the problems involved in smoking. Can't quit, though. When I do, the nerves shrivel up, stomach goes sour. I worry a lot—but we all worry, don't we? I mean, my mother used to worry about the earth slowing down. She read somewhere that between 1680 and 1690 the earth lost twenty-seven hundredths of a second. She said that meant something."

Ashland sighed inwardly. What is it about cocktail parties that causes people you've never met to unleash their troubles?

"You meet a lotta fruitcakes in my dodge," said the pained-looking insurance salesman. "I sold a policy once to a guy who lived in the woodwork. Had a ratty little walk-up in the Bronx with a foldaway bed. Kind you push into the wall. He'd *stay* there—I mean, inside the wall—most of the time. His room-mate would invite some friends in and if they made too much noise the guy inside the wall would pop out with his Thompson. BAM! The bed would come down and there he was with a Thompson subma-chine gun aimed at everybody. Real fruitcake."

"I knew a fellow who was *twice* that crazy."

Ashland looked up into a long, cadaverous face. The nose had been broken and improperly reset; it canted noticeably to the left. He folded his long, sharp-boned frame onto the couch next to Ashland. "This fellow believed in falling grandmothers," he declared. "Lived in upper Michigan. 'Watch out for falling grandmothers,' he used to warn me. 'They come down pretty heavy in this area. Most of 'em carry umbrellas and big packages and they come flapping down out of the sky by the thousands!' This

Michigan fellow swore he saw one hit a postman. 'An awful thing to watch,' he told me. 'Knocked the poor soul flat. Crushed his skull like an egg.' I recall he shuddered just telling me about it."

"Fruitcake," said the salesman. "Like the guy I once knew who wrote on all his walls and ceilings. A creative writer, he called himself. Said he couldn't write on paper, had to use a wall. Paper was too flimsy for him. He'd scrawl these long novels of his, a chapter in every room, with a big black crayon. Words all over the place. He'd fill up the house, then rent another one for his next book. I never read any of his houses, so I don't know if he was any good."

"Excuse me, gentlemen," said Ashland. "I need a fresh drink."

He hurriedly mixed another Scotch at the bar. Around him, the party rolled on inexorably, without any visible core. What time was it, anyway? His watch had stopped.

"Do you happen to know what time it is?" he asked a long-haired Oriental girl who was standing near the bar.

"I've no idea," she said. "None at all." The girl fixed him with her eyes. "I've been watching you, and you seem horribly *alone*. Aren't you?"

"Aren't I what?"

"Horribly alone?"

"I'm not with anyone, if that's what you mean."

The girl withdrew a jeweled holder from her bag and fitted a cigarette in place. Ashland lit it for her.

"I haven't been really alone since I was in Milwaukee," she told him. "I was about—God!—fifteen or something, and this creep wanted me to move in with him. My parents were both dead by then, so I was all alone."

"What did you do?"

"Moved in with the creep. What else? I couldn't make the being-alone scene. Later on, I killed him."

"You what?"

"Cut his throat." She smiled delicately. "In self-defense, of course. He got mean on the bottle one Friday night and tried to knife me. I had witnesses."

Ashland took a long draw on his Scotch. A scowling fellow in shirt sleeves grabbed the girl's elbow and steered her roughly away.

"I used to know a girl who looked like that," said a voice to Ashland's right. The speaker was curly-haired, clean-featured, in his late thirties. "Greek belly dancer with a Jersey accent. Dark, like her, and kind of mysterious. She used to quote that line of Hemingway's to Scott Fitzgerald—you know the one."

"Afraid not."

"One that goes, 'We're all bitched from the start.' Bitter. A bitter line."

He put out his hand. Ashland shook it.

"I'm Travers. I used to save America's ass every week on CBS."

"Beg pardon?"

"Terry Travers. The old *Triple Trouble for Terry* series on channel nine. Back in the late fifties. Had to step on a lotta toes to get that series."

"I think I recall the show. It was—"

"Dung. That's what it was. Cow dung. Horse dung. The *worst*. Terry Travers is not my real name, natch. Real one's Abe Hockstatter. Can you imagine a guy named Abe Hockstatter saving America's ass every week on CBS?"

"You've got me there."

Hockstatter pulled a brown wallet from his coat, flipped it open. "There I am with one of my other rugs on," he said, jabbing at a photo. "Been stone bald since high school. Baldies don't make it in showbiz, so I have my rugs. Go ahead, tug at me."

Ashland blinked. The man inclined his head. "*Pull* at it. Go on—as a favor to me!"

Ashland tugged at the fringe of Abe Hockstatter's curly hairpiece.

"Tight, huh? Really *snug*. Stays on the old dome."

"Indeed it does."

"They cost a fortune. I've got a wind-blown one for outdoor scenes. A stiff wind'll lift a cheap one right off your scalp. Then I got a crew cut and a Western job with long sideburns. All kinds. Ten, twelve . . . all first-class."

"I'm certain I have seen you," said Ashland. "I just don't—"

"S'awright. Believe me. Lotta people don't know me since I quit the *Terry* thing. I booze like crazy now. You an' me, we're among the nation's six million alcoholics."

Ashland glared at the actor. "Where do you get off linking me with—"

"Cool it, cool it. So I spoke a little out of turn. Don't be so touchy, chum."

"To hell with you!" snapped Ashland.

The bald man with curly hair shrugged and drifted into the crowd.

Ashland took another long pull at his Scotch. All these neurotic conversations . . . He felt exhausted, wrung dry, and the Scotch was lousy. No kick to it. The skin along the back of his neck felt tight, hot. A headache was coming on; he could always tell.

A slim-figured, frosted blonde in black sequins sidled up to him. She exuded an aura of matrimonial wars fought and lost. Her orange lipstick was smeared, her cheeks alcohol-flushed behind flaking pancake make-up. "I have a theory about sleep," she said. "Would you like to hear it?"

Ashland did not reply.

"My theory is that the world goes insane every night. When we sleep, our subconscious takes charge and we become victims to whatever it conjures up. Our conscious mind is totally blanked out. We lie there, helpless, while our subconscious flings us about. We fall off high buildings, or have to fight a giant ape, or we get buried in quicksand . . . We have absolutely no control. The mind whirls madly in the skull. Isn't that an unsettling thing to consider?"

"Listen," said Ashland. "Where's the host?"

"He'll get here."

Ashland put down his glass and turned away from her. A mounting wave of depression swept him toward the door. The room seemed to be solid with bodies, all talking, drinking, gesturing in the milk-thick smoke haze.

"Potatoes have eyes," said a voice to his left. "I really *believe* that." The remark was punctuated by an ugly, frog-croaking laugh.

"Today is tomorrow's yesterday," someone else said.

A hot swarm of sound:

"You can't get prints off human skin."

"In China, the laborers make sixty-five dollars a year. How the hell can you live on sixty-five dollars a year?"

"So he took out his Luger and blew her head off."

"I knew a policewoman who loved to scrub down whores."

"Did you ever try to live with eight kids, two dogs, a three-legged cat and twelve goldfish?"

"Like I told him, those X-rays destroyed his white cells."

"They found her in the tub. Strangled with a coat hanger."

"What I had, exactly, was a grade-two epidermoid carcinoma at the base of a seborrheic keratosis."

Ashland experienced a sudden, raw compulsion: somehow he had to stop these voices!

The Chinese gong flared gold at the corner of his eye. He pushed his way over to it, shouldering the partygoers aside. He would strike it—and the booming noise would stun the crowd; they'd have to stop their incessant, maddening chatter.

Ashland drew back his right fist, then drove it into the circle of bronze. He felt the impact, and the gong shuddered under his blow.

But there was no sound from it!

The conversation went on.

Ashland smashed his way back across the apartment.

"You can't stop the party," said the affable fat man at the door.

"I'm leaving!"

"So go ahead," grinned the fat man. "Leave."

Ashland clawed open the door and plunged into the hall, stumbling, almost falling. He reached the elevator, jabbed at the DOWN button.

Waiting, he found it impossible to swallow; his throat was dry. He could feel his heart hammering against the wall of his chest. His head ached.

The elevator arrived, opened. He stepped inside. The doors closed smoothly and the cage began its slow, automatic descent.

Abruptly, it stopped.

The doors parted to admit a solemn-looking man in a dark blue suit.

Ashland gasped. "Freddie!"

The solemn face broke into a wide smile. "Dave! It's great to see you! Been a long time."

"But—you can't be Fred Baker!"

"Why? Have I changed so much?"

"No, no, you look—exactly the same. But that car crash in Albany. I thought you were . . ." Ashland hesitated, left the word unspoken. He was pale, frightened. Very frightened. "Look, I'm—I'm late. Got somebody waiting for me at my place. Have to rush . . ." He reached forward to push the LOBBY button.

There was none.

The lowest button read FLOOR 2.

"We use this elevator to get from one party to another," Freddie Baker said quietly, as the cage surged into motion. "That's all it's good for. You get so you need a change. They're all alike, though—the parties. But you learn to adjust, in time."

Ashland stared at his departed friend. The elevator stopped.

"Step out," said Freddie. "I'll introduce you around. You'll catch on, get used to things. No sex here. And the booze is watered. Can't get stoned. That's the dirty end of the stick."

Baker took Ashland's arm, propelled him gently forward.

Around him, pressing in, David Ashland could hear familiar sounds: nervous laughter, ice against glass, muted jazz—and the ceaseless hum of cocktail voices.

Freddie thumbed a buzzer. A door opened.

The smiling fat man said, "C'mon in, fellas. Join the party."

When I was a boy I bristled with energy. I could be loud and wildly enthusiastic. I had an uncle, on my mother's side, whose nerves had been shattered in the First Great War. When he'd come to visit us, my loud voice and gyrating antics would drive him up the wall. He'd say, "Hush, boy! Can't you just be quiet?" And I'd slink off sulking, to my room. Got so I came to resent his visits, much to my mother's distress.

Thus, my fictional "Uncle Gus" was born in the pages of this story. I combined a much darker version of my real uncle with a sadist who enjoys frightening children. Then I added one of my cats—and I had "Something Nasty."

It was selected as the lead story in the often-reprinted anthology, Gallery of Horror.

It is horrible.

And nasty.

Something Nasty

(Written: April 1982)

"Have you had your shower yet, Janey?"

Her mother's voice from below stairs, drifting smokily up to her, barely audible where she lay in her bed.

Louder now; insistent. "Janey! Will you *answer* me!"

She got up, cat-stretched, walked into the hall, to the landing, where her mother could hear her. "I've been reading."

"But I *told* you that Uncle Gus was coming over this afternoon."

"I hate him," said Janey softly.

"You're muttering. I can't understand you." Frustration. Anger and frustration. "Come down here at once."

When Janey reached the bottom of the stairs her mother's image was rippled. The little girl blinked rapidly, trying to clear her watering eyes.

Janey's mother stood tall and ample-fleshed and fresh-smelling above her in a satiny summer dress.

Mommy always looks nice when Uncle Gus is coming.

"Why are you crying?" Anger had given way to concern.

"Because," said Janey.

"Because why?"

"Because I don't want to talk to Uncle Gus."

"But he *adores* you! He comes over especially to see you."

"No, he doesn't," said Janey, scrubbing at her cheek with a small fist. "He doesn't adore me and he doesn't come specially to see me. He comes to get money from Daddy."

Her mother was shocked. "That's a terrible thing to say!"

"But it's true. *Isn't* it true?"

"Your Uncle Gus was hurt in the war. He can't hold down an ordinary job. We just do what we can to help him."

"He never liked me," said Janey. "He says I make too much noise. And he never lets me play with Whiskers when he's here."

"That's because cats bother him. He's not used to them. He doesn't like furry things." Her mother touched at Janey's hair. Soft gold. "Remember that mouse you got last Christmas, how nervous it made him . . . Remember?"

"Pete was smart," said Janey. "He didn't like Uncle Gus, same as me."

"Mice neither like nor dislike people," Janey's mother told her. "They're not intelligent enough for that."

Janey shook her head stubbornly. "Pete was *very* intelligent. He could find cheese anywhere in my room, no matter where I hid it."

"That has to do with a basic sense of smell, not intelligence," her mother said. "But we're wasting time here, Janey. You run upstairs, take your shower and then put on your pretty new dress. The one with red polka dots."

"They're strawberries. It has little red strawberries on it."

"Fine. Now just do as I say. Gus will be here soon and I want my brother to be *proud* of his niece."

Blond head down, her small heels dragging at the top of each step, Janey went back upstairs.

"I'm not going to report this to your father." Janey's mother was saying, her voice dimming as the little girl continued upward. "I'll just tell him you over-slept."

"I don't care what you tell Daddy," murmured Janey. The words were smothered in hallway distance as she moved toward her room.

Daddy would believe anything Mommy told him. He always did. Sometimes it was true, about over-sleeping. It was hard to wake up from her afternoon nap. *Because I put off going to sleep. Because I hate it.* Along with eating broccoli, and taking colored vitamin pills in little animal shapes and seeing the dentist and going on roller coasters.

Uncle Gus had taken her on a high, scary roller coaster ride last summer at the park, and it had made her vomit. He liked to upset her, frighten her. Mommy didn't know about all the times Uncle Gus said scary things to her, or played mean tricks on her, or took her places she didn't want to go.

Mommy would leave her with him while she went shopping, and Janey absolutely *hated* being there in his dark old house. He knew the dark frightened her. He'd sit there in front of her with all the lights out, telling spooky stories, with sick, awful things in them, his voice oily and horrible. She'd get so scared, listening to him, that sometimes she'd cry.

And that made him smile.

"Gus. Always so *good* to see you!"

"Hi, Sis."

"C'mon inside. Jim's puttering around out back somewhere. I've fixed us a nice lunch. Sliced turkey. And I made some cornbread."

"So where's my favorite niece?"

"Janey's due down here any second. She'll be wearing her new dress—just for you."

"Well, now, isn't that nice."

She was watching from the top of the stairs, lying flat on her stomach so she wouldn't be seen. It made her sick, watching Mommy hug Uncle Gus that way, each time he came over, as if it had been *years* between visits. Why couldn't Mommy see how mean Uncle Gus was? All of her friends in class saw he was a bad person the first day he took her to school. Kids can tell right away about a person. Like that mean ole Mr. Kruger in geography, who made Janey stay after class when she forgot to do her homework. All the kids knew that Mr. Kruger was *awful*. Why does it take grownups so long to know things?

Janey slid backwards into the hall shadows. Stood up. Time to go downstairs. In her playclothes. Probably meant she'd get a spanking after Uncle Gus left, but it would be worth it not to have to put on her new dress for him. Spankings don't hurt *too* much. Worth it.

"Well, *here's* my little princess!" Uncle Gus was lifting her hard into the air, to make her dizzy. He knew how much she hated being swung around in the air. He set her down with a thump. Looked at her with his big cruel eyes. "And where's that pretty new dress your Mommy told me about?"

"It got torn," Janey said, staring at the carpet. "I can't wear it today."

Her mother was angry again. "That is *not* true, young lady, and you know it! I ironed that dress this morning and it is perfect." She pointed upward. "You march right back upstairs to your room and put on that dress!"

"No, Maggie." Gus shook his head. "Let the child stay as she is. She looks fine. Let's just have lunch." He prodded Janey in the stomach. "Bet that little tummy of yours is starved for some turkey."

And Uncle Gus pretended to laugh. Janey was never fooled; she knew real laughs from pretend laughs. But Mommy and Daddy never seemed to know the difference.

Janey's mother sighed and smiled at Gus. "All right, I'll let it go this time—but I really think you spoil her."

"Nonsense. Janey and I understand each other." He stared down at her. "Don't we, sweetie?"

*   *   *

Lunch was no fun. Janey couldn't finish her mashed potatoes, and she'd just nibbled at her turkey. She could never enjoy eating with her uncle there. As usual, her father barely noticed she was at the table. *He* didn't care if she wore her new dress or not. Mommy took care of her and Daddy took care of business, whatever that was. Janey could never figure out what he did, but he left every day for some office she'd never seen and he made enough money there so that he always had some to give to Uncle Gus when Mommy asked him for a check.

Today was Sunday so Daddy was home with his big newspaper to read and the car to wax and the grass to trim. He did the same things every Sunday.

Does Daddy love me? I know that Mommy does, even though she spanks me sometimes. But she always hugs me after. Daddy never hugs me. He buys me ice cream, and he takes me to the movies on Saturday afternoon, but I don't think he loves me.

Which is why she could never tell him the truth about Uncle Gus. He'd never listen.

And Mommy just didn't understand.

After lunch, Uncle Gus grabbed Janey firmly by the hand and took her into the back yard. Then he sat her down next to him on the big wooden swing.

"I'll bet your new dress is *ugly*," he said in a cold voice.

"Is not. It's pretty!"

Her discomfort pleased him. He leaned over, close to her right ear. "Want to know a secret?"

Janey shook her head. "I want to go back with Mommy. I don't like being out here."

She started away, but he grabbed her, pulling her roughly back onto the swing. "You *listen* to me when I talk to you." His eyes glittered. "I'm going to tell you a secret. About yourself."

"Then tell me."

He grinned. "You've got something inside."

"What's that mean?"

"It means there's something deep down inside your rotten little belly. And it's *alive.*"

"Huh?" She blinked, beginning to get scared.

"A creature. That lives off what you eat and breathes the air you breathe and can see out of your eyes." He pulled her face close to his. "Open your mouth, Janey, so I can look in and see what's living down there!"

"No, I won't." She attempted to twist away, but he was too strong. "You're lying! You're just telling me an awful *lie!* You are!"

"Open wide." And he applied pressure to her jaw

with the fingers of his right hand. Her mouth opened. "Ah, that's better. Let's have a look . . ." He peered into her mouth. "Yes, *there*. I can see it now."

She drew back, eyes wide, really alarmed. "What's it like?"

"Nasty! Horrid. With very sharp teeth. A *rat,* I'd say. Or something *like* a rat. Long and gray and plump."

"I don't have it! I *don't!*"

"Oh, but you do, Janey." His voice was oily. "I saw its red eyes shining and its long snaky tail. It's down there all right. Something nasty."

And he laughed. Real, this time. No pretend laugh. Uncle Gus was having himself some fun.

Janey knew he was just trying to scare her again— but she wasn't absolutely one hundred percent sure about the thing inside. Maybe he *had* seen something.

"Do . . . any other people have . . . creatures . . . living in them?"

"Depends," said Uncle Gus. "Bad things live inside bad people. Nice little girls don't have them."

"I'm nice!"

"Well now, that's a matter of opinion, isn't it?" His voice was soft and unpleasant. "If you were *nice,* you wouldn't have something nasty living inside."

"I don't believe you," said Janey, breathing fast. "How could it be real?"

"Things are real when people believe in them." He lit a long black cigarette, drew in the smoke, exhaled it slowly. "Have you ever heard of voodoo, Janey?"

She shook her head.

"The way it works is—this witch doctor puts a curse on someone by making a doll and sticking a needle into the doll's heart. Then he leaves the doll at the house of the man he's cursed. When the man sees it he becomes very frightened. He makes the curse real by *believing* in it."

"And then what happens?"

"His heart stops and he dies."

Janey felt her own heart beating very rapidly.

"You're afraid, aren't you, Janey?"

"Maybe . . . a little."

"You're afraid, all right." He chuckled. "And you should be—with a thing like that inside you!"

"You're a very bad and wicked man!" she told him, tears misting her eyes.

And she ran swiftly back to the house.

That night, in her room, Janey sat rigid in bed, hugging Whiskers. He liked to come in late after dark and curl up on the coverlet just under her feet and snooze there until dawn. He was an easy-going, gray-and-black housecat who never complained about anything and always delivered a small "meep" of contentment whenever Janey picked him up for some stroking. Then he would begin to purr.

Tonight Whiskers was not purring. He sensed the harsh vibrations in the room, sensed how upset Janey was. He quivered uneasily in her arms.

"Uncle Gus lied to me, didn't he, Whiskers?" The little girl's voice was strained, uncertain. "See . . ." She hugged the cat closer. "Nothing's down there, huh?"

And she yawned her mouth wide to show her friend that no rat-thing lived there. If one did, ole Whiskers would be sticking a paw inside to get it. But the cat didn't react. Just blinked slitted green eyes at her.

"I knew it," Janey said, vastly relieved. "If I just don't believe it's in there, then it *isn't*."

She slowly relaxed her tensed body muscles—and Whiskers, sensing a change, began to purr—a tiny, soothing motorized sound in the night.

Everything was all right now. No red-eyed creature existed in her tummy. Suddenly she felt exhausted. It was late, and she had school tomorrow.

Janey slid down under the covers and closed her eyes, releasing Whiskers, who padded to his usual spot on the bed.

She had a lot to tell her friends.

* * *

It was Thursday, a day Janey usually hated. Every other Thursday her mother went shopping and left her to have lunch with Uncle Gus in his big spooky house with the shutters closed tight against the sun and shadows filling every hallway.

But *this* Thursday would be all different, so Janey didn't mind when her mother drove off and left her alone with her uncle. *This* time, she told herself, she wouldn't be afraid. A giggle.

She might even have fun!

When Uncle Gus put Janey's soup plate in front of her he asked her how she was feeling.

"Fine," said Janey quietly, eyes down.

"Then you'll be able to appreciate the soup." He smiled, trying to look pleasant. "It's a special recipe. Try it."

She spooned some into her mouth.

"How does it taste?"

"Kinda sour."

Gus shook his head, trying some for himself. "Ummm . . . delicious." He paused. "Know what's in it?"

She shook her head.

He grinned, leaning toward her across the table. "It's owl-eye soup. Made from the dead eyes of an owl. All mashed up fresh, just for you."

She looked at him steadily. "You want me to upchuck, don't you, Uncle Gus?"

"My goodness no, Janey." There was oiled delight in his voice. "I just thought you'd like to know what you swallowed."

Janey pushed her plate away. "I'm not going to be sick because I don't believe you. And when you don't believe in something then it's not real."

Gus scowled at her, finishing his soup.

Janey knew he planned to tell her another awful spook story after lunch, but she wasn't upset about that. Because.

Because there wouldn't *be* any after lunch for Uncle Gus.

It was time for her surprise.

"I got something to tell you, Uncle Gus."

"So tell me." His voice was sharp and ugly.

"All my friends at school know about the thing inside. We talked about it a lot and now we all believe in it. It has red eyes and it's furry and it smells bad. And it's got lots of very sharp teeth."

"You *bet* it has," Gus said, brightening at her words. "And it's always hungry."

"But guess what," said Janey. "Surprise! It's not

inside me, Uncle Gus . . . it's inside *you!*"

He glared at her. "That's not funny, you little bitch. Don't try to turn this around and pretend that—"

He stopped in mid-sentence, spoon clattering to the floor as he stood up abruptly. His face was flushed. He made strangling sounds.

"It wants out," said Janey.

Gus doubled over the table, hands clawing at his stomach. "Call . . . call a . . . doctor!" he gasped.

"A doctor won't help," said Janey in satisfaction. "Nothing can stop it now."

Janey followed him calmly, munching on an apple. She watched him stagger and fall in the doorway, rolling over on his back, eyes wild with panic.

She stood over him, looking down at her uncle's stomach under the white shirt.

Something *bulged* there.

Gus screamed.

Late that night, alone in her room, Janey held Whiskers tight against her chest and whispered into her pet's quivering ear. "Mommy's been crying," she told the cat. "She's real upset about what happened to Uncle Gus. Are *you* upset, Whiskers?"

The cat yawned, revealing sharp white teeth.

"I didn't think so. That's because you didn't like Uncle Gus any more than me, did you?"

She hugged him. "Wanta hear a *secret,* Whiskers?"

The cat blinked lazily at her, beginning to purr.

"You know that mean ole Mr. Kruger at school . . . Well, guess what?" She smiled. "Me an' the other kids are gonna talk to him tomorrow about something he's got inside him." Janey shuddered deliciously. "Something nasty!"

And she giggled.

I'm an ardent fan of Joyce Carol Oates. Her novels are fine, but as a short story writer, she's unsurpassed in her time. I have all twenty-one volumes of her short fiction, more than 400 stories, and each one is first rate. Marvelous, really.

She and I have shared the pages of many different anthologies, and I was her editor on Urban Horrors, *which I compiled for Dark Harvest in 1990. (I used her superb story, "Have You Ever Slipped on Red Blood?") However, the enthusiasm seems to be one-sided, since I have written her several times without reply. Her lack of response (which bothered me at first) turned out to be a blessing in disguise. It generated the plot of this story, which never would have been written (or never selected, as it was, for* The Year's Finest Crime and Mystery Stories) *if Ms. Oates had replied to my letters.*

So, in retrospect, I'm grateful for her silence. It inspired me to write "An Act of Violence."

An Act of Violence

(Written: July 1994)

June 20, 1994

To Janice Coral Olinger,

Having read every word you've written, I feel I know you well enough to address you as "Dearest Janice," but of course this would not be socially appropriate. I'm a fellow writer who stands in your very tall shadow—but (to my honor and delight) we *have* shared many an anthology contents page together. Thus far, nine of my humble tales have been selected for anthologies in which your fine work has appeared. But I doubt that you read my contributions or even know I exist, since you probably have no time for the work of obscure writers such as myself. (I know how busy you are: *Conversations with Janice Coral Olinger* lists 98 books in a 30-year career span, and at least 25 of these are major novels. Amazing output!) But, hey, you don't have to know me because this letter will serve to introduce me to you.

My reason for writing at this time is to extend my sincere and heartfelt condolences on the very recent death of your husband, Theodore N. Olinger. I know that you and "Ted" were both very devoted to one another and that his sad passing (isn't cancer a bitch!) was a severe blow to you emotionally. Ted (if I may so refer to him) was a wonderful poet and an astute critic, and I realize that you both shared an intellectual and creative seedground as well as an abiding physical attraction. Your sex life with Ted is naturally none of my business, but a strong sexual bond was evident from your mutual behavior in public. The way you held hands and *touched* each other at that P.E.N. awards dinner made this very clear to me. (Yeah, I was there.)

Anyhow, please accept my deepest sympathy at this immense and tragic loss in your life. I trust that once you have weathered your period of mourning you will again return to the role you were born for: that of a supreme artist of the written word.

> With profound respect and good wishes,
> Alex Edward

P.S. My address is on the envelope in case you wish to reply—and I *do* hope you will wish to do so.

July 30, 1994

Dear Janice Coral Olinger,

Well, the Great Wheel of Time grinds ever onward and I see that more than a full month has gone by without a reply from you to my missive of 20 June. That's fine, really it is. I had, of course, hoped for a reply, but I am certainly not surprised that I failed to receive one. In view of your personal family loss, this is quite understandable, and I bear you no malice. I'm sure your mail has been piling up from many other devoted readers and that you simply have not been up to answering it. (Bet you get a *ton* of letters!)

However, now that you have been granted suitable time to pull yourself together, I *would* ask that you be kind enough to honor me with a personal reply.

I'm excited about your latest novel, WHOSE BLOOD IS IT, ANYHOW? (what a bold and splendid title!) which I have had the pleasure of reading as they say "cover to cover." (In fact, I was up most of last night lost in those final, dynamic chapters!) May I say that I am truly awestruck at the passion and artistry evident on every page of this epic work. Your short stories are marvelous watercolors, but your novels are many-layered oil paintings. (At least, that's how I think of them.) And your dialogue . . . wow! No one in America today handles dialogue with your deft, incisive touch. Just one example (of oh, so many!): when your dying politician, Arthur (invoking shades of Camelot, right?) bids his final farewell to Morgana (a clever reversal of character names in terms of darkness and light), their exchange left me literally breathless. The entire scene was illuminated by your brilliant dialogue. Viva! Bravissimo!

I could go on for pages about BLOOD, but I'll let the critics rave for me—as they most certainly will. Let me just say how much your work has inspired my own, how your fire and passion have transformed my life. I am a better man, a better human being, because of Janice Coral Olinger. Salud!

By the way, to prove whereof I speak, I have every one of your books in mint first editions, with each dust jacket carefully protected by a clear plastic cover.

As a writer, you are numero uno. No one else has your heart, your spirit, your expansive imagination. I stand in humble awe of your powers.

Enough. Write to me soon and let me know your reaction to this letter. I eagerly await your response.

With sincere admiration,
Alex Edward

August 25, 1994

Dear Janice Coral Olinger,

I'm frankly perplexed. All these weeks have gone by and I haven't heard a peep out of you. I know you received my letters since my return address was plain on each and I never got them back from the post office. Have you been ill? On a trip? Away on a lecture tour? What's the problem? All I have asked is that you take a few minutes to reply to someone who has shown his deep and sincere respect for your boundless creative gifts. Truly, I don't see why you can't write me a letter (however brief) acknowledging my existence. Why do you continue to ignore me in this disturbing fashion when it is obvious I so greatly admire you? (It seems that common courtesy alone would dictate a reply.) I repeat, what's the problem?

Last night I reread your short story, "The River Incident"—which rightfully earned the O. Henry prize in '82 (go, Janice!). And once again I was struck with your employment of raw violence within the context of a higher sense of morality. Your characters *transcend* death, even though they may themselves die or cause others to die. In "The River Incident," when Cara shoots her father on the river bank, her act is not an act of violence, but of release. (Obviously, this is what the O. Henry judges realized.) Knowing there is no hope for the old man's future, knowing that life has become a terrible burden on him, Cara sends a .45 slug into his brain, allowing him ultimate freedom and a release from the crippling cage of his body. (Which is exactly what the great lady poet Sylvia Plath accomplished with her suicide; I *know* you agree.) "Go, my father, go," she says, pressing the barrel against his temple and pulling the trigger. She is sending him on a wondrous journey. Thus, her act is one of great compassion.

I am curious. What was your motivation for this story? Did it come out of your own life—or did you hear about an incident like this when you were growing up in that house by the river in Maryland? (The story has a ring of stark truth which cannot be denied.) Or did it all flow from your incredible imagination? Please, write and let me know.

Devotedly yours,
Alex Edward

September 2, 1994

Dear (silent) Janice Coral Olinger,

Here we are into September and I've had *no* word of any kind from you. I am baffled (and, I must confess, somewhat hurt) by your continued silence and lack of human response. Why are you treating me in this manner? Why are my letters to you being ignored? Why am *I* being ignored? It is obvious from what I've written how much I admire you and your works. I have made this abundantly clear. Why, then, have you chosen to bypass me utterly, as if I don't exist? I simply do not understand why you cannot spare a few random minutes for me (no matter *how* busy you may be).

This is not like you, not in character with your

work. Your books, for all their overt violence, are extremely humanistic at their core, and I know you to be a gentle, caring person, a creature of warm compassion. (What was it Ted said of you in that *Newsweek* piece? . . . that you were "a vessel of tenderness.") One look into those round dark luminous eyes of yours clearly reveals your compassionate soul. Well, what about sending some of that compassion in my direction? I could *use* a little. All I'm asking of you is a simple note, after all. A few kind words, letting me know you appreciate my devotion as a dedicated reader. Is this too much to ask? I think not. Right now, with my letter before you, write and let me know you *care*.

Vaya con Dios!
Alex Edward

October 15, 1994

Janice Coral Olinger,

I find that I can no longer address you as "Dear." Your cold, unresponsive silence has rendered such a salutation impossible. I checked my files today and find that I first wrote you a letter (and a fine, warm one it was!) on 20 June—almost *four full months ago*! I followed up this initial missive with those of 30 July, 25 August, and 2 September, all without a *single word* back from you. There is no excuse for this kind of rudeness. You insult me with your stubborn refusal to respond to my letters. It is no longer possible for me to maintain positive feelings toward you. Your cruelty has also tainted your work, and this is most unfortunate. I now look at your shelved books and mourn the past. You have wounded me deeply. Additionally, you have made me look like a fool. I wrote to praise you and got nothing back. I'm becoming very angry at you, Ms. Olinger—or however the hell you like to be addressed. Just who do you think you are, some Goddess living up in the clouds? You live right here on good ole Mother Earth, just like I do. We both breathe, eat, and shit, like everybody else on this lousy planet. You're no Goddess, lady. You may know how to write novels and stories, but you sure don't know much about common courtesy.

And what do you say to this?

In frustration,
Alex Edward

December 10, 1994

Olinger bitch . . .

Again, you have chosen to callously ignore my letter of 15 October. You obviously don't give a flying fuck about me, or my opinions, or my words, or anything else having to do with Alex Edward. Normally,

I'm a real easygoing guy, patient, reasonable, quick to forgive and forget—but you've gone over the line. Your snotty silence is just too fucking much. I will *not* be treated this way. Not by you or by anybody. Let me state my position loud and clear: either I get a letter of apology from you within the next ten days or I'll be over to your house in Baltimore to give you a Christmas present you *won't* like. Remember what the witch said to Dorothy in that Oz film . . . "and your little dog, too!" Well, I'll also have a present for that witless little pansy poodle you lug around in your arms for all those dust jacket photos. I think you should know that what you are doing is directly promoting an act of violence. You are really one rude bitch and if I don't hear from you this time, I'm sure as hell going to pay you a personal visit.

Think I'm bluffing? Just blowing off steam? Think I won't act? Then think again, sister, because you are dealing with a guy who has your number. The way you mistreat people means you don't *deserve* to go on living.

It's like in that *Harper's* story of yours, "Dark Angel." Take my word, unless your apology is in my mailbox by 20 December I'm *your* Dark Angel come Christmas.

This is one letter you better not ignore.

Alex E.

PRESS ANNOUNCEMENT—FOR IMMEDIATE
RELEASE

On the morning of December 26, 1994, in the den of a private home at 6000 Roland Avenue, Baltimore, Maryland, the body of noted writer Janice Coral Olinger was discovered by neighbors. She had been shot once in the left temple and had died instantly. Her white poodle, "Snowball," was found lying beside her. The dog had also been shot to death.

Local police were called to the scene. Lieutenant Angus Campbell of Baltimore Homicide has issued this public statement:

"Several handwritten letters, dated from June into December of this year, were found on the desk of the deceased. They were all signed 'Alex Edward.'"

"Ms. Olinger's father, A. E. Coral, was for many years a prominent Baltimore banker, and was known to have a violent temper. Police records show that he had frequently been cited for physically abusive incidents involving his wife, Barbara, as well as Janice Coral (later Janice Coral Olinger), their daughter. Records indicate that Janice Coral left the family home as a teenager and apparently never saw her father again. His initials, A. E., stand for Alexander Edward, which correlate with the signatures on the letters.

"In the opinion of Dr. Thomas F. O'Rourke, a respected Baltimore psychiatrist, the emotionally shattering death of her husband, noted poet Theodore Olinger, caused a fracture in Janice Coral Olinger's personality. She took on a second, wholly separate identity based on the male persona of her violent father and, as 'Alex Edward,' wrote the series of deranged letters leading to the tragedy.

"Her death, by gunshot, was apparently self-inflicted. The police department theorizes that she first shot her pet, then put the weapon to her own head. Dr. O'Rourke explained it as an 'acting out of what her father might have done to her had she remained in the family home.' (The banker was later jailed for attempting to murder his wife, Barbara Coral, and is now serving a term in the Maryland state prison.)

"The death of Janice Coral Olinger is tragic and senseless, the product of what Dr. O'Rourke describes as 'a lingering and ultimately fatal childhood trauma.' Funeral arrangements are pending."

This one, happily enough, was chosen for Best of Cemetery Dance and resulted directly from a long-delayed reading of Dostoyevsky's Crime and Punishment. (I have all these classics sitting on shelves in my library, and suffer periodic guilt over the fact that I've read so few of them.)

All contemporary writers are affected by what other writers have written in the past. I know that a single reading of William Faulkner's The Sound and the Fury changed my creative life. He demonstrated just how far you can climb out on a literary limb without having it break under you. Faulkner gave me "permission" to be bolder, to take more creative chances and, thus, stretch my talent to its limit. Dostoyevsky did the same with Crime and Punishment. His spirit lives within the pages of this story.

Thanks, Fyodor. I owe you one.

Fyodor's Law

(Written: February 1994)

They were at nearly every street corner in Greater Los Angeles, standing or sitting cross-legged in their ragged, dirt-stiffened clothing, their faces stubble-bearded, eyes slack and defeated, clutching crude, hand-lettered cardboard signs:

HOMELESS!
HUNGRY!
WILL WORK FOR FOOD
PLEASE HELP???
GOD BLESS YOU!!!

Today he would help one of them as he had helped many others. He took no credit for this; it was simply his way, his personal contribution. He felt a real sense of pity for them. Society's outcasts. The dispossessed. The lost ones.

Dostoyevsky's children.

The one he selected was standing on the south corner at Topanga Canyon and Ventura, in front of a hardware store. He was very tall, well over six feet, and of indeterminate age. Under his ragged hat and twist of beard he could be thirty, or forty, or even fifty. They *all* had old faces; they'd lived too long on the dark side, seen too much, experienced too many horrors. The pain of existence etched their skin.

He pulled the long blue Cadillac to a whispered stop at the curb and ran down the passenger window, beckoning to the tall man. "Over here," he called, waving. The sun flashed rainbow colors from the diamond ring on his left hand.

The ragged figure approached the car.

"Get in . . . I have work for you." The driver's name was Conover—James Edward Stanton Conover—and he lived alone in a hillside home on the other side of the Santa Monica Mountains in Bel Air. He was wealthy by inheritance, had no need for work, and although he considered himself a professional artist, had never attempted to sell any of his creations. Every other year he traded in his Cadillac for the latest model. He always drove Cadillacs; his family had never driven anything else. His great-grandfather, in fact, had owned the first Cadillac in Los Angeles.

"You gonna help me, huh, mister?" The bearded man was leaning down to peer inside the car at James Conover.

"Right, I'll help you." Conover opened the passenger door. "Please, get in. We'll drive to my place. I have some work for you."

"I can fix anything," declared the tall man, tossing his hat and grimed knapsack into the seat behind him. "Do your plumbing. Repair your roof. Tile your patio. Weed your garden. Paint or plaster. You name her, mister, and I can do her."

Conover smiled at the man as he put the blue Cadillac into drive, rejoining the eastbound traffic stream along Ventura Boulevard. "You're a regular Jack of all trades," he said.

"*That's* my name," said the ragged man. "Jack. Jack Wilbur."

"How did you acquire all these remarkable skills, Mr. Wilbur?"

"From my Pap," replied Jack Wilbur. "We come here from Tennessee, me an' my Pap, after Ma took sick an' died. My brother an' little sis, they stayed on in Willicut, but we come out here to the Coast, the two of us." He stared at Conover. "Ever hear of Willicut?"

"Can't say that I have."

"It's fifty miles north of Chattanooga. Little bitty runt of a town, but full of good folks. My brother, he owns a feed store back in Willicut. That's how come he stayed there."

"Where's your father now?"

"Pap's in jail," said Jack Wilbur. "He done a violent act, an' they arrested him."

"What kind of violent act?"

"Well, ole Pap, he drinks some. We was in this pool hall in North Hollywood, an' Pap was takin' on whiskey. He gets mean when he drinks, an' pretty soon he's into a bustup with a trucker over one of the pool hall ladies. Killed him, Pap did. Just smashed his head right in."

"And you witnessed this?"

"Sure as hell did. But I couldn't stop what Pap done. All happened too fast. One minute the pair of 'em are yellin' over this blondie, an' the next ole Pap is layin' this pool stick alongside the fella's head. Split it open like you do a cantaloupe. It was a sight, I'll tellya. Blondie was screamin' like she was havin' a fit an' the police come an' hauled Pap off and now he's in jail."

"How did you end up on the street? It would seem that a man with your variegated skills could support himself."

"Well, I sure tried. But unless you work for some company it's tough findin' jobs that pay much. Since I lack me any kinda formal schoolin', no company will take me on. Believe me, mister, I'm no bum by nature. No siree, not Jack Wilbur. Back in Willicut I worked regular from when I was just a nipper, an' I had respect. Nobody called Jack Wilbur a bum in Willicut."

"After your father's incarceration, why didn't you return home—to be with your brother and sister?"

"Naw!" The bearded man shook his head. "I can't go back now. For one thing, I gotta earn enough money to show all them locals I amounted to somethin' worthwhile out here in California. Our family's always had a lotta pride, an' I can't go low-tailin' home like some kinda whipped hound. It's bad enough, what happened to Pap."

"I understand," nodded Conover. "I really do."

They were on the freeway, taking the connector to the southbound 405, headed for Bel Air. The sleek blue car purred along at sixty, smooth and steady.

"Real nice machine you got here," said Jack Wilbur. "I plan to buy me one a'these soon as I get back on my feet so to speak."

"You seem confident that it will happen."

"Betcha. Man like me, with all my talents, I'm fair bound to come out a winner. Just a matter of time. An' I'm only thirty, so I *got* me some time."

"I take it you've never been married."

"Nope—but I come real close once. There was this

sweet little thing over to Haines—that's near Willicut—an' she just about roped me for sure, but I slipped away clean. Lucky I got shut of her when I did. Hell's bells, marriage should be for when you're ready to settle down and raise a flock a'kids." He chuckled. "Me, I'm a natural born ramblin'. man. Been through sixteen states. That's another reason I don't want to go back to Willicut. It's what's on the other side of the hill that always takes my fancy."

"I admire your spirit," said Conover.

"What kinda work you got for me?"

"I live on a steep hillside," said Conover. "Lots of thick, fast-growing brush and trees up there. Dangerous in the fire season. I need this brush cut back from the house."

"I can do that easy," said the bearded man. He hesitated. "But I got no cuttin' tools. You got those?"

Conover nodded. "Everything you'll need is in the garage. Don't worry."

Jack Wilbur grinned. "Hell's bells, mister, that's one thing I *never* do—is worry. With me, things always have a way of workin' out fine."

And Conover repeated: "I admire your spirit."

James Conover's angular, flat-roofed, two-story house, at the top of Bel Air road, hovered at the edge of a heavily brushed canyon like some huge stone-

and-glass animal. Below the overhanging cast-steel deck the ground fell away in a steep drop that made Jack Wilbur dizzy.

"Geez!" he muttered, peering down. "Aren't you scared?"

"Of what?" asked Conover, standing beside him on the deck.

"Of this whole shebang ending up at the bottom of the canyon! I mean, a big quake could be murder."

"This structure is supported by steel construction beams sunk deep into granite, considerably below the surface soil. There's no need to fear earthquakes, let me assure you."

"Well, I'd say you got some guts, livin' in a place like this. Fine for an eagle maybe, or a buzzard."

Conover smiled thinly. "I happen to appreciate the view. On a clear day you can see forever."

Wilbur shrugged; it was apparent he didn't recognize the classic reference. "'Bout time for me to get crackin' on that job you mentioned."

"No rush," said Conover. "I spend a lot of hours alone up here and I could use some company. How about a drink before beginning your labors?"

Wilbur looked uncertain. "Pretty early in the day for booze," said the tall man. "I usually don't start till the sun's down."

"Then make an exception," urged Conover. "I have some excellent imported brandy. Aged to perfection." He saw Jack frown. "You *do* drink brandy?"

Again, Wilbur shrugged, uncertain. "Hard whiskey's more my style."

"All right, then, I have some Black Irish that should be suitable." He moved to the tinted glass door leading into the den and slid it back. "Please . . ." He waved Wilbur inside.

The den was richly paneled in carved oak with a fully stocked bar at the far end. Conover nodded toward a leather-topped stool as he moved behind the bar to fix their drinks.

Jack Wilbur scowled at his image in the bar mirror, rubbing a slow hand along his bearded chin. "Boy, I look kinda ragged. Need me a trim."

"Here you go, Jack," said Conover, placing a glass of Black Irish whiskey in front of Wilbur. He walked around the bar with his own drink, moving to a deep red-leather couch. "Let's make ourselves comfortable."

They settled into the couch and Conover, after a sip of whiskey, asked Wilbur if he had ever met any professional artists.

"You mean guys that do pictures?"

"In general, yes."

"Well, I never met none personal. Artists don't

show up much in Willicut, I guess. Pap told me once that when he was in Chicago, he shook hands with the comics guy who did *Dick Tracy*."

Conover smiled. "If you'll wait here," he said, "I have something to show you."

He walked out of the den and returned with a thick scrapbook handsomely bound in levant morocco. He placed the book, unopened, on the coffee table in front of Jack Wilbur. Then he resumed his seat on the couch, taking another sip of Black Irish.

"What's in there?" asked Wilbur. "Pictures of your family?"

"Not exactly," Conover replied. "But they are photos. Of my art."

"So *you're* an artist, huh?"

"Correct." Conover smiled. "But not in any conventional sense of the term."

"What does that mean?"

"It means I'm not a painter or a sketch artist. I do montages."

Wilbur looked confused. "Mon what? I never heard of 'em."

"A montage is made up of various separate components. The artist uses these components to achieve a particular design. Actual three-dimensional objects are often utilized in the overall work."

"You're way over my head," said Jack Wilbur.

"You'll understand exactly what I'm referring to when I show you the photos."

"Well, I'm not much for art an' that's a fact. Never been in no museum." He hesitated. "Do these . . . mantoges of yours . . . do they hang in museums?"

"No, I destroy the originals after I photograph them," said Conover. "They exist only in this book."

"Well, I admit you got me curious. Let's have a look at 'em."

"In due course," Conover told him. "First, I must explain certain things."

"What things?" asked Jack Wilbur, taking a solid belt of whiskey.

"Let me begin by outlining a unique personal philosophy." He leaned forward, eyes bright, excited. "Have you ever heard of Dostoyevsky?"

"Nope. He an artist, too?"

"Indeed, yes—and a very great one—but his art was that of the printed word. Fyodor Mikhailovich Dostoyevsky. Eighteen twenty one to eighteen eighty-one. Critics have called him Russia's greatest novelist."

"Russian, huh?" Wilbur shook his head. "No wonder I never heard of the guy. Hell, the only book writer I know about is Ernie Hemingway an' I never actual read anything of his—but how I know about him is because of his boozing. He sure loved to get smashed, Ole Ernie did."

"True enough. Many great writers have fallen prey to the evils of alcohol."

Jack held up his whiskey glass, now three-quarters empty. "If this stuff is evil, then I guess I'm one bad dude." Grinning, he took another swallow.

"Of course, a multitude of critics have attempted to define the essence of Dostoyevsky's work, but the most perceptive analysis comes from a gentleman whose name I fail to recall at the moment. His words, however, are very clear in my memory: 'The extremes of man's nature, his spiritual duality, the conflict between conventional morals and the overwhelming urge to move beyond such constrictions, forms the core of all of Dostoyevsky's major novels.' Beautifully put, I'd say."

"This kinda talk is givin' me a headache," declared Jack Wilbur.

Conover smiled. "Bear with me, Jack. There's a point here that applies directly to both of us—but I have to reach it in my own way. Will you indulge me?"

"Go ahead," said Wilbur.

"Dostoyevsky's greatest work, in my opinion, is the novel he published in eighteen sixty-six, *Crime and Punishment*."

"The title sounds okay," admitted Wilbur. "You do a crime, you get punished for it—like my Pap."

"The novel's lead character," continued Conover, "is an embittered scholar named Raskolnikov. He murders two women, one of them for money. At least that's what he thinks is his motive: However, money is not Raskolnikov's true reason for the crime. In fact, he hides the stolen loot and never profits from it."

"That's crazy," declared Jack Wilbur. "If he went to all the trouble of knockin' off some dame for her dough, then why didn't he spend it? Sounds like the guy was a real dummy."

"On the contrary, he was a brilliant man," said Conover. "His violent action perfectly reflected the author's personal philosophy. It was through Raskolnikov that Dostoyevsky developed what I choose to call 'Fyodor's Law.' You know, when the novel appeared, it was considered quite controversial. It shocked many people."

"How come?"

"Dostoyevsky boldly declared that truly extraordinary people are not bound by conventional moral standards. He wrote of a higher 'law of nature' unknown to the untutored mass of humanity. This law permits the extraordinary individual to commit violent acts, including murder, in order to advance beyond, to transcend ordinary boundaries."

"That's a hell of a thing to put in people's heads."

"Allow me to quote directly from memory," Conover continued, ignoring Wilbur's negative comment. "Raskolnikov speaks of a 'right to crime,' and adds: 'If such a one is forced, for the sake of his idea, to wade through blood, he can find within his conscience, a *sanction* for wading through blood.' The author, of course, was not advocating such extreme behavior for everyone—only for the truly extraordinary individual."

"Horseshit," muttered Jack Wilbur.

Undeterred, Conover went on: "If the individual is clever enough, his actions will never be discovered by the law. For one thing, a dead body is the primary proof of murder. But what if the body simply vanishes?" He spread his hands. "No corpse, no provable crime."

"Bodies don't vanish."

"Ah, but they *can*," argued Conover. "All one need do is saw the corpse into small parts and then burn each part to a fine grey ash. Quite simple, actually."

Jack Wilbur stared intently at him. "This is pretty heavy stuff," he said slowly.

"It's time to open my scrapbook," said Conover. He flipped back the heavy cover to reveal, within the book's pages, a variety of color photos—of human body parts arranged on brightly painted boards in bizarre designs.

"My art," Conover declared proudly. "Unfortunately, for obvious reasons, I am unable to preserve the originals. Sadly, I am forced to burn each montage after I have completed it. But at least I have this book of photographs. Arms, legs, hands, ears, noses . . . they all comprise my basic artistic materials."

"Christ!" breathed Jack Wilbur, staring at one of the photos. "That's a guy's dick!"

"Yes," nodded Conover. "I am sometimes able to utilize genitalia to splendid effect. But *every* body part is potentially usable." He pointed to another photo. "Here we have a loop of bowel tract, actually part of the small intestine, surrounding a freshly-severed heart. Quite original, don't you think?"

Jack Wilbur stood up, backing away from his host. "What I think, mister, is that you're one sick son of a bitch!"

"Sit down, Jack," said Conover sharply. "I laced that drink of yours with a potent pharmaceutical drug that will render you totally helpless within a very short period."

"I don't believe it," said Wilbur.

"Trust me. I'm quite adept at this by now. Very soon your lungs will begin to tighten. With every breath they will expand less, restricting the oxygen available to you. Then black spots will appear before your eyes as you gasp for air. You'll fall to the floor and lie there for a minute or two, conscious but unable to move. And then your heart will stop and it will all be over."

"You plan to cut me up in pieces an' use me for one of your damn pictures?"

"Precisely," nodded Conover. "I'm actually doing you a service—helping you to make something special out of your otherwise miserable life. You shall serve the cause of true artistic expression. A noble end to your mundane existence."

"How can you just go around killing people?" gasped Jack Wilbur. His skin was red and flushed with heat.

"After the first time it becomes quite easy. One's first murder is always somewhat disturbing. Now all I feel is a sense of exhilaration." He checked his wristwatch. "Time's up, Jack. The poison kicks in very suddenly. No use your attempting to fight it. Just let . . ." He stood up eyes wide. "Just . . . let it . . ."

James Conover staggered, clutching at his throat. He choked, gasping for breath. Then he fell to his knees, toppling sideways to the polished peg floor of the den. Lying on his back, he stared sightlessly at the ceiling, conscious but totally paralyzed.

"Well, Mr. Conover," said Jack Wilbur as he removed the fallen man's wallet and slipped the diamond ring from the middle finger of his left hand, "your back was to me when you put that stuff in my glass, but I could see what you was doing in the mirror. When you went to fetch your book of sicko pictures I switched glasses. Guess the joke's on you, huh?"

There was no physical response from Conover, but Jack caught a faint flicker of shocked understanding in the dying man's eyes. Then they began glazing over. Conover had, at best, another few seconds of life.

Jack Wilbur bent over him, leaning close, smiling. "Fuck you, Mr. Conover," he said softly.

He removed the man's car keys and gold wristwatch, walked out to the shiny blue Cadillac, and motored away down the hill, whistling.

The sun was very bright and the Los Angeles air was smogless and sweet.

Jack Wilbur felt "truly exraordinary."

This story began as a television outline in the spring of 1977. I was working on the manuscript of Logan's World in a rented apartment on Coronado Island, just across the bay from San Diego, when I got a phone call from a producer who wanted me to write an original Movie of the Week for him featuring a strong female lead. I came up with a plot concept I called "Return to Yesterday," about a woman who goes back to her home town to face some startling changes—my version of the old cliché, "You can't go home again."

The producer didn't feel it worked for him so the project died and I went back to Mr. Logan. But the idea stayed with me. Years later, when Carol Serling (Rod Serling's widow) wanted new fiction for a book she was editing, Journeys to the Twilight Zone, I got out my plot notes on "Return to Yesterday." I'd known Rod as a friend back in his Zone days, had sold him a teleplay (alas, unproduced), and was frustrated at not being more active in his series. Now I had a chance for my own return to yesterday.

The result of all this was "On Harper's Road."

The story was just what she wanted. Carol was sure that Rod would have loved it. I'd like to think she's right.

This one's for you, ole buddy.

On Harper's Road

(Written: August 1991)

Joanna Morland was a cynic. Her cynicism had been born when she was very young, amplified by unloving parents and nurtured by a town that didn't seem to give a damn about her. She had never believed in Santa Claus. Or the Easter Bunny. To her, fairy tales were nonsense and the classic Disney films saccharine and ridiculous. In *Bambi*, when the young deer's mother was shot to death by the hunters, and the other children in the theater were all sobbing around her, Joanna was tearless; the death of her own mother, some years later, left her equally unmoved.

Her parents were, in fact, totally alien to her. She had never been given proper care or attention. Her father was a ruthless, poorly educated man who had financially destroyed his longtime partner in order to gain control of a small local hardware store. Her mother, cut of the same amoral cloth, always agreed with her father; he totally dominated her life. Joanna harbored a cold contempt for them both. In the family, she loved only her "Gramps," Joanna's grandfather on her mother's side. (Her father's parents were both deceased.) He, too, felt alone in the world, his wife having died in 1961, the same year in which Joanna was born. When things got too bad at home, Joanna would run over to Gramps' house and he would soothe and comfort her.

She had only one school friend, Linda Whittaker, and in no way were they like other teenagers. Both of them hated popular music and had no interest in going to movies. They refused to "run around" with the local boys (whom they considered to be "terminally stupid"). Instead, they spent their time together playing classical music (Linda was crazy for Bach; Joanna favored the Hungarian rhapsodies of Franz Liszt). And they would read the short stories of Ernest Hemingway aloud to one another. They liked Hemingway because his stories had the ring of hard truth about them, at least the early ones did, the stories he wrote in Paris.

Joanna had grown up in Oakvale, a small town east of Kansas City in the Missouri heartland, and for the first eighteen years of her life had seldom ventured beyond the town limits. (She'd been to Kansas City just twice, on trips with her father.) When both of her parents were killed in a highway car crash in 1975, and her grandfather expired of a heart attack shortly after the accident, Joanna found herself suddenly alone in the ugly, drafty house on Flora Avenue. She had inherited no money, only the house and her father's debts at the store.

By then, she had come to detest the stifling, mean-spirited atmosphere of Oakvale and (in desperation) had married Jack Bryson, a big-boned, gawky boy she'd known since grade school. There was no love involved, at least not on Joanna's part. Jack had been promised a foreman's job in his father's Chicago refrigeration plant, and shortly after high school graduation in 1979 he took his new bride with him to Illinois.

Life in the big city was exciting for Joanna, but Jack wasn't. He was a bully, and he drank too much. They got a divorce two years after their arrival in Chicago. Joanna had worked, during the marriage, as a low-paid ad writer for a very small city newspaper, the kind you pick up free in all night coffee shops. She went to New York to join an agency that specialized in auto accounts, starting as a secretary. But her ability to write outstanding copy was quickly recognized and, on her thirty-first birthday (in early October of 1992), she was promoted to the position of senior vice president.

That was the same day Joanna saw the Gypsy fortune teller in Greenwich Village. She was visiting the old woman as part of a research project, her "crystal ball ad campaign" for the Ford Motor Company ("You are destined to own a new Ford!"). Madame Olga startled Joanna by telling her that, within the month, she'd be "going home."

"Me? Go back to Oakvale? That's ridiculous. I haven't gone back since I left thirteen years ago. There's nothing for me in Oakvale."

The old woman raised her shadowed eyes, scanning Joanna's face. "Yet I *see* you there . . . on Harper's Road . . . trapped in a storm."

Joanna smiled. Impossible. Harper's Road had been permanently closed when she was still in high school. Although it led from the main highway directly into town, the road was impassable in heavy rains; the surface quickly turned to sticky gumbo and cars would mire down, buried to the bumpers in thick yellow mud. Faced with the expense of paving Harper's Road, the City Council had voted to close it, and heavy wooden gates had been placed at each end, sealing it off to traffic. Some of the local kids would come in from the open fields flanking the road and race their bicycles over the dirt. More often than not, they were caught by the police and taken home to angry parents. By now, thought Joanna, the old road would be so overgrown that driving on it would be out of the question. (It had taken on a legendary status in Oakvale. "Odd" things were said to have happened there. Kids and animals were rumored to have disappeared during storms in the area—but Joanna had never believed any of these fanciful tales.)

Naturally, she dismissed the Gypsy's prediction. Joanna was far too cynical to believe in fortune telling. But she did get some good photos of the old crone gazing into a crystal ball. She'd turn these over to a sketch artist at the agency with her ideas for rough copy.

It would all work out fine.

That night she had the dream again. About her mother's red necklace. The dream was always the same . . .

She was running. In darkness. In a fierce thunderstorm. Rain slashed down at her like a thousand tiny knives, sharp enough to cut her flesh. Lightning forked the sky, sizzling silver bolts of electricity, reminding her of Frankenstein's castle—the one in the late night movie she'd seen on TV. Wet grass whipped at her legs and the ground was soft and spongy beneath her running feet, like the body of an immense animal.

Then, suddenly, the way things happen in dreams, she was inside some vast structure with the rain fisting the roof, trying to reach her, to cut her with its sharp, daggered drops. She was trapped here, in this dim, openfloored structure (a garage, perhaps?), totally vulnerable, quaking with fear.

A figure advanced toward her—her mother—unclipping a heavy red-bead necklace, the one she usually wore when they went out. Someone behind Joanna grabbed her, pinning her arms. She screamed as her mother looped the necklace around Joanna's neck. Then, relentlessly, her mother began to tighten the loop, eyes fired with fierce determination. Joanna felt the beads of the necklace bite deeply into her flesh.

At this point in the dream she would abruptly awaken, hands to her throat, gasping and choking, tears running down her face. And it was like that now. She sat up in bed, shaking from the horrible intensity of the nightmare.

She got up. It was two a.m. A clear night, with the stars out. Joanna walked into the bathroom to wash her tear-streaked face, then returned to bed. But she couldn't sleep for the remainder of the night.

At the agency the next morning she received a phone call. From Jason Whittaker, Linda's father. His voice was low and strained. "Linda's in the hospital," he told her, "dying of cancer. The doctor says she won't last out the week. She's been asking for you. You're the only one she wants to see."

Joanna didn't hesitate. She booked the next flight

to Kansas City. Oakvale didn't have an airport, and trains no longer stopped there. She planned to rent a car in K.C. and drive out.

It was only when she was on the plane, airborne, that she thought of Madame Olga.

Just as the old Gypsy had predicted, Joanna Morland was "going home."

The sky above Kansas City was gray and somber with the threat of an oncoming storm when Joanna drove away from the airport in her rented Ford Probe.

She headed due east, driving fast, her mind tracking memories of Linda . . . of the long sunlit afternoons when they played chess in Joanna's small bedroom on Flora . . . of the school production when Joanna had been in charge of the ketchup for Shakespeare's bloody *Macbeth* and Linda had played Macbeth's treacherous wife ("Out, out, damned spot!") . . . of Linda's rapturous smile as they listened to one of Bach's Brandenburg concertos . . . of the Sunday picnic when a line of ants had climbed under Linda's skirt when she was dozing in the sun. (Oh, how she'd hopped and danced around slapping at those ants!)

And now she was dying at thirty-one in a bed at Oakvale Hospital. My God, why hadn't they at least sent her to a modern facility in K.C. for treatment?

It was late afternoon when Joanna encountered the paint-flaked metal sign on the outskirts of town:

WELCOME TO OAKVALE!
HEART OF THE GREAT MIDWEST
A FRIENDLY TOWN OF FRIENDLY FOLKS

Joanna had always found the sign ironic, with its bright words of good cheer in sharp contrast to the meanness of spirit lurking beneath Oakvale's placid surface.

Then, instead of turning left onto the two-lane access highway leading into town, she found herself accelerating, heading toward the old route. . . .

Toward Harper's Road.

This is crazy, Joanna told herself. Why are you doing this when Linda is dying at the hospital and might not last out the day? Joanna couldn't justify her action; there was no rational way to explain this sudden, overwhelming impulse.

I have to see it again. Have to.

At the gate blocking the entrance to Harper's Road (WARNING! THIS ROAD IS CLOSED! NO TRES-PASSING!) Joanna got out of her car, opened the trunk, and removed the tire iron. With this, she smashed at the large metal padlock securing the gate. Three blows did the job and the rusted lock snapped open. Struggling against the heavy brush that had grown around it, she strained at the wooden gate. Pushed it wide. There! Done!

But why? Why are you doing this?

Without attempting to give herself an answer, Joanna got back into the Probe and drove onto Harper's Road.

Trees lined it to either side, next to a sagging split-rail wooden fence—solid black oaks and heavy maples, their fat limbs scraping the top of the Ford as Joanna drove deeper into the storm-threatened afternoon. The day had turned dark and ominous, with swollen rainclouds now cloaking the sky.

She had been right about the years of unchecked growth. The road was wildly overgrown and full of deep ruts. Navigating it, the Ford wallowed and pitched like a ship in choppy seas.

Then the October storm that had been hovering over the area since she'd left Kansas City broke with a tigerish roar of thunder and savage, down-rushing sheets of steel-colored rain. A ragged spear of lightning split the stretched fabric of sky, like the flash-bulb on a giant's camera.

Another few minutes of this and the packed dirt under her tires would turn to clinging sludge, as treacherous as a bed of quicksand.

Joanna still had time to put the car into reverse and

back out to the paved highway. But she didn't. It was as if she were compelled to fulfill the old Gypsy woman's prediction ". . . on Harper's Road . . . trapped in a storm."

The wheels of the Probe were rapidly losing traction, the tires beginning their whining spin in the mud. Soon she'd be completely mired down; it was now too late to reverse direction.

Then she remembered the old Hennessey place. An abandoned farm, with the main house fallen to ruin, but with the feed barn intact. At least, it would serve to shelter her until the storm passed.

Within moments, she saw it ahead of her—a tall, age-slanted wooden structure a few hundred feet left of the road.

Joanna pulled to a stop, cut the engine, and eased out into the mud. Immediately, she sank to her ankles, with the cold rain pelting her skin. The wild grass was waist high, clinging and slapping at her as she cleared the fence and ran awkwardly for the barn.

Forcing open the wide door, she ducked inside. Countless gaps in the badly-weathered roof admitted chilled gusts of rain; a damp odor of mold permeated the barn's interior.

Maybe I should have stayed in the car, she told herself. This place is—

Her thoughts were abruptly shattered by a cannon

blast of thunder, followed by an impossibly bright radiance; the crackling explosion from above told Joanna that a bolt of lightning had struck the barn, deflected and been absorbed by the rooster-shaped lightning rod mounted on the roof.

Instinctively, she had closed her eyes against the fierce assault, and when she opened them again . . .

The storm had gone.

No rain.

No thunder.

Nothing but silence.

No! This was beyond logical reason. A major rainstorm doesn't blow over in an instant.

Yet when Joanna stepped into the outside yard a full moon rode the clear evening sky and a net of silver stars shimmered above her.

Stunned, she walked back to the rail fence, slipped through it, and climbed behind the wheel of the Ford. Joanna started the engine, engaged gear, and the car began rolling forward.

Harper's Road was now passable. The surface on this end stretch was stable, providing ample traction for the tires. And the road was oddly free of overgrowth. She didn't question this. It seemed right somehow. Then she remembered that Linda was waiting for her at Oakvale Hospital.

She had to hurry.

* * *

The road took her straight into town. (No gate at the other end; perhaps it had been vandalized.) Oakvale's only hospital was a three-story building of smoked red brick topping the hill at Wornell and Prospect. Joanna had been born there.

Crossing the lobby, she approached a dour-faced nurse at the reception desk.

The nurse didn't look up. She kept writing in a small white pad, her head down as she spoke to Joanna. "May I help you?"

"I've come to see Linda Whittaker. It's urgent."

"Does she work here at the hospital?" Head still lowered over the pad. Scribbling.

"No, no. She's a cancer patient. In critical condition. You've probably got her in Intensive Care. She's been asking to see me."

The nurse finally looked up, sighed, pushed aside the pad, and began leafing through the admissions book. "We have no patient here named Whittaker."

"You must have. There's some mistake."

The nurse stared at her. "There's no Whittaker here," she repeated.

Had they taken Linda to Kansas City after all? But not now. Not with her *dying!*

Joanna decided the best thing to do at this point

was to go see Linda's father. After all, Jason Whittaker was the one who'd phoned her.

The house was just seven blocks from the hospital, on Harrison, a big Southern-style mansion, set well back from the street, with a white wooden veranda built around its exterior. The yard was beautifully kept, the bushes neatly trimmed—the work of a full-time gardener. Mr. Whittaker was President of the Oakvale Bank, and the family had always been well off.

When the door opened, Jason Whittaker was there behind the screen, looking not a day older than the last time she'd seen him. Well, some people don't age as fast as others.

He scowled at her over his reading glasses. "If you're selling anything, we don't—"

"I'm Joanna," she said. (After all, it *had* been thirteen years.) "I came as soon as I could get a flight to Kansas City—right after your call. But Linda wasn't at the hospital. Did you have her moved?"

Whittaker looked confused. "Call? Hospital? I don't know what the devil you're talking about, young lady. And I sure don't know you."

"But you phoned me in New York about Linda— about her cancer—that she was asking for me."

Whittaker stared at her. "My daughter is in perfect health—and I've no time for this nonsense." He stepped back from the screen, firmly shutting the heavy oak door.

Joanna hesitated, then stumbled down the veranda steps. Dazedly, she returned to the Ford, wondering if this was another of her nightmares. Am I just *dreaming* I've come back to Oakvale?

No, dammit! This is all real. The street, house, the car—*all real*.

But the ultimate reality lay ahead. . . .

Keying the ignition, Joanna put the Probe in gear and drove toward Flora Avenue. Toward the shoddy, one-story frame house she had abandoned thirteen years ago. She'd never tried to sell it after the death of her parents; even when they were all living there together it had needed major restoration. Joanna hadn't cared to spend the money to have it fixed properly. Cheaper to have the house torn down and put the lot up for sale. Someday she intended to do that. But, for now, it was a boarded-over, time-weathered relic of her past.

Except it *wasn't*.

She parked directly in front of the house, staring at it. No boards on the windows. A trimmed yard. Lights glowing warmly from the living room in the late evening's darkness.

Suddenly chilled, Joanna crossed the yard and mounted the wooden porch steps. She stood there, feeling lost and helpless. Somehow, she couldn't bring herself to knock at her own door.

She'd been heard. The porch light bloomed to life and the inner door opened. A heavyset woman peered at her from behind the locked screen. "Who's *out* there?"

Her mother. Alive! Exactly as Joanna remembered her.

She didn't know how this could be, how such an impossible situation could exist—but she *accepted* it. And, in that instant of acceptance, she felt that in order to survive, to keep from losing her mind, she must establish her own individual identity, her own subjective reality.

"I'm your daughter," she told the woman behind the screen. "I'm Joanna." She paused, searching for words of explanation. "I—I came here from . . . your future . . . from 1992 . . . through some kind of . . . I don't know . . . a kind of 'time gate,' I guess . . . out on Harper's Road." She drew in a nervous breath. "Mama, I swear I'm telling you the truth. I swear it! I *am* your daughter."

"You're crazy, is what you are," snapped Doris Morland. "I got me just one kid, an' she's eleven years old. Up to her room right this minute, doin' her studies. Now, you get the hell off this porch or I'll call the law!"

"Shut up and let her in!" Joanna recognized the

harsh voice from the dimness of the hallway. A dark figure was silhouetted against the wash of yellow light from the living room.

"Daddy . . . is that *you*?"

"Yeah, it's me all right." He stepped forward to unlatch the screen. "C'mon in, girl."

He was precisely as she remembered him: tall and angular, with hard eyes and a tight, cruel mouth. "Well, don't just *stand* there. C'mon inside."

Joanna stepped into the house, into her past, into a world she had always hated and feared.

She was baffled at her father's casual acceptance of this incredibly bizarre situation. It was almost impossible for *her* to accept, despite all the tangible evidence. But her *father* . . .

Ned Morland smiled, showing the gold tooth in his upper jaw. There was no warmth in the smile, only a cool irony. "You're wondering how come I believe you so quick an' easy. That right, girl?"

"Why *do* you?" she asked. "I wouldn't—in your place."

"I been expectin' ya, *knew* you'd show up." He nodded, sitting down on the overstuffed living room sofa (it still needed upholstering) while she remained standing near the hallway door. Her mother hovered at Ned's shoulder, pale and quiet. "Last summer, at the county fair," Ned Morland continued, "I went into this little tent they had set up, with an old Gypsy woman inside who told fortunes. Called herself Madame Olga."

Joanna felt a sharp chill sweep through her. The *same* woman! How could it be?

"She had me sit down at a fancy table in front of this big shiny crystal ball an' she told me all about you . . . how you'd be comin' home from the future to Oakvale. In the fall, in October, she said. You'd take old Harper's Road an' it would send you right home. Way she said it, the way her eyes locked inta me, I knew it would happen. Yessir, just damn well knew it. Some things ya just don't question."

"You and Mama . . ." Joanna spoke slowly. "You both died—"

"—in a car crash." He nodded again. "In 1975, three years from now. That's when the old Gypsy said it was gonna happen." He rubbed a fist thoughtfully along one side of his stubbled cheek. "Unless, that is . . ."

"Unless what?"

"Unless I stop it. Keep it from happenin'."

Joanna stared at him. "What are you saying?"

"I'm sayin' you got to die, girl. To save us, me and your Mama here." He reached up to squeeze his wife's hand. "It's real plain, how the Gypsy spelled it all out. We kill you now an' that car crash don't happen. What we do here in your past changes *our* future. You die an' we go on livin'. Just like the Gypsy said."

"That's *insane!*" gasped Joanna, backing away. "My death won't save you."

"How do you know that?" asked Ned Morland. He stood up, his hands fisted, walked over to her. "If everythin' else that old Gypsy bitch said come true, an' it *has*, then why not this, too? Makes sense ta me." He swung his head back toward his wife. "What about you, Dorry?"

Doris Morland nodded slowly, eyes bright as a bird of prey. "I don't claim to understand none a' this, not a whit, but . . ." She peered closely at Joanna. "You know best, Ned. You always know best. I'll do what you think we ought." And she fingered the red-bead necklace at her fleshy throat.

"Me an' your Mama here was about to go out," he said. "Figgered to look around the new shopping center some, then get us a bite to eat. But all that can wait." He put a big-knuckled hand on Joanna's shoulder. "Right now, let's just us all take a little ride in that fancy car a' yours." And once again, he smiled. "Out to Harper's Road."

* * *

They forced Joanna to drive. Her father sat next to her, with her mother in the back seat.

Joanna was rigid with fear. She had always been afraid of her parents. They were violent, cruel people who had never shown tenderness or compassion. For her, or for anyone else. But the idea that they were willing to commit *murder*—to kill their own daughter—was beyond comprehension.

Yet it was happening.

The Probe bumped its way onto Harper's Road, tires digging into the packed dirt.

"Head for the old Hennessey place," her father told her. "It's got to be done there in the barn. Just like the Gypsy said." He nodded. "Gotta do this proper."

Despite her fear, Joanna was taut with anger. "You're just as I remembered you, Daddy," she said. "You're a miserable bastard! Never wanted me, never loved me or did anything to make me love you. And Mama always siding with you against me—just the way she's doing tonight."

"Wife's gotta stand by her husband," nodded Doris Morland. Her voice was soft, placid. "Ned's the man a' the house—an' I was taught a woman stands by her man."

Joanna glared at her. "Even when it comes to murder?"

"Well, my goodness, honey," declared her mother, "it's not really murder. You don't *exist*—not here in 1972 you don't. So how can we be killin' a person who don't exist?"

"Your mama's right," agreed Ned Morland. "Way I figger things, the Gypsy sent you back to us so's we could stay alive." He grinned in the darkness. "Shoot, maybe we'll end up bein' immortal! Never *been* a case like this—chance to change the future an' all. No sir. Never been."

The car jolted to a stop. Just beyond the fence, the tall bulk of the Hennessey barn loomed against the sky.

They got out. The night air was cold. A wind was rising. Another storm was due to break.

"You first under the fence," said Joanna's father, directing her with a flashlight. "Your Mama an' me, we'll be right behind ya."

Joanna decided to run. But where? To Gramps! Impossible. To him, she was an eleven-year-old child. He'd never believe her story about coming here from the future. But she *had* to try.

Had to.

And she ran.

Her father caught her easily, just beyond the rail fence. Ned Morland gripped her arm hard, digging into her flesh. He hurried her toward the barn. Joanna moved mechanically, fear numbing her. The door was opened and she was pushed inside.

With the door closed behind them, Ned gestured to his wife. "This is where you do it, Dorry."

"Me?" Doris Morland looked uneasy. "I thought you was gonna do it."

"The Gypsy said you was to be the one to strangle her. With that." And he pointed to her heavy red-bead necklace.

Now, finally, Joanna understood her dream. *This* was the killing place! Dark, with open flooring all around. Not a garage . . . a barn.

"Well," sighed her mother, unclipping the necklace, "if this is the proper way. . . ."

Frantically, Joanna looked around for a weapon, something with which to defend herself. A pitchfork stood in one corner, near the hayrack, its tines glimmering faintly in the illumination from Ned Morland's flash. If she could just reach the *pitchfork* . . .

But her father's rough-fingered hands closed on her arms, pinning them, holding her vise-tight. "All right, Dorry. Let's get to it."

As she had always done in her nightmare, when the bead necklace was looped around her, Joanna screamed.

Her mother said, "Hold her, Ned. She's squirmin' like a fish!"

The beads of the necklace bit deeply into Joanna's neck as her mother tightened the loop.

Then the storm hit.

Thunder like a collision of freight trains. Rain assaulting the roof in blowing, savage gusts.

And lightning.

It was the lightning that did it. To Doris and Ned. Stabbing down from the sky in jagged fury, blasting them to the barn floor in mounds of writhing, sizzling flesh. The interior of the barn danced with electrical energies, bright as day.

Joanna reeled back, squeezing her eyes shut against the dazzling illumination.

Then darkness again.

And silence.

Joanna opened her eyes.

The barn floor was empty.

The rain had stopped.

The storm was gone.

She ran wildly for the road, thrashing her way through the high grass, slipped under the rail fence, pulled herself, sobbing, gasping, almost breathless, into the Ford, fired the engine, began roaring forward . . . stopped . . .

She knew that there would now be a locked gate at the town end of Harper's Road.

Joanna put the Probe into reverse and backed out. The highway gate, with its broken padlock, stood open for her.

It was over. She had returned from her nightmare.

No . . .

Joanna looked down at the red-bead necklace still clutched in her right hand.

. . . not a nightmare.

Reality.

This story has a twin. It evolved from intensive research into the lives and career patterns of a number of serial killers. I wanted to find out what forces drove them to murder . . . again . . . and again . . . and again. During the 1989 World Fantasy Convention in Seattle, in order to test my work on a live audience, I read this story aloud. Writer-editor Joe Lansdale was there. After my reading he told me he absolutely loved the story—right up to the ending. He disliked the fantasy element I'd closed it with. Even so, he'd be willing to use my story in his new anthology, Dark at Heart. *Sorry, I told him. I'd already sold it to* Whispers.

Joe said, "Look, I've just gotta have this. Revise it, put in a new, non-fantasy ending, and I'll buy it. You can still have the original version printed in Whispers."

So that's what happened. This version, the one you are about to read, appeared in Best of Whispers. *The revised version, "Hi, Mom!," was included in Joe's anthology. Thus, my serial killer research gave birth to twins.*

Which one do I prefer? Hey, I'm the father. Please don't ask me to choose between my children.

I'm very fond of them both.

The Francis File

(Written: August 1988)

Among the items found in the apartment of Francis Scott Francis, 1318 W. Franklin, Hollywood, California:

ITEM: A human head. Female. Not identified. Used as dartboard by F.S.F.

ITEM: A pair of pink baby shoes, identified as belonging to F.S.F. and worn by him as infant.

ITEM: A carpenter's claw hammer, with human hair adhering. Bloodstains on hammer from victims various.

ITEM: A photo of F.S.F. as a young child standing beside his mother, Mrs. Alma Hastings Francis. The mother's features (Caucasian) have been defaced by knife cuts across photo. Word "Bitch!" written in red ink by

F.S.F. in adult hand with arrow pointing to mother.

ITEM: A page torn from a blue-lined school tablet, undated. On page, in adult hand of F.S.F.:
I am a nothing.
I don't exist.
There is no me.

ITEM: A snapshot of Mr. and Mrs. Francis seated on wooden porch (location not identified) with F.S.F. as small baby in arms of Mrs. Francis. Father is black. (His full name: Leonard Kippard Francis.) Written across back of this photo, in adult hand of F.S.F.:
Never knew my father, but know he hated me. Left us when I was 2. I hope he got cancer. Would kill him if I ever saw him.

ITEM: A school report sent to Mrs. Francis from teacher Edna Vann in 1966 when F.S.F. was eight years of age. Frank is a very difficult child, and is prone to violent temper outbursts. He resists proper discipline, has no friends, and struck another child today with a rock in the school playground. I am sending him home with this note, and I recommend that he be soundly punished. If his behavior does not improve he will be expelled from school.

F.S.F. has added, in red ink:

Mother beat me real bad for this. My head hurt for a long time and I was dizzy and spit blood.

ITEM: A membership card in the American Nazi Party, undated. The card is stamped "Cancelled" with hand notation: "Not Caucasian."

ITEM: A nose, recently severed (female), in ziplock plastic bag.

ITEM: A poem, undated, written by F.S.F. on torn section of a brown paper sack:

> Drums of beaten flesh
> Sun scars eating worms
> of Hate,
> and icy dreams of blood.

ITEM: A newspaper clipping (loose) from *The Kansas Star*, Lawton City, Kansas, dated June 2, 1968:

POLICE FIND DEAD PETS

Responding to a neighbor's phone call, authorities entered the home of Mrs. Alma Francis on Forest Road today to discover the bodies of more than a dozen cats and dogs listed as missing from the neighborhood over the past year. The dead pets were found buried in the basement of the house. Mrs. Francis' 10-year-old son, Frank, has admitted slaying the animals. He is now at Juvenile Hall.

ITEM: A child's drawing (done by F.S.F. in grade school). Drawing, in colored crayons, depicts a row of houses on a hill with orange-and-red flames coming from each roof. Scribbled beneath the drawing, in a crude child's handwriting, are the words:

    I LIKE FIRE

ITEM: An untitled child's story, written in a notebook. Not dated.

    Once upon a time there was a little boy named Frankie who had a father who ran away who was a black man they call a niger and a Mommy who hit him a lot who was a white lady. Frankie did not know if he was a niger like people called him sometimes or if he was a white boy like his Mommy said so he wanted to run away and live with a curcus and have his face painted like a klowns is, all colors.

ITEM: A human skull (female) with the top half of the skull cut away to form an ashtray. Used in kitchen by F.S.F. and found filled with cigarette butts.

ITEM: A copy of the Lawton City High School Yearbook for 1975. On page 76 (corner turned down), a school photo of F.S.F. with printed note below:
"Frankie"
Offbeat. Outside the crowd. Likes boxing and wrestling. (Don't get him mad!) Interested in the occult world. Ambition: to be a TV celebrity.

ITEM: A reel-to-reel home tape recording.

TAPE BEGINS.

YOUNG WOMAN'S VOICE: Are you recording this?

VOICE OF F.S.F.: Yes.

WOMAN: Well turn it the fuck off. I don't like
              being recorded.

F.S.F.: No. It stays on.

WOMAN: Then I'm splitting. I don't even know
              you anyway. I don't dig freaky guys.

F.S.F.: No, you're not leaving.

(SOUND OF STRUGGLE.
BREAKING GLASS.)

F.S.F.: You're never going to leave me again, Alma!

WOMAN: (terrified now) I'm not Alma. Who the
              shit is Alma?

F.S.F.: Sargoth wants you dead. He asked me to
            kill you.

(WOMAN SCREAMS. SOUND OF BLOWS.
SCREAMING STOPS.)

TAPE ENDS.

ITEM: A woman's silk undergarment (panties). Bloodstained.

ITEM: A letter, hand-written, postmarked Chicago and dated Sept. 5, 1983 from ex-convict Edward Williams to F.S.F. in Indianapolis.

Dear Frankie,

Hey, buddy, how are things in your neck of the woods??? You said you'd write me when we left the joint. Some writer you are! (Ha, ha!) As for me, I am back in Chicago working as a mechanic for Don like I did before. How are things with you? I am with my old girl friend again and getting laid plenty like old times. Are you getting any nookie? (Ha, ha!) I hope you are getting some. Why don't you come to Chicago? Did you see the 500 Mile Indy Race there yet? I hear it is great to see it, with lots of smashups. Well, take it easy, Frankie, and write to a pal, huh.

Your friend, Eddie

P.S. I hope you find your old lady. As for me, I don't ever want to see my Mom again. She never done nothing good for me or Pop neither.

ITEM: Tearsheets of a magazine article titled "Profile of a Serial Killer" by Frank Anmar. From *Esquire,* dated October 1985. Following paragraph was underlined in red by F.S.F.:

> Therefore, with each of his murders, the serial killer is repeating a ritual that can only end in death (often by suicide) or imprisonment. He is not capable of stopping this cycle of violence since the elements leading up to his string of murders are beyond his conscious control.

ITEM: A list, written on a sheet of white notepaper:
> Enter house by sliding door (break lock).
> Kill dog.
> Kill her.
> Cut off hands (save thumbs).
> Burn house.

ITEM: A scrapbook of pasted-in news clippings on murders committed by F.S.F. Among the headlined stories:

> WOMAN BEATEN TO DEATH IN PARKING LOT
>
> MOTHER OF FOUR SLAIN IN BED-

ROOM OF HER HOME
HAMMER KILLER STRIKES AGAIN
HAMMER MURDERS BAFFLE POLICE

ITEM: A clothbound book, *Demons Conjured!* by Craig Graham. On page 103 (corner turned down) is a woodcut of a horned demon: SARGOTH, THE DESTROYER. The author warns that this demon is particularly dangerous but that it can be contained within a pentagram drawn in human blood. (Illustration shows pentagram.)

ITEM: A postcard from F.S.F. dated February 3, 1984, sent to his mother at a motel in Florida. The card was returned, marked "ADDRESS UNKNOWN." On the card, F.S.F. has written:

> Long time no see. How are you??? I am OK, except for bad dreams all the time. I need to see you.
>
> Your son, Frank

ITEM: A necklace, woven from human hair (female).

ITEM: A poem, written by F.S.F. on the back of an envelope.

> The flower of death
> opens its petals with teeth of acid.
> I need to enter death's
> dark garden
> and let its teeth
> devour me.

ITEM: Last two pages of typed transcript of a television interview, dated July 1987.

TRANSCRIPT SEGMENT BEGINS:

INTERVIEWER: And even though you told the prison psychiatrist that you were dangerous to society and could not function in the outside world, the parole board nevertheless released you?

F.S.F.: That's right. The prisons in this country are all overcrowded, so they don't care who they let go. But I tried to warn them that . . . that I wasn't ready to leave.

INTERVIEWER: Are you saying you *like* being in prison?

F.S.F.: No, not that. It's just that being in prison keeps me from . . . doing bad things.

INTERVIEWER: What things, Frank?

F.S.F.: I can't say what. I could get into a lot of trouble. They don't know who I really am. I got put in jail for breaking and entering and for assault. But I never got caught for what I really done.

INTERVIEWER: Are you presently, as a free man, a danger to society?

F.S.F.: I am. I know I am.

INTERVIEWER: What do you want to do with your life now, Frank?

F.S.F.: End it. I just want to be dead is all. That's the best thing for everybody, me being dead.

INTERVIEWER: But don't you have people who
care about you? What about your
mother? I know you told us that
your father deserted you and your
Mom when you were very young,
but she's still alive, isn't she?

F.S.F.: I guess so. I never hear from her. I tried to
find her for awhile. Now I don't care.

INTERVIEWER: But wouldn't *she* care if you died,
Frank?

F.S.F.: I don't think she cares about anything I do.
She used to beat me all the time when I was
a kid. I got scars. I got a terrible skull fracture from her and couldn't think straight for
days. That happened twice. I wanted to find
her and tell her how much I hated her but
now I just don't care anymore.

INTERVIEWER: I see. (long pause) Why did you
volunteer to come on this show
today, Frank?

F.S.F.: To let people know that these parole boards
let people out of prison even when they

should not be let out on the public street
and that it's wrong. It's a wrong thing to do.

INTERVIEWER: Well, we certainly thank you for
your candor here today, Frank,
and we surely appreciate the
courage it took to tell your story.

F.S.F.: I didn't tell it all. There's a lot you don't
know about. I belong dead. I really do
belong dead.

TRANSCRIPT SEGMENT ENDS

NOTE: When police arrived and entered the apartment of Francis Scott Francis on April 6, 1989, they
found that he was deceased. The living room rug had
been pulled aside and a crude design (pentagram)
was drawn on the wooden floor in what appeared to
be human blood. Mr. Francis was lying inside the
pentagram and appeared to have been attacked by
some particularly savage animal. The head of the
deceased was nearly severed from his neck, and there
were deep lacerations on the torso. Inexplicably,
nearly every bone in the body had been broken.

I wrote this one for free. No payment. It was for a good cause as part of The Touch, a book published to benefit Health Education and the Foundation for Advancement in Cancer Therapy.

"Freak" was deliberately written in the style and mood of Logan's Run. Swift. Compact. Action-packed. A kind of "throwback" to the golden age science fiction I enjoyed in the 1950s.

This printing marks its first appearance in one of my collections.

I think it belongs here.

Freak

(Written: April 1998)

He was brought into the building by an Enforcer who waited in the long sterile corridor while Kal Adams faced the Compdoctor.

He knew he'd end up here. It was inevitable, given his shattered emotional state. His rage had been steadily increasing and he was very near Breakpoint. And why not? It was a near-miracle that he'd endured this long.

He'd been forced to wear a Skinsuit since he was one. Which was unheard of, since the Depriver Syndrome seldom manifests itself before puberty, and *never* during infanthood. Except in his case.

Except for Kal Adams.

During his first birthday party Kal's mother had kissed her baby son in happy celebration, and was instantly struck blind. Not for hours or days, but permanently. For the next three years, until she died with his father in a gyro crash, she had remained utterly sightless.

"I was too young to remember it," Kal said, sitting

on a steel chair directly in front of the Compdoctor. "I only know how I was treated. They put me in a Suit and I've never experienced a human touch since that day."

"I can understand," said the doctor. "I know just how difficult it has been for you."

"No, you don't," said Kal flatly. "You're a machine . . . lights and circuits and relays. You can't appreciate what it means to be afflicted as I am."

"You are quite wrong, Mr. Adams," said the doctor. "I have been *programmed* to understand."

"It's not the same," said Kal, staring dully at the audiowall. Its banked lights glimmered and flashed in pulsing rhythms.

"You are obviously a very disturbed young man," said the wall.

"I'm twenty now," said Kal. "For the past nineteen years I've been isolated, denied genuine human contact. I've never held a woman's hand . . . felt the warmth of her skin . . . caressed her face. I feel as if I'm buried in a pit of darkness."

"Unfortunate," said the wall.

"Why *me*?" asked Kal. "Why did this awful thing happen to me?"

"Every Depriver asks, 'why me?' It is a universal question."

Adams shook his head. "I'm not like other

Deprivers. They've all had normal childhoods, years of human contact before their affliction set in. But I've been inside this Suit all my life, wrapped in my protective cocoon." Kal lifted his right arm, shiny and layered; lights gleamed from the Suit's armored surface.

"And you are bitter regarding your condition," stated the wall.

"Damn right I am! It's all I think about anymore, the cruel injustice of it . . . the *horror* of it."

"It is good that you are here," said the Compdoctor. "You have reached a state of potential violence."

Kal glared at the wall. "Society did this to me."

"Not so," the doctor declared. "Society is not responsible for your genetic structure."

"I don't understand this world," Kal said, a hopeless note in his voice. "We've got a space station on the Moon. We've built hive units on Mars. We're at the technical edge of star travel. Yet . . . still no cure for Deprivers."

"Science does not have all the answers," said the wall. "There are problems that are unsolvable."

"I don't believe that," said Kal Adams. "This society doesn't *want* to find a cure for people like me. The world needs a minority to kick around and Deprivers fit the bill. Most people feel smug and superior to us. We're the underdogs, the scapegoats."

"That is, of course, neurotic nonsense," said the

wall, "stemming from your aberrated mental condition."

"I'm not insane," Kal protested. "But I *am* enraged. My God, I was just twelve months old! I was robbed of my childhood."

"And now you feel like striking out," the wall said. "You are at Breakpoint."

"Which is why they brought me here, right?"

"That is correct. When a Depriver reaches Breakpoint he or she is sent to me for help."

Kal laughed harshly. "Help? No one can help me, least of all a talking wall."

"You are mistaken, Mr. Adams," declared the Compdoctor. "I shall administer a tranc dosage that will lower your emotional drive level."

"You intend to numb my mind . . . put me into Sleepstate?"

"That is the only remedy," said the wall.

"And what if I don't want to be drugged? What if I refuse medication?"

"You have no choice," the wall told him. "You should have remained in D-Colony. Most Deprivers are content to be among their own kind."

"That was agony," said Kal. "I couldn't take it."

"You are a misfit," the wall declared. "A man on the verge of committing an anti-social act. Sleep is better than Termination."

"Not for me, it isn't," said Kal.

"I repeat, you have no choice in the matter."

A silver panel opened in the wall directly in front of Kal Adams, and a long metalloid tube snaked out, capped by a glittering needle.

"This injection will solve all of your emotional conflicts," said the wall. "Hold out your right arm. And do not be concerned about the Suit. The needle is designed to penetrate."

Adams stood up. "To hell with you! I won't be drugged!"

"Then I shall summon an Enforcer and he will—"

Kal Adams picked up the steel chair and smashed it into the wall. Lights exploded. Circuits shorted out in sizzling, sparked showers. An alarm bell keened.

The exit door was flung open by an armed Enforcer who brought his laser to firing position as Kal slammed him across the skull with the steel chair.

The Enforcer went down and Kal grabbed his laser. He brought down a second Enforcer with a cutbeam blast from the handweapon.

The Suit was restricting his movement, and Adams used the laser to carefully cut it away from his body. Now he wore only boots and a waist tunic. For the first time in his life he was able to feel the stir of air on his bare skin. Marvelous!

Enforcers were closing in from both ends of the

corridor. They'd terminate him. He knew that. But he had no regrets. He wasn't afraid of Termination. Better than Sleep. At least he'd die with his mind intact.

Then, a female voice from a side door: "Hurry! *This* way!"

A woman in a light blue flogown was gesturing to him from mid-corridor. Adams ran to her and she waved him through the door, slam-bolting it behind them. "In here," she snapped. "Quickly!"

The room had served as a sensory lab. Crowded with open Thinktanks and exotic equipment.

"Who are you?" Kal stared at her. Stunning. Young. Beautifully-figured. Dark-eyed.

"I'm Zandra, and I can get us out of this building."

"All the main exits are blocked by now," said Adams. "There's no way out."

"But there *is*," countered the girl. "Trust me."

They moved through another door into a narrow transport corridor. She sprinted ahead, urging him to follow.

"Why are you doing this?" he asked. "Why risk your life for me? I'm a Depriver."

"I know who you are," she said as they raced along the narrow passage. "You're Kal Adams."

"But how—"

"You're one of a kind. Unique. I heard about you, got curious and comped your statrecords."

"You work here?"

"Not exactly. I'm part of a lab experiment. But there's no time for talk. We have to escape."

"There's no escaping the Enforcers," said Kal. "Even if we manage to get out of the building they're bound to find us. Enforcers are everywhere. They'll terminate us both."

"Just do as I say," she told him. "Here . . ." She was tugging at a panel in the flooring. "Help me with this."

Together, they loosened the panel, pulling it free. A flight of metalloid steps spiraled downward. "There's a maintenance tunnel below that leads to the street."

"How do you know?"

"Because I've been planning a way out." she said. "I comped the blueprints, and they show this tunnel running under the length of the building."

They hurried down the twisting stairs and began to move cautiously along the dim-lit passageway.

"I've been in comp-contact with a group called the Outsiders," Zandra told him. "Do you know about them?"

"I've heard rumors," said Kal. "Anti-system rebels. Operating against the state."

"They'll help us," she said. "They hate the Enforcers . . . hate what the system is doing to block the cure."

"What cure?"

"For Deprivers. They're working on a cure for the affliction. And they're close to a breakthrough."

"My God, that's wonderful!"

"After we made contact I told them I wanted out of the experiment, and they agreed to help. I planned on making my run this weekend—until you popped up. I recognized you from your statshot, and I knew why you were here. For Sleep."

"Yes." Kal nodded. "And I refused."

"I'm just glad I came along when I did."

Kal smiled at her. "I'm beginning to think we have a chance."

"We *do*," she said vehemently.

They'd reached the end of the tunnel. A steel ladder angled up to an exitplate.

"Once we're on the street," said Kal, "what then? Where do we go?"

"I know where," she said. "I'll take you."

Kal didn't argue. Maybe this remarkable young woman *could* lead him to the Outsiders. Why not take the gamble? Most certainly he was doomed without her.

They exited the tunnel at a street level some three hundred feet beyond the rear of the building. No Enforcers were in sight.

"They won't expect us to come out at this point," declared Zandra. "They'll figure we're still trapped inside."

"So we have breathing space," said Kal. "But my statshot will be all over the city by now. They'll be watching every possible escape route."

"I have a plan," she said. "If it works we'll be clear of the city."

"Well, I just hope—"

Kal's words were cut off by a sizzling burst of laser fire that chopped the grass inches from his left foot. A second beam caught him in the left shoulder.

"Take cover!" yelled Kal, diving behind a transit vehicle and pulling Zandra in close behind him. Another beam scored the roof of the truck.

Ahead of them, across a grassed verge, three Enforcers were advancing at a run. Kal scrambled into the truck's controlseat with Zandra.

"Can you drive this thing?" Her tone was desperate.

"Just keep your head down." Kal powered the truck forward in a skidding arc that quickly separated them from the trio of Enforcers.

"Tell me!" snapped Kal. "Which way now?"

"Stanton Square. The park . . . behind the old carousel."

"They'll have ground units out," said Kal. "Don't know if we can make it."

"*Try*, dammit! It's not that far." Then her voice softened. "How's your shoulder?"

The laser had cut deeply into Kal's flesh; the wound was raw and bleeding.

"I'm all right," he said.

Ten minutes later Kal pulled the truck to a stop in Stanton Park. To their left, the silent carousel baked in the heat of day, its mirrors shattered, painted wooden horses cracked and fading, with the floorboards of the abandoned ride warped by wind and rain.

A door opened at the inner section of the carousel, and a tall, sour-looking man in black came out to meet them.

To Zandra: "I see you arrived safely. Who's your friend?"

"Kal Adams," she told him. "He's a Depriver."

The hard-faced man looked at Kal. His eyes narrowed. "I've heard about you, Adams. Afflicted from infanthood. Unique case. What are you doing with Zandra?"

"Trying to stay alive," said Kal. "When I wouldn't accept Sleep they were going to Terminate me. Zandra got me into the clear." He hesitated. "Are you an Outsider?"

"That's what I'm called by the system. My name's Hollister."

"I won't shake your hand," said Kal.

Hollister nodded. "Follow me," he said, entering an overgrown section of heavy-growth woods.

In a small clearing, under a protective cover, a twin-thrust gyro was waiting for them, its rotor blades turning lazily in the heated air.

"This will take you to our headquarters near Bend City in New Oregon," said Hollister. "You'll be safe there."

"What about Airscouts?" asked Kal. "They'll be on full patrol."

"We're invisible on their scanners," said the tall man, helping them aboard the gyro. "We'll be well under their flight-detect range. Believe me, they won't even know we're in the air."

"Looks as if you've got everything figured out," said Kal.

"Not everything," said Hollister, strapping himself into the controlseat, "but we're making progress. One step at a time."

The canopy rolled back and they lifted away, rotor blades slicing the sky.

In the passenger section Zandra opened a side panel and removed a flesh-repair kit. "Now . . . let's see about that shoulder."

Kal flinched back. "Don't touch me!" he warned her.

"Afraid I'll go blind?"

"God knows I wouldn't want to do that to you," he said.

"Not to worry. I'll be fine." And before he could stop her she'd laid the wound bare, spreading a healing paste over the laser cut.

"I don't understand," he said. "You're touching my skin, and yet—"

"And yet I'm not afflicted," she said. Zandra smiled, continuing to work on his shoulder. "I'm in no danger. Only humans are affected by Deprivers."

He stared at her. "You mean . . . that you're a . . . a *machine?*"

"Not quite," she told him. "I'm a freak . . . a Composite. Parts of me are robotic, but my main components are human tissue. Muscles . . . skin . . . bones. I'll age normally, grow old and die someday. Just as you will. But I'm not human in the exact sense you are. And I'm immune to affliction."

"Incredible," Kal murmured.

"After I was born . . . constructed might be a better term . . . they were going to experiment on me. That's when I began planning my escape. Fortunately, I was able to take you with me."

She finished with his shoulder, sealing the wound. The skin looked pink and fresh.

"There," she said. "You're good as new."

"I . . . I don't know how to thank you," he said. "There's no way I can—"

She put a finger to his mouth. "Hush!" And, slowly, she caressed his cheek.

He took her firmly into his arms. "I've never kissed a woman . . . never felt a woman's lips on mine. And—" he hesitated, trembling "—suddenly, I'm . . . I'm afraid."

"Don't be," she said, pressing her body to his.

She kissed him. Deeply. Warmly.

And the world became a very bright place for Kal Adams.

I liked "The Pool" well enough to use it as the model in a step-by-step construction of a horror story for my book, How to Write Horror Fiction (Writer's Digest, 1990).

The concept came to me when my pal Richard Matheson proudly showed me his newly-landscaped backyard swimming pool. He had completely transformed its appearance. It now looked wild and primitive, with small trees, brush, and boulders enhancing its woodland effect. Matheson's pool had taken on an unfamiliar and alien character.

People keep asking me, "Where do you get your ideas?" The answer is simple.

From other writers' swimming pools.

The Pool

(Written: May 1980)

As they turned from Sunset Boulevard and drove past the high iron gates, swan-white and edged in ornamented gold, Lizbeth muttered under her breath.

"What's the matter with you?" Jaimie asked. "You just said 'crap,' didn't you?"

"Yes, I said it."

"Why?"

She turned toward him in the MG's narrow bucket seat, frowning. "I said it because I'm angry. When I'm angry, I say crap."

"Which is my cue to ask why you're angry."

"I don't like jokes when it comes to something this important."

"So who's joking?"

"You are, by driving us here. You *said* we were going to look at our new house."

"We are. We're on the way."

"This is *Bel Air,* Jaimie!"

"Sure. Says so, right on the gate."

"Obviously, the house isn't in Bel Air."

"Why obviously?"

"Because you made just $20,000 last year on commercials, and you haven't done a new one in three months. Part-time actors who earn $20,000 a year don't buy houses in Bel Air."

"Who says I bought it?"

She stared at him. "You told me you *owned* it, that it was yours!"

He grinned. "It is, sweetcake. All mine."

"I hate being called 'sweetcake.' It's a sexist term."

"Bull! It's a term of endearment."

"You've changed the subject."

"No, *you* did," he said, wheeling the small sports roadster smoothly over the looping stretch of black asphalt.

Lizbeth gestured toward the mansions flowing past along the narrow, climbing road, castles in sugar-cake pinks and milk-chocolate browns and pastel blues. "So we're going to live in one of these?" Her voice was edged in sarcasm.

Jaimie nodded, smiling at her. "Just wait. You'll see!"

Under a cut-velvet driving cap, his tight-curled blond hair framed a deeply tanned, sensual actor's face. Looking at him, at that open, flashing smile, Lizbeth told herself once again that it was all too good to be true. Here she was, an ordinary small-town girl from Illinois, in her first year of theater arts at UCLA, about to hook up with a handsome young television actor who looked like Robert Redford and who now wanted her to live with him in Bel Air!

Lizbeth had been in California for just over a month, had known Jaimie for only half that time, and was already into a major relationship. It was dreamlike. Everything had happened so fast: meeting Jaimie at the disco, his divorce coming through, getting to know his two kids, falling in love after just three dates.

Life in California was like being caught inside one of those silent Chaplin films, where everything is speeded up and people whip dizzily back and forth across the screen. Did she *really* love Jaimie? Did he *really* love her? Did it matter?

Just let it happen, kid, she told herself. Just flow with the action.

"Here we are," said Jaimie, swinging the high-fendered little MG into a circular driveway of crushed white gravel. He braked the car, nodding toward the house. "Our humble abode!"

Lizbeth drew in a breath. Lovely! Perfect!

Not a mansion, which would have been too large and too intimidating, but a just-right two-story Spanish house topping a green-pine bluff, flanked by gardens and neatly trimmed box hedges.

"Well, do you like it?"

She giggled. "Silly question!"

"It's no castle."

"It's perfect! I hate big drafty places." She slid from the MG and stood looking at the house, hands on hips. "Wow. Oh, wow!"

"You're right about twenty-thou-a-year actors," he admitted, moving around the car to stand beside her. "This place is way beyond me."

"Then how did you . . ."

"I won it at poker last Thursday. High-stakes game. Went into it on borrowed cash. Got lucky, cleaned out the whole table, except for this tall, skinny guy who asks me if he can put up a house against what was in the pot. Said he had the deed on him and would sign it over to me if he lost the final hand."

"And you said yes."

"Damn right I did."

"And he lost?"

"Damn right he did."

She looked at the house, then back at him. "And it's legal?"

"The deed checks out. I own it all, Liz—house, gardens, pool."

"There's a *pool*?" Her eyes were shining.

He nodded. "And it's a beaut. Custom design. I

may rent it out for commercials, pick up a little extra bread."

She hugged him. "Oh, Jaimie! I've always wanted to live in a house with a pool!"

"This one's unique."

"I want to see it!"

He grinned and then squeezed her waist. "First the house, *then* the pool. Okay?"

She gave him a mock bow. "Lead on, master!"

Lizbeth found it difficult to keep her mind on the house as Jaimie led her happily from room to room. Not that the place wasn't charming and comfortable, with its solid Spanish furniture, bright rugs, and beamed ceilings. But the prospect of finally having a pool of her own was so delicious that she couldn't stop thinking about it.

"I had a cleaning service come up here and get everything ready for us," Jaimie told her. He stood in the center of the living room, looking around proudly, reminding her of a captain on the deck of his first ship. "Place needed work. Nobody's lived here in ten years."

"How do you know that?"

"The skinny guy told me. Said he'd closed it down ten years ago, after his wife left him." He shrugged. "Can't say I blame her."

"What do you know about her?"

"Nothing. But the guy's a creep, a skinny creep." He flashed his white smile. "Women prefer *attractive* guys."

She wrinkled her nose at him. "Like *you*, right?"

"Right!"

He reached for her, but she dipped away from him, pulling off his cap and draping it over her dark hair.

"You look cute that way," he said.

"Come on, show me the pool. You promised to show me."

"Yes, madame . . . the pool."

They had to descend a steep flight of weathered wooden steps to reach it. The pool was set in its own shelf of woodland terrain, notched into the hillside and screened from the house by a thick stand of trees.

"You never have to change the water," Jaimie said as they walked toward it. "Feeds itself from a stream inside the hill. It's self-renewing. Old water out, new water in. All the cleaning guys had to do was skim the leaves and stuff off the surface." He hesitated as the pool spread itself before them. "Bet you've never seen one like it!"

Lizbeth never had, not even in books or magazine photos.

It was *huge,* at least ten times larger than she'd expected, edged on all sides by gray, angular rocks. It was designed in an odd, irregular shape that actually made her . . . made her . . . suddenly made her . . .

Dizzy. I'm dizzy.

"What's wrong?"

"I don't know." She pressed a hand against her eyes. "I . . . I feel a little . . . sick."

"Are you having your . . ."

"No, it's not that. I felt fine until . . ." She turned away toward the house. "I just don't like it."

"What don't you like?"

"The pool," she said, breathing deeply. "I don't like the pool. There's something wrong about it."

He looked confused. "I thought you'd *love* it!" His tone held irritation. "Didn't you just tell me you always wanted—"

"Not one like this," she interrupted, overriding his words. "Not *this* one." She touched his shoulder. "Can we go back to the house now? It's cold here. I'm freezing."

He frowned. "But it's *warm,* Liz! Must be eighty at least. How can you be cold?"

She was shivering and hugging herself for warmth. "But I am! Can't you feel the chill?"

"All right," he sighed. "Let's go back."

She didn't speak during the climb up to the house.

Below them, wide and black and deep, the pool rippled its dark skin, a stirring, sluggish, patient movement in the windless afternoon.

Upstairs, naked in the Spanish four-poster bed, Lizbeth could not imagine what had come over her at the pool. Perhaps the trip up to the house along the sharply winding road had made her carsick. Whatever the reason, by the time they were back in the house, the dizziness had vanished, and she'd enjoyed the curried chicken dinner Jaimie had cooked for them. They'd sipped white wine by a comforting hearth fire and then made love there tenderly late into the night, with the pulsing flame tinting their bodies in shades of pale gold.

"Jan and David are coming by in the morning," he had told her. "Hope you don't mind."

"Why should I? I think your kids are great."

"I thought we'd have this first Sunday together, just the two of us; but school starts for them next week, and I promised they could spend the day here."

"I don't mind. Really I don't."

He kissed the tip of her nose. "That's my girl."

"The skinny man . . ."

"What about him?"

"I don't understand why he didn't try to sell this house in the ten years when he wasn't living here."

"I don't know. Maybe he didn't need the money."

"Then why bet it on a poker game? Surely the pot wasn't anywhere near equal to the worth of this place."

"It was just a way for him to stay in the game. He had a straight flush and thought he'd win."

"Was he upset at losing the place?"

Jaimie frowned at that question. "Now that you mention it, he didn't seem to be. He took it very calmly."

"You said that he left after his wife split. Did he talk about her at all?"

"He told me her name."

"Which was?"

"Gail. Her name was Gail."

Now, lying in the upstairs bed, Lizbeth wondered what had happened to Gail. It was odd somehow to think that Gail and the skinny man had made love in this same bed. In a way, she'd taken Gail's place.

Lizbeth still felt guilty about saying no to Jaimie

when he'd suggested a post midnight swim. "Not tonight, darling. I've a slight headache. Too much wine, maybe. You go on without me."

And so he'd gone on down to the pool alone, telling her that such a mild, late-summer night was just too good to waste, that he'd take a few laps around the pool and be back before she finished her cigarette.

Irritated with herself, Lizbeth stubbed out the glowing Pall Mall in the bedside ashtray. Smoking was a filthy habit—ruins your lungs, stains your teeth. And smoking in bed was doubly stupid. You fall asleep . . . the cigarette catches the bed on fire. She *must* stop smoking. All it took was some real will power, and if . . .

Lizbeth sat up abruptly, easing her breath to listen. Nothing. No sound.

That was wrong. The open bedroom window overlooked the pool, and she'd been listening, behind her thoughts, to Jaimie splashing about below in the water.

Now she suddenly realized that the pool sounds had ceased, totally.

She smiled at her own nervous reaction. The silence simply meant that Jaimie had finished his swim and was out of the pool and headed back to the house. He'd be here any second.

But he didn't arrive.

Lizbeth moved to the window. Moonlight spilled across her breasts as she leaned forward to peer out into the night. The pale mirror glimmer of the pool flickered in the darkness below, but the bulk of trees screened it from her vision.

"Jaimie!" Her voice pierced the silence. "Jaimie, are you still down there?"

No reply. Nothing from the pool. She called his name again, without response.

Had something happened while he was swimming? Maybe a sudden stomach cramp or a muscle spasm from the cold water? No, he would have called out for help. She would have heard him.

Then . . . what? Surely this was no practical joke, an attempt to scare her? No, impossible. That would be cruel, and Jaimie's humor was never cruel. But he might think of it as fun, a kind of hide and seek in a new house. *Damn him!*

Angry now, she put on a nightrobe and stepped into her slippers. She hurried downstairs, out the back door, across the damp lawn, to the pool steps.

"Jaimie! If this is a game, I don't like it! Damn it, I *mean* that!" She peered downward; the moonlit steps were empty. "*Answer* me!"

Then, muttering "Crap!" under her breath, she started down the clammy wooden steps, holding to the cold iron pipe rail. The descent seemed even more precipitous in the dark, and she forced herself to move slowly.

Reaching level ground, Lizbeth could see the pool. She moved closer for a full view. It was silent and deserted. Where was Jaimie? She suddenly was gripped by the familiar sense of dizzy nausea as she stared at the odd, weirdly angled rock shapes forming the pool's perimeter. She tried to look away. And *couldn't.*

It wants me!

That terrible thought seized her mind. But what wanted her? The pool? No . . . something *in* the pool.

She kicked off the bedroom slippers and found herself walking toward the pool across the moon-sparkled grass, spiky and cold against the soles of her bare feet.

Stay back! Stay away from it!

But she couldn't. Something was drawing her toward the black pool, something she could not resist.

At the rocks, facing the water, she unfastened her nightrobe, allowing it to slip free of her body.

She was alabaster under the moon, a subtle curving of leg, of thigh, of neck and breast. Despite the jarring hammer of her heart, Lizbeth knew that she had to step forward into the water.

It wants me!

The pool was black glass, and she looked down into it, at the reflection of her body, like white fire on the still surface.

Now . . . a ripple, a stirring, a deep-night movement from below.

Something was coming—a shape, a dark mass, gliding upward toward the surface.

Lizbeth watched, hypnotized, unable to look away, unable to obey the screaming, pleading voice inside her: *Run! Run!*

And then she saw Jaimie's hand. It broke the surface of the pool, reaching out to her.

His face bubbled free of the clinging black water, and acid bile leaped into her throat. She gagged, gasped for air, her eyes wide in sick shock.

It was *part* Jaimie, part something else!

It smiled at her with Jaimie's wide, white-toothed open mouth, but, oh God! only *one* of its eyes belonged to Jaimie. It had three others, all horribly different. It had *part* of Jaimie's face, *part* of his body.

Run! Don't go to it! Get away!

But Lizbeth did not run. Gently, she folded her warm, pink-fleshed hand into the icy wet horror of that hand in the pool and allowed herself to be drawn slowly forward. Downward. As the cold, receiving waters shocked her skin, numbing her, as the black liquid rushed into her open mouth, into her lungs and stomach and body, filling her as a cup is filled, her final image, the last thing she saw before closing her eyes, was Jaimie's wide-lipped, shining smile—an expanding patch of brightness fading down . . . deep . . . very deep . . . into the pool's black depths.

Jan and David arrived early that Sunday morning, all giggles and shouts, breathing hard from the ride on their bikes.

A whole Sunday with Dad. A fine, warm-sky summer day with school safely off somewhere ahead and not bothering them. A big house to roam in, and yards to run in, and caramel-ripple ice cream waiting (Dad had promised to buy some!), and games to play, and . . .

"Hey! Look what I found!"

Jan was yelling at David. They had gone around to the back of the house when no one answered the bell, looking for their father. Now eight-year-old Jan was at the bottom of a flight of high wooden steps, yelling up at her brother. David was almost ten and tall for his age.

"What is it?"

"Come and see!"

He scrambled down the steps to join her.

"Jeez!" he said. "A pool! I never saw one *this* big before!"

"Me neither."

David looked over his shoulder, up at the silent house.

"Dad's probably out somewhere with his new girl-friend."

"Probably," Jan agreed.

"Let's try the pool while we're waiting. What do you say?"

"Yeah, let's!"

They began pulling off their shirts.

Motionless in the depths of the pool, at the far end, where rock and tree shadows darkened the surface, it waited, hearing the tinkling, high child voices filtering down to it in the sound-muted waters. It was excited because it had never absorbed a child; a child was new and fresh—new pleasures, new strengths.

It had formed itself within the moist deep soil of the hill, and the pool had nurtured and fed it, helping it grow, first with small, squirming water bugs and other yard insects. It had absorbed them, using their eyes and their hard, metallic bodies to shape itself. Then the pool had provided a dead bird, and now it had feathers along part of its back, and the bird's sharp beak formed part of its face. Then a plump gray rat had been drawn into the water, and the rat's glassy eye became part of the thing's body. A cat had drowned here, and its claws and matted fur added new elements to the thing's expanding mass.

Finally, when it was still young, a golden-haired woman, Gail, had come here alone to swim that long-ago night, and the pool had taken her, given her as a fine new gift to the thing in its depths. And Gail's long silk-gold hair streamed out of the thing's mouth (one of its mouths, for it had several), and it had continued to grow, to shape itself.

Then, last night, this man, Jaimie had come to it. And his right eye now burned like blue phosphor from the thing's face. Lizbeth had followed, and her slim-fingered hands, with their long, lacquered nails, now pulsed in wormlike convulsive motion along the lower body of the pool-thing.

Now it was excited again, trembling, ready for new bulk, new lifestuffs to shape and use. It rippled in dark anticipation, gathering itself, feeling the pleasure and the hunger.

Faintly, above it, the boy's cry: "Last one in's a fuzzy green monkey!" It rippled to the vibrational splash of two young bodies striking the water.

It glided swiftly toward the children.

The story was selected for the 8th Annual Year's Best SF *although it has nothing to do with science fiction. It's a lightly-disguised study of madness. On a surface level, "One of Those Days" is wildly humorous, but the style is deceptive. Here, suddenly, reality is fractured. The world around my luckless protagonist is no longer real. He is beyond hope.*

Join him for a trip into bedlam.

One of Those Days

(Written: January 1959)

I knew it was going to be one of those days when I heard a blue-and-yellow butterfly humming *Si, mi chiamano Mimi*, my favorite aria from *La Boheme*. I was weeding the garden when the papery insect fluttered by, humming beautifully.

I got up, put aside my garden tools, and went into the house to dress. Better see my psychoanalyst at once.

Neglecting my cane and spats, I snapped an old homburg on my head and aimed for Dr. Mellowthin's office in downtown Los Angeles.

Several disturbing things happened to me on the way . . .

First of all, a large stippled tomcat darted out of an alley immediately after I'd stepped from the bus. The cat was walking on its hind legs and carried a bundle of frothy pink blanketing in its front paws. It looked desperate.

"Gangway!" shouted the cat. "Baby! Live baby here! Clear back. BACK for the baby!"

Then it was gone, having dipped cat-quick across

the street, losing itself in heavy traffic. Drawing in a deep lungful of air, smog-laden but steadying, I resumed my brisk pace toward Dr. Mellowthin's office.

As I passed a familiar apartment house a third-story window opened and Wally Jenks popped his head over the sill and called down to me. "Hi," yelled Wally. "C'mon up for a little drinkie. Chop, chop."

I shaded my eyes to get a clearer look at him, and yelled back: "On my way to Mellowthin's."

"Appointment?" he queried.

"Spur of the moment," I replied.

"Then time's no problem. Up you come, old dads, or I shan't forgive you."

I sighed and entered the building. Jenks was 3G, and I decided to use the stairs. Elevators trap you. As I reached the second-floor landing I obeyed an irresistible urge to bend down and place my ear close to the base of the wall near the floor.

"You mice still *in* there?" I shouted.

To which a thousand tiny musical Disney-voices shot back: "Damned *right* we are!"

I shrugged, adjusted my homburg, and continued the upward climb.

Jenks met me at the door with a dry martini.

"Thanks," I said, sipping. As usual, it was superb. Old Wally sure knew his martinis.

"Well," he said, "How goes."

"Badsville," I answered. "Care to hear?"

"By all means. Unburden."

We sat down, facing one another across the taste-fully furnished room. I sipped the martini and told Wally about things. "This morning, 'bout forty min-utes ago, I heard a butterfly humming Puccini. Then I saw a cat carrying what I can only suppose was a live baby."

"Human?"

"Don't know. Could have been a cat-baby."

"Cat say anything?"

"He shouted 'Gangway!'"

"Proceed."

"Then, on the way up here, I had a brief conversa-tional exchange with at least a thousand mice."

"In the walls?"

"Where else?"

"Finish your drinkie," said Jenks, finishing his. I did so.

"'Nother?" he asked.

Nope. Got to be trotting. I'm in for a mental purge."

"Well, I wouldn't worry too much," he assured me. "Humming insects, talking felines and oddball answering mice are admittedly unsettling. But . . . there *are* stranger things in this world."

I looked at him. And knew he was correct—for old

Wally Jenks had turned into a loose-pelted brown camel with twin humps, all stained and worn looking at the tops. I swallowed.

"See you," I said.

Wally grinned, or rather the camel did, and it was awful. Long, cracked yellow teeth like old carnival dishes inside his black gums. I gave a nervous little half-wave and moved for the door. One final glance over my shoulder at old Jenks verified the fact that he was still grinning at me with those big wet desert-red eyes of his.

Back on the street I quickened my stride, anxious now to reach Mellowthin and render a full account of the day's events. Only a half-block to go.

Then a policeman stopped me. He was all sweaty inside his tight uniform, and his face was dark with hatred.

"Thought you was the wise one, eh Mugger?" he rasped, his voice venom-filled. "Thought you could give John Law the finger!"

"But officer, I don't—"

"Come right along, Mugger. We got special cages for the likes a you."

He was about to snap a pair of silver cuffs over my wrists when I put a quick knee to his vitals and rabbit-punched him on the way down. Then I grabbed his service revolver.

"Here!" I shouted to several passers-by. "This man is a fraud. Killed a cop to get this rig. He's a swine of the worst sort. Record as long as your arm. Blackmail, rape, arson, auto-theft, kidnapping, grand larceny, wife-beating, and petty pilfering. You name it, he has *done* it."

I thrust the revolver at a wide-eyed, trembling woman. "Take this weapon, lady. And if he makes a funny move, shoot to kill!"

She aimed the gun at the stunned policeman, who was only now getting his breath. He attempted to rise.

"OOPS!" I yelled, "he's going for a knife. Let him have it! Quick!"

The trembling woman shut her eyes and pulled the trigger. The cop pitched forward on his face.

"May heaven forgive you!" I moaned, backing away. "You've killed an officer of the law, a defender of the public morals. May heaven be merciful!"

The woman flapped off. She had turned into a heavy-billed pelican. The policeman had become a fat-bellied seal with flippers, but he was still dead.

Hurrying, and somewhat depressed, I entered Dr. Mellowthin's office and told the girl at the desk it was an emergency.

"You may go right in," she told me. "The doctor will see you at once."

In another moment I was pumping Mellowthin's hand.

"Sit down, boy," he told me. "So—we've got our little complications again today, have we?"

"Sure have," I said, pocketing one of his cigars. I noted that it was stale.

"Care to essay the couch?"

I slid onto the dark rich leather and closed my eyes.

"Now tell us all about it."

"First, a butterfly sang *La Boheme,* or hummed it rather. Then a tomcat ran out of an alley with a baby in its paws. Then some mice in an apartment house yelled at me. Then one of my oldest and dearest friends turned into a camel."

"One hump or two?" asked Mellowthin.

"Two," I said. "Large and scruffy and all worn at the tops."

"Anything else?"

"Then a big pseudo-Irish cop stopped me. His dialogue was fantastic. Called me Mugger. Said I was fit for a cage. Started to put cuffs on me. I kneed him in the kishkas and gave his gun to a nice trembly lady who shot him. Then she turned into a pelican and flapped off and he turned into a seal with flippers. Then I came here."

I opened my eyes and stared at Dr. Mellowthin. "What's the matter?" he asked, somewhat uneasily.

"Well," I said, "to begin with, you have large brown, sad-looking liquidy eyes."

"And . . ."

"And I bet your nose is cold!" I grinned.

"Anything else?"

"Not really."

"What about my *overall* appearance?"

"Well, of course, you're covered with long black shaggy hair, even down to the tips of your floppy ears." A moment of strained silence. "Can you do tricks?" I asked.

"A few," Mellowthin replied, shifting in his chair.

"Roll over!" I commanded.

He did.

"Play dead!"

His liquidy eyes rolled up white and his long pink tongue lolled loosely from his jaws.

"Good doggie," I said. "Nice doggie."

"Woof," barked Dr. Mellowthin softly, wagging his tail.

Putting on my homburg, I tossed him a bone I'd saved from the garden and left his office.

There was no getting around it.

This was simply one of those days.

Bob Bloch was a longtime pal of mine. He wrote a wonderful Afterword to one of my books and we often talked about the power of icons. "You'll always be 'Robert (Psycho) Bloch' and I'll always be 'William F. (Logan's Run) Nolan.' Even though we've both written a ton of other stuff."

He shrugged. "So what's so terrible about that? How many writers can you name who've created a world icon in their careers? Let's be grateful for the success. Logan's Run is your lifelong calling card, and Psycho is mine. We're lucky to have them."

Which is why Bob called his best anthology Psycho-Paths. It fit his iconic label.

He wanted a Nolan story for the book. I gave him this one.

Him, Her, Them

(Written: July 1989)

HIM

He walked in darkness.

He was quite tall, with startling blue eyes and a sleek, strong body that he was proud of, that he worked on constantly, the way a mechanic works on the engine of a fine automobile. All the stomach muscles were sharply defined, and the biceps were terrific. (That's what one of his women had told him: "You have terrific biceps.")

He liked women, enjoyed the thrill he got out of them, but he didn't respect them. Women were, by nature, cheats and liars, and you could never dare to trust one. They never say what they really mean. Men are usually more honest and direct. *Real* men, that is. It disgusted him to think of Rock Hudson. The rugged actor had been one of his top favorites, especially in Westerns. He liked Westerns. Lots of shooting but very little blood.

He hated blood.

Blood made him sick, the sight of it. You want to kill a chicken, you wring its neck. Hands are extremely effective instruments. Strong, muscled hands.

He had become very angry at Hudson when he found out that the Rock (the way he used to refer to him) was actually homosexual. Doing it with other men! A real shock, finding out a thing like that about the Rock. Well, at least Hudson was dead now. God's vengeance. The fruits of perdition. Ha! Double meaning there.

He didn't actually believe in any *particular* God, just God in general. He could envision a kind of white-bearded old gentleman in a flowing robe seated on a golden throne with lightning bolts coming out of each extended hand, out of the fingertips. Blue and silver lightning that kills. Without blood. You don't screw around with the Old Man.

He liked to walk at night. Darkness soothed him; it was soft and inviting. Really exciting things happen in the dark. Daylight was harsh and unforgiving; the sun stabbed at his pale blue eyes. ("You have eyes just like Paul Newman," a woman told him at a motel in Detroit. She was really attractive, but quite stupid. And, she'd doused herself with cheap perfume that made him want to throw up. But he got the thrill out of her, so it was okay. Getting the thrill was all that counted!)

He always wore his shades in daylight to protect his delicate eyes—but at night he was like a hunting cat; he could see extraordinarily well in the dark. One of his gifts. From the Old Man. From God. Ha!

He had weights in the back of his van and he worked out with them for at least an hour each morning. This way he was able to build muscle mass and maintain the basic strength of body necessary to survive. He needed strength in his arms to handle the big, cross-country rigs he'd driven. And in his shoulders and back for construction jobs. And in his legs for warehouse work. And in his hands . . .

Men are strong. Women are weak. His mother used to tell him that. She was an invalid. Stayed in bed most of the time. He'd go into her room that smelled of medicine and dead flowers and she'd read to him from the Bible every day when he was a kid. Now he couldn't remember a single word from the Good Book. She'd never held him or kissed him or told him she loved him; she read all those Bible words to him instead. Her way of expressing love, God's love, through the Good Book. That's when he began thinking of God as the Old Man. When she was gone the Old Man would be looking out for him.

His own father had never looked out for him. His

father was a cold bastard. Never spoke to his mother, once she got sick. Blamed her for it. His parents were like two strangers living in the same house. And they died in that house without ever saying goodbye. To each other, or to him. No goodbyes.

He was thirty-six and had never been married. Never in love, so why get married? Women had always been attracted to him, to his smile and intense blue eyes and muscled body. And he was good at telling jokes. Could make a woman laugh like a loon. ("Guy couldn't afford to buy any cheese for his mouse trap, so he cut out a *picture* of some cheese and used that in the trap. Guess what he caught? He caught a *picture* of a mouse!") Trouble was, they were ugly when they laughed, their red mouths too wide. You could see their repaired teeth and their fat tongues all coated with saliva. He'd never liked to tongue-kiss. Exchanging all that saliva. Ugh!

But he liked them for the thrill. They gave him that, each of them—in hotel rooms across the country, in their bedrooms, in motels and the backs of vans and sometimes in their cars. The place didn't much matter, so long as it was at night. In the dark, always, with the lights out and his hands on them . . .

Then he saw her, crossing at the far corner and heading for an all-night drugstore. He knew right away that *she* was the one. It was an instinct he had, a kind of gut reaction that he always trusted. Never doubt your instincts. His mother had told him that.

His pale eyes studied her as she entered the drugstore.

She was young, maybe twenty or so. With a good, firm body, and a lovely soft fall of blond hair along her back—like burning gold.

He went in after her.

She was standing near the front counter, her back to him. The overhead lights shone on her hair. "Do you have *Cosmo*?" she asked the clerk who hardly glanced at her. Probably a homosexual.

"We're all sold out," he told her, fiddling with something behind the counter. "New issue comes in next week."

"Then I'll just take a pack of Camels," she said, handling him a five-dollar bill.

He was over by the candy display, watching as she got her cigarettes and change. Smoking was really bad for her, and she was a fool to smoke. But then, he thought, with a faint smile, most women are fools. This one was a lovely young fool with burnt-gold hair and all he wanted from her was the thrill. So it didn't matter if she smoked Camels. He disliked those billboards with a camel all dressed up like James Bond in a tux, smoking and trying to look super-cool. A camel was ugly; it could never look like James Bond.

The suave secret agent was a passion of his. The way 007 handled women excited him. Bond was rough with them. Just took what he wanted and left them flat. He had never read the books, but he'd seen all the movies. His favorite was *Goldfinger,* had seen it four times. He liked the way the girl died, all covered in gold paint. That was very exciting.

Now she glanced in his direction as she moved toward the door with her cigarettes. He could tell she was instantly attracted to him. There was sudden electricity in the air between them, sparked by his Newman-blue eyes. Hers were brown, like the eyes of a fawn.

He followed her outside. She looked back at him as he approached her.

"Pardon me, but I know where you can get a copy of *Cosmopolitan,*" he said.

She looked amused, standing by the door of her orange Honda Civic. "You heard me ask for it?"

He nodded, smiling. (He had a terrific smile.)

"It's got an article on Meryl Streep," she told him.

"Probably the best actress in films today," he said.

The young woman shrugged. "Well, *do* you?"

"Do I what?"

"Know where I can get the latest issue?"

"Oh, sure. Sure I do." He moved closer to her, close enough to detect the subtle fragrance of her hair. The scent excited him. "All-night newsstand. On Nelson at Fifth."

"I've just moved here," she said. "Afraid I don't know where—"

"I can show you. It's really not far."

She hesitated, then unlocked the passenger door. "Climb in. After I buy the issue I'll drive you back here again. Will that be all right?"

"Fine," he said. "That'll be fine."

As they drove away into the darkness, he was thinking how simple it was for him to deal with women, once that initial attraction was established. It was always so easy, picking them up. He'd read in the papers about how careful women were being these days, with all the rapes and murders happening in the big cities, and maybe *some* women were like that, very careful about meeting strange men. But he'd never had any problems along this line. Maybe it was his smile.

"You live here in town?" she asked, flicking her soft brown eyes at him.

"No, I'm just passing through," he told her. "I like to keep on the move. Natural traveling man."

"A salesman?"

"I've sold things. But not often. Mostly I just work at whatever comes along. Guess you could say I've done a little of everything." ·

What he'd said made her suspicious. "If you're just passing through town, how do you know where the all-night newsstand is?"

"I read a lot of newspapers—from different cities," he said. "So I check the phone book. I always look up the biggest newsstand when I come to a new place."

"Why do you read so many papers?"

"I just like to keep up with things," he said. "Habit I got into."

"Don't you watch the news on TV?"

He shook his head. "No. It's too thin and superficial. Newspapers cover things in depth. Television goes for surface sensationalism."

They were moving along Nelson when he pointed ahead. "There's Fifth Street, at the next corner."

She pulled the Honda to a stop in front of Al's All-Night Newsstand, cut the engine. She smiled at him. "This is real nice of you. I'll only be a minute."

"Take your time. I got nowhere to go."

He watched the way she walked, watched her buy the magazine, watched the way her body moved under the tight blue dress, smooth and silky-sexy. The dress was snug across her buttocks and he watched the play of muscle. Tight and fine. Her legs were firm, long thighed, the way he liked.

This one would give him a real thrill, all right. All

he had to do was play it cool. Guess the Old Man was still looking out for him.

When they were driving down Nelson again he said, "Where you from? Before you came here."

"Indianapolis. Native Hoosier. Love basketball, but I hate Indiana winters."

"Yeah, I know what you mean," he said. "Cold cuts right through you like a knife. Chicago's even worse."

"That's where you're from . . . Chicago?"

"I grew up in Waukegan. Guess you could say it's part of Greater Chicago."

"I've heard of it. Wasn't Hemingway born there?"

He laughed. "No, that's Oak Park. But you're close. They're both part of the same general area. And the winters are murder."

"So we're both summer people," she said, smiling. Her teeth were white and perfect in the faint reflected light from the dash. He liked perfect teeth.

"What do *you* do?" he asked.

"I'm a legal secretary. Just started this new job, but it looks like it's going to be a good one. Kind of a challenge. I like challenges."

So do I, he thought. What he said was, "You're not married then? I mean, you don't *sound* married."

"Nope. Mr. Wonderful hasn't stopped by to tap on

my door yet. Someday, maybe." She flashed her brown eyes at him. "You?"

"The same. I never met a woman I wanted to marry."

"Maybe we're both too particular," she said.

"Listen," he said, leaning across the seat as she drove, close enough to catch the scent of her brushed-gold hair. "I've got a challenge for you."

"What's that?" she said.

"I challenge you to have a drink with me. You're fun to talk to."

"So are you," she said, turning her head to look into his eyes. "Where?"

"There's bound to be a bar along here if we keep driving."

"I hate bars," she told him. "They're always too noisy and I wind up with a headache. Why not have a drink at my place?"

"Great," he said. And his lips curved in a faint smile of triumph. This was working out just the way he hoped it would. Her place. Perfect.

Just perfect.

She stopped the Honda on a side street next to a tall pink stucco two-story building with a clipped hedge. Town house. Classy.

They got out, walked up a short flight of outside

steps, and she keyed open a side door, waving him inside. A light was on in the kitchen and it made her skin seem phosphorescent.

Once the door was closed, she turned to him, pushing back her hair. Her forest eyes were shining. She raised her hand, gently touched his cheek.

He leaned forward to meet her, took her confidently into his arms. The kiss was deep, intense. He could feel her body tremble.

She was his.

He felt the soft pressure of her full breasts pressing into his chest. Heat seemed to shimmer from her skin. She wants it, he thought. She can't wait for it.

Like most women, she didn't turn on the light in the bedroom. They undressed in darkness. Not total darkness; he could see the white of her curved body as she turned to him.

"Wow," she said softly, her voice a deep cat-purr. "You must work out." She traced a slow finger along his muscled shoulder. "You must work out a *lot*."

"I do," he said. "My body is my temple."

He picked her up, walked to the bed, lowered her onto the soft flowered sheets. She was ready.

Vulnerable.

Open.

Ready.

He entered in a single, deep, hard-thrusting movement, igniting the sensual thrill that only a willing woman could provide.

A deep guttural sound issued from her throat, exciting him. "Wait . . . before . . ." She thrust up against him, her hips seeking, greedy. "I have something . . . be good for us both . . ." Her right hand was fumbling in the drawer of the night table next to the bed.

Drugs, he thought. She has something to give us an extra jolt.

"Try this," she said—and plunged the slim silver ice pick solidly into his back, skillfully penetrating his central heart muscle.

He heard three more words from her before he died.

"You were easy," she said.

HER

The next afternoon, a Saturday, she went to a horror movie. Got in for the matinee price. She had a genuine passion for horror on the screen, an addiction that began when she was ten and her mom had taken her to see Vincent Price in a movie about a wax museum where really frightening things happened.

There was a fire and all the people melted, their skin boiling and blistering and rippling away, glass eyes sliding down their cheeks, hands and feet shriveling and curling . . . That film had given her nightmares for a month, and she had felt her own skin melting from her bones in the darkness of her bed. She'd wake up screaming, heart pounding.

Daddy was furious with her mom for taking her to see such a scary movie. They had a terrible, shouting fight over it, one of the many fights they had. Daddy always won because he could shout louder—and once he pointed a loaded gun at her mom. It was that one time, with the gun, that made Mom divorce him.

That afternoon she was scanning the local news in a coffee shop downtown when she saw the announcement. In the entertainment section:

MEET TERRY CARTER!

Today
From 1 P.M. to 5 P.M.
B. Dalton Book Store
In the Magic Mall

TERRY CARTER
will be here to sign copies
of his new book.

Come and join us.
Meet the Master of Mayhem
and have him personally autograph
a copy of his latest shocker . . .
DEATH DEVILS!

She was suddenly flushed and shaking. What a marvelous opportunity—the chance to meet a genius whose mind spawned epics of terror, who understood the true power of darkness and death. Besides, she'd have a brand-new Carter book to read. She'd heard he was working on a new one, and here it was. What an opportunity!

She checked her watch: 3 P.M. Still plenty of time. The Magic Mall was just two blocks away, opposite the Federal Building. Easy walking distance. Should she go home first and shower? Put on fresh makeup, change her clothes? No, she'd just walk right over there as she was. No delays. She didn't have much patience for delays.

As she walked she thought about her parents . . . By the time she was in high school, Daddy had moved to Kansas City and she saw him only on vacations. He looked worse each time, drinking the way he did. His face began to look melted, like the figures in the museum.

Mom enjoyed being single again; she dated a new man every weekend, and most of them spent the night. Her mom told her she felt "free."

Now, as a grown woman, she didn't see her mom anymore. Didn't care to. Didn't love her. Didn't love her daddy, either. As a child, she'd been just one more thing for them to argue over, an object more than a person. So there wasn't any love among the three of them. She knew her parents never really gave a damn about her, and the feeling was mutual.

She had a pretty face and a sexy body (terrific boobs at thirteen!) and guys liked her. She never dated boys her own age. At fifteen, she was sleeping with a thirty-five-year-old man. Young boys were boring, and they never had enough money to give her a good time.

She was hit on constantly—at the movies, in stores, at the shopping mall, and often at the gym where she worked out to maintain her figure. She was obsessive when it came to her figure; if she gained a pound or two she'd live on water and grape-fruit until the extra weight had vanished.

She was puzzled about why she could never seem to fall in love. Maybe it was because there had never been any love in her childhood and she didn't know *how* to love someone. She felt desire, sexual excite-ment, but that wasn't the same.

She began to see men as predatory animals, on the hunt for physical delights, using her to obtain these delights. Just an object—as she'd always been from childhood.

She hated being used.

The great thing about horror movies was that death solved all the problems. The monster came along and chopped everybody up and got away neat to come back in the next picture and do it all over again. As she watched, she always cheered the monster on. Oh, yeah! *Do* it to them! Go, big Daddy! Slice 'n' dice!

Love was an axe, or a knife, or an ice pick.

She especially enjoyed watching Freddy in that *Nightmare on Elm Street* series, with his razor-gloved hand and his glittery pig eyes and fire-ravaged skin. Freddy was great. He liked to make little jokes before he slashed up his victims. He was a riot! Great sense of humor. Freddy was always able to crack her up, the things he said. She'd laugh so hard sometimes the tears would come to her eyes—and then quite suddenly she'd be crying. She didn't know why she did that, why she cried after laughing. But both things would happen at once. Weird.

She liked to read horror books almost as much as seeing horror movies. Had a complete collection of Stephen King paperbacks. He was her favorite. In fact, his book *The Shining* was a whole lot scarier than the movie. In the movie you didn't get to see those animals made out of bushes, didn't get to see them come to life the way they did in the book. Now every time she walked by the high, trimmed hedge outside her building she imagined it was moving, growing teeth and eyes, getting ready to attack her. It was a scary feeling, but it was also kind of *delicious*.

Of course, she knew it couldn't really happen, that a hedge creature could never slash her flesh, so the fear was never tangible, never truly real.

Still, it was a lot of fun to think about stuff like that.

Beyond Stephen King, her second-favorite horror writer was Terry Carter. What a warm, happy name for the man called the Master of Mayhem. That's how his publishers described him in the ads for his books: "Another Tour into Terror from the Master of Mayhem!"

She'd read every one of his four best-sellers (devoured was more the word for it): *Slash by Night, Slaughter Sisters, Bloodaxe,* and *The Nightstabbers.* The last one was really frightening, about this gang of kids who started out human and gradually turned into alien things who slashed up everybody they met, then ate them, even their bones. There would just be this little pile of clothing left on the street for the cops to find. Certainly, it was Carter's best novel, no doubt about that. When she read about gangs in the papers she always thought about the Nightstabbers.

She walked faster. Even this short trip to the mall was torture. Knowing that Terry Carter was waiting for her was enough to set her pulse racing.

Questions burned in her mind. Could she lure him to her bed as she had lured so many others? Would he be attracted to her? Would her body serve to draw him to her as the fly is drawn to the web? It wouldn't be enough, just meeting Terry Carter.

Not nearly enough.

B. Dalton's was crowded as usual on a Saturday, and a line had formed at the rear of the store. Mostly women. Giggling nervously. Clutching their newly purchased copies of *Death Devils*. Waiting to get a personal autograph from the Master of Mayhem.

The procedure was to pay for the book, then line up for an autograph. She couldn't see what Terry Carter looked like; the line forked around a corner where he was seated at a desk. But that was all right. First she wanted to examine his latest book. She picked up a copy from the tall stack on the display table.

The dust jacket pictured a blazing-eyed Hell Crea-ture crouched over a screaming young woman who was spread-eagled on a lab table. The demon was in the process of clawing the clothes from her body. His fingernails were long daggers (like Freddy's glove!) and he had already ripped away most of her blouse.

She noted that the illustration was in good taste since a swirl of hellish steam obscured the victim's naked breasts (you couldn't see the nipples). The colors were bright and garish, emphasizing the red veins in the terrified girl's popping eyes.

Obviously, another Carter classic.

When she rounded the fork in the line and got her first sight of Terry Carter she was shocked. And amused. Now she could understand why no photo of him had ever been used on the jackets of any of his books—because he was *not* what his readers would have expected. Terry Carter was anything but sinister. He was, in fact, a mild, gentle-faced man. Perhaps thirty-five. With a full head of dark hair and tranquil gray eyes. An easy-smiling man in a dark blue, neatly pressed suit and cream-colored button-down shirt, and wearing a classic red striped tie. Could have been dressed for a Yale college reunion. No monster. Just a pleasant fellow who spoke softly and acknowledged each compliment with a warm smile.

In the line, she'd been framing the words she would say to him; it was important that she make a strong initial impression.

"Every one of your books is a masterwork, and your characters are totally alive on the page. I think you write better than Edgar Allan Poe."

He looked up at her with a degree of amazement, taking the copy of *Death Devils* from her slim-fingered hand. "That's wonderful to hear," he said, his voice smooth and deep-toned. "No one has ever told me I write better than Mr. Poe. I'd like to believe you."

And he gave her one of his warmest smiles.

"Could you personalize the inscription?" she asked.

"Of course." His black felt-tip was poised above the title page. "I'll need your name."

"Judy," she said. "Just make it Judy."

And he wrote, in a flowing scrawl across the page: "Happy Nightmares to Judy, from Terry Carter."

At first, she hadn't been certain she could pull it off, seducing this quiet man in his conservative suit—but as he handed the book to her their eyes locked and held. And she knew he was hers. Her prize. All hers.

To do with as she desired.

It was in his eyes. His surrender was implicit—and total.

*　　*　　*

She was waiting for him just after five outside B. Dalton, watching him shake hands with the store manager, a flustered, middle-aged woman. The woman's smile was strained and her hand shook. Genius and fame can intimidate.

He left the store carrying a scuffed leather briefcase, and she walked up to him just as he reached the elevators.

"Remember me?" she said brightly. "Judy?"

The warm smile. The flash of eyes. "Of course. How could I ever forget you?" he said. "The perceptive lady who tells me I write better than Poe."

"You're on a book tour, right? One town to the next?"

"That's right. I'm due in Des Moines tomorrow morning."

"And you're traveling alone?"

"Unhappily, yes."

"And you have nowhere in particular to go? Tonight, I mean?"

"Right again." He smiled.

"I think you deserve some company. I'm volunteering." She canted her head, pushing a strand of hair away from her face. "I hate to see a man like you eating all alone."

He nodded, smiling again. "That's very sweet of you, to care about a stranger."

"You're no stranger to me," she told him. "I've read all your books at least three times. I feel as if we're old friends."

"I know what you mean. I've always felt there's a special bond between writer and reader. A bond of . . . intimacy, perhaps."

"Then you'll let me take you to dinner?"

"So long as you allow *me* to pay for it. My publisher is footing the bills for this tour."

"Okay, Mr. Carter, we've got a deal." And she put out her hand.

He took it gently, turning the handshake into a kiss. His lips pressed her fingers. "Please . . . call me Terry. After all, as you point out, we're really old friends."

She drove him to one of the town's best seafood restaurants. (A friend at work had mentioned the place, giving it high marks.) They both admitted to a passion for sand dabs with hollandaise sauce.

The food was superb.

Over wine, at the end of the meal, she leaned toward him: "There's something I've always wanted to know about you."

"Ah." He tipped back his head. "Which is?"

"Well . . . I've read all the bios on the dust jackets

of your books, and I read that article on you in *Writer's Digest* last year . . ."

"I'm afraid I sounded a bit pompous in that one."

"Not at all," she said. "It was a wonderful interview. I just wondered why you've never married. I know it's none of my business, and very personal, but—"

"Oh, I don't mind talking about it. The truth is, I was, in fact, married once. To a girl I met in college. We fell in love and married right after graduation. But it didn't last long." His voice dropped. "She died in an accident. I've just found it too painful to discuss with interviewers, so I leave out that part of my life. At least for public consumption. Understand?"

"Absolutely," she said, pressing his hand across the table. "And I'm so glad you were willing to confide in me."

It was easy, getting him to stop at her place for a nightcap before he returned to his hotel. And it was easy to get him into bed.

She was about to add the Master of Mayhem to her list of conquests.

"I have something here in my purse for you," she said. "I think it will be a surprise."

"Wonderful," he said, reaching into his briefcase

by the side of the bed. "But I have something I think will surprise *you*."

And he removed the hunting knife his father had given him on his sixteenth birthday and plunged it into her throat.

Judy's purse tipped sideways and the small vial of cocaine rolled to the floor.

She bled a lot, but he didn't mind. His wife had been like that, after he'd done her. A bleeder. And there were so many others along the way. A lot of blood.

He was smiling when she died.

THEM

They had met in Des Moines where his tour took him next. She had driven there in the Honda after quitting her job with the law firm.

She'd delivered her last victim to a garbage dump at the outskirts of town before she headed to Iowa. The police would eventually find the corpse, but there was no possible way to connect her to the murder. She was always careful about details. (She ascribed this to her astrological chart. Out of ten major natal positions, she had seven in Virgo.)

The guy was so easy. At least he'd shown her where

to buy a copy of *Cosmo*. The Streep article had been really good.

He had chopped up Judy's body for easier transport and had buried her in a lime pit. The lime would take care of the body parts. As he boarded the plane for Des Moines he dismissed Judy from his thoughts. Well, not entirely, since he planned to use the entire incident in his next novel.

Hemingway had expressed it beautifully: "Live it up, write it down." Splendid advice for any professional writer. Maybe Terry Carter's books were not great literature (he knew Judy was bullshitting him about Poe) but they were, at the very least, *authentic*. He'd dispatched more than a dozen women. Each one snuffed out in a different way. And with none of the murders connected to the mild, self-effacing author of best-selling novels.

"Tell us, Mr. Carter, where on earth do you get those weird, murderous ideas of yours?"

"Oh, that's an easy one to answer." And he would smile warmly at the questioner. "I just go around killing people and then write it all down."

That answer always got a big laugh. A real crowd-pleaser. Then he'd follow it with a broad wink at his interviewer. A horror writer with a wry sense of humor. His fans loved him.

The first thing he'd noticed about her, when they met in a downtown seafood restaurant (both of them waiting for a table), was the lovely burned-gold hair, which reminded him of a lion's mane. It occasioned his first words to her.

"You have beautiful hair. I hope you don't mind my saying so."

"Not at all." Her smile was radiant. "And you, sir, have wonderfully soft gray eyes."

"So long as you drop the 'sir,' and call me Terry, I think we're off to a great start."

"Terry." Her voice was husky. "A name to match your eyes."

And she stood very close to him, pressing her thigh against his.

It was going to be an interesting evening for them both.

Back in Kansas City, in the 1940s, I chanced upon a copy of Weird Tales *at a local newsstand. In those teen years, I was an avid horror/fantasy buff, and I welcomed the opportunity to add more chills to my life.* Weird Tales *provided them. It was here, in these gaudy pulp pages, that I discovered the work of Ray Bradbury. I began dreaming that someday I, too, would see my name in this wondrous publication.*

That dream came true in the winter of 1990, when Weird Tales *printed "Gobble, Gobble!" Better yet, in the fall of 1991, an entire issue of the magazine was devoted to my work, with a novella, a short story, my artwork, an essay, a poem, and an interview—all included in this special "Nolan Issue." It was a highlight of my career.*

Here, then, the story that a teenaged boy in Missouri once dreamed about seeing in print.

Gobble, Gobble!

(Written: July 1988)

Right now I'm a young, healthy female human being. I haven't always been human (didn't start that way) and I probably won't stay human for too much longer, but I'm having fun these days so I'll stick with it for awhile. Not that I'm from outer space or anything, but in human terms I'm an alien organism.

What I am is a feeder.

I don't feed very often—maybe once every six months or so—but when I do get hungry it takes a lot to satisfy me. But that's cool. I can always find things to eat.

And each time I feed, I change. But I'll get to that. Guess my changing can seem kind of icky, kind of a grossout, but it's really cool. Hey, I *know* I use the word cool too much, okay? But so do all of my friends.

If I sound like a dippy high school chick writing in her school notebook or something, well, that's what I am right now. That's the latest me. Sixteen and pretty. I mean, not an absolute knockout, not like some cheerleaders I know with super boobs and real cute butts, but pretty enough to make the guys go for me. Sharp looking. And I dress sharp. Plenty of boys ask me out. To dances and parties and stuff. (And to a lot of dumb movies!)

Of course, I don't eat what my friends do: gooky burgers with fries (heavy on the ketchup), jelly doughnuts and candy and junk like that. Most of my girlfriends scarf down Big Macs and pizza like mad, and a lot of them drink beer. That's sicko stuff as far as I'm concerned. Sure, I can *fake* eating junk like that (and I have to) but there's no real food value in any of it. I go for basics. I seem to get extra hungry around the holidays, especially Thanksgiving (gobble, gobble!).

My pattern as a feeder has been pretty consistent. I select a town, and a species, move in, live with them for six months or so, do my feeding (yum, yum) and then move on to another place. (I really dig France. Had me some good eating in Paris, you bet!)

I've been a bird and an insect (beetle) and a dog and an ant (African) and once I was a male housecat named Ari. Since I was "fixed" (you know, like no balls!) I didn't go around chasing females. I was real skinny, with all the little knobs on my backbone, sticking out. Vet said I was hyperthyroid and I had to swallow pills with my catfood. Real drag.

You're mixed up, right? About my feeding. Look, I didn't say I never ate "normal" food when I go between feedings; it's just that I don't *like* it and have to fake liking it.

After a few months I start to get bored, no matter what change I've made. But by the time the boredom really sets in I'm usually like *starved*. So I feed, change, and move on. (Usually eat more than once, when I begin a feeding, but I'll get to that later.)

I guess you figure I'm a creep, huh? Just because I'm different. I'm with my girlfriends at a movie and this guy in a ski mask chops off a nice lady's head with an axe and we go, ugh, that's *gross*. So I guess, to you, I'm in the same bag. A gross old feeder.

Old. That's an interesting word. How old am I? Who the freak knows? I've been around a long time, that's for sure. Feeders just keep going. We don't age like you do because we keep adapting and we're never the same long enough to get old. So I don't really have any idea of how old I am. Or care, for that matter.

Right now (existential time), as Jody Ann Singer, I'm sixteen. And I live in Lawton City, Illinois. In a green, quiet little town of three thousand. And I go to Lawton High where I'm president of the Drama Club (I'm good at acting roles, been doing it all my life).

Being female again is a blast (as my pals say). Last

three times I fed I was a male and I like being female better. Everything is *softer,* somehow. It's a silky feeling, being female. Males have hard edges; they live in a rougher world. But I'd freak out, having to stay one or the other. We feeders have a choice.

Well, I guess I've done enough rambling. Since this is what I call an alien record then I'd better start recording, eh? Instead of just blah, blah, blah on paper. Get down to the important stuff. The nitty-gritty.

Okay, then. I'll start by telling you about Rick. He's my latest boyfriend. Been going steady with him for just over three months. Do we *do* it? Sure. He's cool. Safe sex, right? Anyhow . . .

Rick's on the football team. Not captain yet, but he could be next year. And he also plays basketball and baseball. All-round jock. I go to a *lot* of games, take my word!

Football is cool, with all the guys bashing away at each other. Blood sport. Basketball's okay, too, but baseball's a drag. The pits. Bore-ing.

One of our fun things to do is go to the drive-in on Fridays in Rick's yellow Mustang convertible. We put the top up (for privacy) and just make out like crazy for most of the dumb movie. Unless it's an Arnold Schwarzenegger.

I always have Rick cool down when big Arnold's

doing his thing. And he doesn't mind, really. He digs Arnold, too, just like me. That's when we actually *watch* the movie.

So it's Friday night and Rick asks me to go to the drive-in with him to a horror flick called *The Blood-suckers* about a bunch of vampires on Fifth Avenue in New York who suck blood out of rich people who live in million-dollar townhouses or condos or whatever.

I dig horror flicks because I can do a lot of screaming and Rick thinks it's neat, my screaming and grabbing at him. Actually, vampires don't scare me. First of all, they don't exist and if they did they'd be real easy to fight off with garlic and crosses (two crossed tablespoons will do) and holy water and all like that. But I *do* like to watch the stakes get hammered into their chests (spurt, spurt!). That's neat.

So off we go to the Big Clock Drive-In to see this new bloodsucker movie, and right away Rick gets real attentive. You know, he's hot to trot. We haven't made it in about two weeks and he's all steamed up about the idea of being with me in my tight black-leather outfit. Boots and the whole bit. Rick's a freak for black leather. Wears it himself when he rides his Honda. (Yeah, he's a biker, too. Macho man!)

They know us at the Big Clock. We go there a lot (no other drive-ins in Lawton) and the ticket guys know us and when they see me in some of my sexy outfits they kind of drool, you know. ("Way to go, Ricko! Way to go.")

Rick keeps the Mustang real cherry. Wax job every other Sunday. It's a classic, and he treats it like one. Like he treats me. (Thinks he knows me. Oh, wow, does he ever *not* know me!)

It's dark now and we've got the top up and the black metal speaker's inside so we can hear the soundtrack, and we're eating popcorn. (Well, *he* is; I'm faking.)

Then Rick goes, "Today my parents told me they want me to go to UCLA in California for college. Wha'dya think?"

And I go, "It's a neat school. And I hear that L.A. is neat, too."

"My ole man went to UCLA so he wants me to go there." Rick leans in close. "Will you go with me?"

"In a year? You kidding? I never plan ahead that far."

"Hey, I don't want to go unless you do."

"I'll think about it. Yeah. Maybe I'll go to California. Who knows?" I giggle. "Quit being so serious. We're here to see some vampires, right?"

And he goes, "Right," and gives me a squeeze as the screen noise starts and the previews come on.

It's really dark now, the kind of deep dark you get in an Illinois summer, and pretty soon the chief bloodsucker is sinking his fangs into the throat of some blonde rich bitch who owns a lot of Texas oil and wears a ton of diamonds around the house.

That's when I realize I haven't fed in over six months, when this ham actor is scarfing away at the blonde's neck.

Hungry. It always hits me sudden like this. I never plan a feeding, it just happens. Like pow! One second I'm doing my act, as a human or whatever, and the next I'm like into my feeding mode.

When the time comes to feed, look out world! The hunger just *consumes* me, like a wave washing over a shore. And right then, watching the rich blonde getting fanged by this chief vampire . . . I . . . am . . . suddenly . . . *starved!*

Rick goes, "You look funny, Jode."

And I go, "Yeah? Funny how?"

"Your eyes. The way you're staring at me. Kind of super intense. What's with you?"

"It's time to eat is all. I'm hungry. Gobble, gobble!"

"Eat? We ate before we came here, remember? At the break I'll get some chili dogs an' Cokes, like always. How come all of a sudden you're hungry?"

"It's been almost six and a half months," I tell him.

He goes, "Huh?" Real surprised at what I just said.

Which is when I went for him. Like that shark went for the swimmer at the beginning of *Jaws*.

I've got a lot of inner strength. All feeders do. We can summon it up when we need it. And my teeth are sharp.

But this is for the record, so I don't want to mix you up about what happened to Rick.

I'm Rick now. I mean, after we left the drive-in I was behind the wheel of the Mustang and Jody Ann Singer was inside me, all part of the change, okay?

Let me try and explain. I don't feed like you'd think I would. I don't just go around gobbling up people and things the way girls at the school do Big Macs. That's not how a feeder operates.

We absorb.

We go inside and eat out the whole center of our victims (if you want to call them that), kind of leaving them hollow but still looking and acting ordinary on the outside.

And we usually go for two or three at once. At least I do. You know, I told you how it takes a lot to satisfy me once I really settle down to feed after maybe half a year. I'm starved, for sure.

So Rick wasn't enough. He was like the first course of the meal. I was still real hungry.

His parents were home, watching TV, when I

parked the Mustang outside their house and used Rick's key to get in.

They're in the living room, watching a Late Night movie about some lady doctor who was saving babies in Calcutta.

I go, "Hi!" giving them a smile.

They make me wait for the next commercial before they'll talk to me.

"You're home early, son," goes Rick's father.

And his mother goes, "Yes, where's Jody?"

I shrug. "She's dead."

They go all pale.

"My God!" says Rick's old man, standing up from the couch. "Did you have an accident?"

"Nope." I walk over and switch off the TV. "No accident. She just isn't around anymore."

"You're not making sense," says Rick's mother.

I smile at her. I walk toward her. I'm strong and I'm fast and I'm *still* very hungry.

"Gobble, gobble!" I say.

Another experimental effort in style and content. I had enjoyed the pre-Comics Code horrors of the E.C. magazines where sly artists and writers conspired to gross out the reader with severed heads, rotting zombies, and fanged ghouls.

"Fair Trade" was a sheer kick to write and could have served as the lead story in any one of the old E.C. comics. It features split-apart coffins, risen corpses, and dark woods laced with storm lightning.

Can the dead walk?

Oh yes, they can!

Fair Trade

(Written: March 1981)

He tole me to speak all this down into the machine, the Sheriff did, what all I know an' seen about Lon Pritchard an' his brother Lafe an' what they done, one to the other. I already tole it all to the Sheriff but he says for sure that none'a what I tole him happened the way I said it did but to talk it all into the machine anyhow. He figgers to have it all done up on paper from this talkin' machine so's folks kin read it an' laugh at me I reckon. If you don't believe it why should I talk it all down I wanted to know but he says it's for legal when they stan' me afore Judge Henry for Lon Pritchard's killin' which I sure never done. I witnessed it done, with the blood an' all, but I never done it personal.

Well, anyways, here goes . . .

First, my name is Jace Ridling. I guess that's Jason but none as ever called me the name formal. I was born right here in this part'a Virginia where I been all my life but I'm not rightly sure about my years due to my bein' alone an' all with no kinfolk alive to testify my age. I don't recall I ever had no blood kin-folk—'cept my Ma and my Pappy an' I never knew 'em proper. Not enough to hang a recollection on 'em. They both took off when I was a tad an' left me at the county home an' I run away an' jus growed as best I could, livin' off the woods an' what you find there. Guess I've et everthin' that grows there in my time—grub worms an' wiggly bugs under dead logs an' squinch owls an' frogs an' crickets an' skittery squirrils an' what all else I can't rightly recall. Don't matter none to this story, 'cept that's why I saw what I did. Livin' out in deep woods like I do I see what goes on when town folk are abed of a night. Lotsa funny things go on in deep woods if yer a mind ta look for 'em.

Like I tole Sheriff Meade this here story begun a week back, at the tail end'a that real mean rain spell we had. Hard black rain, the worst anybody kin rec-ollect, worst ever in this county, slicin' inta that yella clay out there on Cemetery Ridge, makin' the ground all soft an' slidey. It was the rain, jes comin' down an' comin' down what done it—what caused the box they had Lafe Pritchard nailed inside to bust open at the bottom'a Calder's Hill. Rain loosed it— an' that wet clay run like yella blood down the hill, carryin' the box hard onto the rocks. Knocked the top clean off, lettin' the rain in onto Lafe an soakin' his nice black fifty-dollar store-bought suit, the one they buried him in.

Now comes the part Sheriff Meade says is looney talk—but as the Lord A' mighty is my witness it happened jes like I tole him it did. 'Bout Lafe Pritchard I mean, 'bout how the rain—God's Tears some call it— come peltin' down into that cold split-open wood box an' woke ole Lafe till he rose up to sit straight as a soldier there in his fine black suit . . .

I was no more'n ten feet away—huggin' the side'a the hill the way I was to shelter me some agin' the storm—with my shiny rain slicker curled 'round me like a tent there in the blowin' dark—watchin' that dead man blinker his dead eye an' move his dead mouth like he was testin' 'em to see if they still worked proper.

I was down wind'a him—an' even past the smell'a the rain I caught his scent, strong as sin on Sunday. I could nose him plain, all sour an' gone to rot, the kinda smell a crushed rat gives off inside a barn after the wagon wheel has run him over an' him bein' there on the barn floor a while.

For sure, I was scart. Never seen me no livin' dead men afore, but I'd heard tell of 'em a'plenty an' knew it could happen, that the dead could raise up if they had a mind to do so. An' a *reason*. They's a reason behind everythin' men do, livin' an' dead. An' Lafe, he sure *had* hisself a reason. The rain was the thing that woke him from his uneasy rest, gave him the chance to do what he had to do. It jes happened I was there to see it.

I tole myself Jace, you calm on down now, boy, 'cuz Lafe was yer friend an' it don't figger he means to harm ya none. Jes speak up to him kindly.

Lafe, I say . . . standin' close to him an' lookin' down at him sittin' there in that cold wet box with his rain-slicked hair all plastered along the dead white of his face. His one eye rolls up to look me over. There's jes a hole where the other was. Worms got it likely. His face is half gone. Parts of him have fell off, parts'a his nose is missin' an' his upper lip is been most et away till the teeth shine out at me like he's smilin' even when he's not.

He's a plain fright, Lafe Pritchard is—but I say to him, Lafe, oh sweet Jesus, Lafe, you're the first livin' dead I ever come across. What brung ya back?

He don't answer right off. First, he stands up slow, looks around with that one eye at the dark on Calder's Hill an' up at the other graves on Cemetery Ridge an' at the wind-shook trees an' he stretches like a long-asleep cat, his arms up above his head, stretchin' those dead muscles an' I stand there a'side him wonderin' if there's still any blood in him. For sure not. But *somethin'* keeps him there, tall in the dark. Somethin' fires his dead flesh an' moves those long arms a'his.

Lon. He says that name to me, soft an' raspy, deep as a well. It's Lon I want to see. Where's Lon?

To home, most likely, on a night like this I say back to him.

Lon. I must see my brother Lon, he says. Can't sleep proper till I do. That voice a'his was somethin' to remember. Like no voice I ever heard a'fore or since or ever will agin' I'd guarantee.

Can the dead walk? Can they move through hollers an' gullies an' through deep woods? Oh *yes* they can!

Lafe did, that night, walkin' his dead legs along steady as you please past drippin' oak and evergreen, through tangle-weeds an' waist-high grass, his shoes suckin' at yella clay or lost in leaf loam an' me with him an' the black rain peltin' down like buckshot on us both an' neither of us sayin' nary a word as it final gave way to a smoky-burnt sun which come up slow over the trees.

Sure enough, the storm was over. Over an' spent, jes like it had stayed long enough to wake ole Lafe an' havin' done that job took off for other woods. A bird, kingfisher most likely, sang high an' sweet for us, an' frogs moved morning-soft in the marsh.

We're almost into town, I say to Lafe.

He nods an' I step back a mite from the scent of him. The sun makes him smell worse as it heats him up. Already our wet clothes is steamin' like smoke.

I ask him do you aim to walk right down the main street? Somehow it don't seem proper to me.

I aim to, he tells me in that raspy voice that sounds like it comes from inside a holla log.

What'll folks say, seein' as how you look an' all? Seein' as how they know you belong dead an' buried on Cemetery Ridge?

They'll be none up to say, he tells me. They'll most be abed.

You intendin' to go straight through town to Lon's?

Straight through. That's my proper intent.

Now he stops at the edge of the wood, lookin' toward the town with that one spit-shiny eye, with his teeth gapin' an' his dead white skin all flaked half away to raw bone.

I coulda cut an' run, right then. I didn't hafta go in an' see what I saw, witness what I witnessed, an' sure as God's grace I'd be safe off this minute in the deep woods if I'd done jes that 'stead'a bein' here inside this jailhouse talkin' at this machine an' not bein' believed by nobody. But I never run.

I went in with Lafe.

The town was dawn-silent 'cept for a big splotchy dog that came snuffin' an' barkin' outa Red's Cafe toward us, till he got a whiff'a Lafe an' down-tailed it quick back inside. Lafe paid him no mind.

We walked the length'a that street to Lon's house at the far side where the road turns back to deep wood. Lon he's lived there alone since Lafe died. Nice, with climbin' vines along one side an' big sunny windas.

I had no fear in me then, jes a burnin' curiosity to see what Lafe would do when he found Lon, an' what Lon would do when he laid sight'a him seein' his own dead brother standin' there fresh from the grave.

Jace boy, I tole myself, keep yer eyes wide open 'cuz it ain't never 'afore happened that a dead man walks bold as brass beside you toward a brother he hated more than Satan himself 'afore he died.

Because see, it was *hate* that brung Lafe here, hate fer Lon that druv him up from that coffin to walk the woods here to face the brother that deviled his woman an' ruint his life an' drove him to fire that bullet into his own heart.

Hate was the blood that filled Lafe Pritchard's body that mornin'—hate was the coal that fed the furnace of him.

What you gonna do when you find Lon to home I asked?

You'll see, Lafe says to me an' knocks on that door as calm as you please, a dead man knockin' to be let in an' Lon comin' up from sleep in his gray long-johns to open the door an' seein' his horror of a brother standin' there—an' screamin' like a stuck pig as Lafe reaches out to take him by the throat.

It all happened fast.

Lon claws at those bone-white fingers an' staggers back inside, eyes bugged, an' Lafe, all swole up an' stinkin' from the sun havin' been at him, drags Lon down the hall by the neck, me follerin' to the kitchen. Not a word betwixt 'em. Just the horror of it, the stench of it, in that dark mornin' room with the shades down an' the light still outside.

Now comes the part that got me sick, so I don't rightly want to dwell on it.

Sheriff Meade says he's certain convinced that what I'm really doin' here is confessin' up to killin' Lon Pritchard an' that this is my way'a tryin' to slip past the law's penalty by blamin' a dead man for what I done.

He's wrong. Lafe done in Lon, right there in front'a me that mornin' in that kitchen an' it was Lafe that cut the hole in him with the carvin' knife. I didn't do it. I jes watched it gettin' done, gaggin' the while, sick with the raw sight of it all, yet with my gaze plain fixed to it.

After it was done Lafe steps back an' says to me, we're even now, me an' Lon. I got what I come fer. I can sleep proper now. It's a fair trade. He owed me an' I collected.

So that's all there is to it. If you don't believe me you go out an' see fer yourself. Out to Cemetery Ridge where he's sleepin' now inside that box agin with the lid nailed shut an' a fresh hole dug an' him at the bottom where he asked me to put him.

I done it fer a friend. I buried him proper so's he could finally rest easy.

I don't judge him fer what he done. Lon Pritchard was bad clean through, we all knew that. Stealin' other folks wommin, an' cheatin' at his store business an' gettin' sod-drunk on God's Sunday. Deserved what he got, if truth be tole. It's the Lord's own justice what Lafe done to him.

An' the trade's been made. You'll find it in there, in the box with him. He's a'holdin' it fast in those bony fingers, claspin' it to his bosom like a lost pup. I didn't take it. Not me. Nosir. It's down there with him—the thing that was missin' when Sheriff Meade found the deceased.

Lon Pritchard's heart.

Challenges, faced and overcome. That's what good writing is all about. I like to keep "pushing the envelope" with my fiction, seeing how far I can go with a new idea, how different I can make it. This one is a good example of what I mean. I wanted to dramatize a woman's disintegration within a very compressed time frame. What sudden event could tip her over the edge—and what would be the result?

Richard Chizmar wanted a story for his Cold Blood anthology. I turned out "Babe's Laughter" in a single session.

Another challenge met.

And the story is cold-blooded.

Babe's Laughter

(Written: May 1990)

She was in the motel shower when she thought of the Hitchcock scene with the knife. That was a very disturbing movie, and the shower scene terrified her. She couldn't sleep for two nights after seeing that movie, and she didn't take a shower with the door closed for a month. But she got embarrassed thinking that her father could see her naked and that made her start shutting the door again.

Her father's dying was why she was here, in this motel. His dying at the Franklin Hospital in Oak Park, where he'd been for the last month, failing fast, getting thinner and weaker. His face looked like a death's head when she came to visit him from St. Louis. They'd lived in the same house for fourteen years after her mother died, and then he'd been forced to go to Chicago for advanced treatment for the cancer. The shitty damned cancer! Ate him up inside, just hollowed him out until he was nothing but a shell. No hair left. Cheeks sagging, sunken. Coughing up blood near the end. She would see him weekends, when she had time off from her job, stay in Chicago at a motel, then fly back to St. Louis. Expensive, but you don't count dollars when someone you love is dying. He had his insurance, so that end of it was taken care of at least.

This was the last weekend she'd spend in Chicago. She hated the town. It smelled of death. Of cancer. They'd asked her, at the hospital, what she wanted done with the body. (That's all he was now—the body.) And she told them to cremate him. Fire purifies. The grave rots you. Food for the worms.

She hated graves.

He'd been holding her hand when he died. Tight. Real, real tight—as if death couldn't take him if he held tight to her. But he died anyway. With a little gasp and a gargling sound deep in his throat. They'd warned her he wouldn't last through the night.

Once it was over she'd accepted his death, rejoiced in it, actually, for his sake; no one wants to go on living looking and feeling the way he did toward the end. No one.

Then, in the shower, she thought about the girl in the Hitchcock movie dying under the spray, with the blood from the knife wounds running down the drain, and she felt suddenly vulnerable. Her skin tingled and little waves of apprehension rippled through her.

She carried a knife in her purse. From her Girl Scout days. But of course she'd never killed anyone in a shower with it.

Getting out, folding herself into the big white terry cloth robe, she felt dizzy. Kind of giddy. Not sad. Not how she thought she'd feel when his death was real and not something coming at them. She was lightheaded, the way she got when she drank three Manhattans in a row. Giddy and lightheaded.

She brushed her hair, using hard firm strokes. Then she got dressed. Tight green skirt. White blouse with ruffled lace at the neck. Kind of old-fashioned, but she liked the effect against her pale skin. Black stockings. High heels.

Sitting in front of the dresser she found, to her surprise that she felt wonderful. My God! Not sad at all. Liberated and wonderful. The dark weight of her father's illness had been lifted from her shoulders. He was gone now, and she could do anything.

Anything.

She put on her makeup, carefully applying just the right amount of eye shadow and making sure her lipstick was perfect. But, shit, she didn't need to be perfect anymore. Nothing about her needed to be perfect.

On the way out to her rented car she killed the motel manager.

For no particular reason—except that maybe he looked something like the doctor who'd first told her that her father had terminal cancer. There *was* a definite resemblance. In the cheekbones and along the jawline.

She'd cut his throat.

She still felt lightheaded when she got into her car. It was good doing just what she felt like doing for a change after holding back all these years—being the perfect daughter. (Being perfect is a real bitch.) His blood, the motel manager's, was on her coat and blouse. Mostly on her coat. Didn't matter.

Nothing mattered.

Which was kind of wonderful.

The car smelled of cancer. The smell from the hospital from her father's skeletal body. Sour and intense.

She rolled down all the windows before she started the engine. To air out the car.

Then she drove away from the motel. The night air was cold against her skin.

She wondered what the police would say about the motel manager. But who cared? Who gave a flying fuck *what* the police said or thought or did?

It was a long drive to the bar-restaurant—from Oak Park to the Loop. On Michigan Avenue, a place called Charlie's. Dave would be waiting for her there.

She'd called him from the motel and suggested they get together for a late drink. Old Davy boy. His hair had been thinning last time she'd seen him. He was probably bald by now.

She and Dave had a few heavy dates the summer she spent her vacation in Chicago. He'd wanted to take her to bed, but she hadn't gone to bed with him. Or anyone else. Her father didn't like her seeing men.

Maybe she'd go to bed with Dave tonight. Maybe she'd let him do all the things to her that her father warned her against. The nasty things.

Maybe she would.

Charlie's was crowded, which surprised her. Somehow, she had expected to walk through the door and see Dave sitting alone in a corner booth, and they'd just stare hotly across the empty room at each other. But it wasn't like that at all. It was a Saturday night, and the place was filled with smoke and loud voices and a mass of people who flowed around her as she looked for Dave.

He was on a stool at the bar. And mostly bald, like she'd figured. In some kind of a shiny polyester suit that looked crummy on him. He'd grown a beard since she'd seen him. To make up for the hair loss on top; lots of men do that. (How would a beard feel between her legs?)

"Hello, Dave," she said, slipping out of her coat.

"Hi, Babe." (He always called her that and she'd hated it, his not using her name. Tonight she didn't mind.)

He gave her a tight hug and a kiss on the cheek.

"I got a table for us," he said. "Near the back."

"Fine," she said.

"Great to see you," he told her when they were seated. "Been a while."

"Six years this summer," she said. And ordered a Manhattan, no ice. He asked for a gin and tonic.

He looked steadily into her face. "I'm curious."

"About what?"

"About why you called me tonight."

"My father died a few hours ago. At the hospital in Oak Park. Of lung cancer. I thought I'd like some company."

"Jesus!" he said softly. "I'm sorry, Babe."

Their drinks arrived. She raised her glass.

"Here's to better times," she said.

"Jesus," Dave repeated softly. "I should hope."

"I guess you think I ought to be mourning," she said.

"No . . . oh, no. It was just . . . I mean, if my old man—"

"Didn't anyone ever die of cancer in your family?"

"Uh, sure. An aunt in Cincy. Aunt Martha. She was my Mom's sister. She died. About a year ago."

"It hits every family," she said. "My father got it from smoking too much. Four packs a day. I never smoked. He didn't like to see girls smoking."

"And you always did just what Daddy told you to do," said Dave.

"How do you know that?"

"He didn't want you to see me. You said so in the letter I got from you after that summer. Said you didn't want to get him all upset, so we'd better knock it off. Tell you the truth, I never expected to hear from you again."

"Well . . . you did. And here I am."

He was staring at her in the hazed dimness of the bar.

"The front of your blouse," Dave said. "That . . . dark stain."

"It's dried blood," she found herself admitting. (Why the hell not?) "There's more on my coat. A lot more."

And then she couldn't help herself, just couldn't, because of the way his face looked. (Like her father used to look when she'd tell him about some awful thing she'd been thinking about.) She didn't want to, it wasn't appropriate, but she couldn't stop herself.

From laughing.

From howling with laughter.

She just couldn't.

I could never write this story today. Why not? Because (along with my wife) I've turned into a confirmed cat lover. Beginning in 1980, a succession of furry felines entered our lives. Once you discover how mysterious, fascinating, and loving cats can be, you're hooked. They don't live with you—you live with them. We've had a total of ten. Seven have gone to cat heaven, and we cherish the three that remain.

When I wrote this story in 1967 I had no problem in creating a cat-hating protagonist who believed that all felines were evil. The story worked fine on its own terms, and still does, but right now I don't sympathize with a damn word of it.

If you ask me, Frederick Baxter got what he deserved.

And shame on him!

He Kilt it With a Stick

(Written: January 1967)

A mild night in June.

Louise away, visiting her parents. The house on Gillham Avenue empty, waiting.

Warm air.

A high, yellow moon.

Stars.

Crickets thrumming the dark.

Fireflies.

A summer night.

Fred goes to the Apollo to see a war film. It depresses him. All the killing. He leaves before it has ended, walking up the aisle and out of the deserted lobby and on past the empty glass ticket booth. Alone.

The sidewalk is bare of pedestrians.

It is late, near midnight, and traffic is very sparse. The wide street is silent. A truck grinds heavily away in the distance.

Fred begins to walk home.

He shouldn't. It is only two blocks: a few steps to

the corner of 40th, then down the long hill to Gillham, then right along to his house at the end of the
block, near 41st. Not quite two blocks to walk. But
too far for him. Too far.

Fred stops.

A gray cat is sleeping in the window of Rae's Drugstore. Fred presses his hand against the glass.

*I could break the window—but that would be useless.
The thing would be safe by then; it would leap away and
I'd never find it in the store. The police would arrive
and . . . No. Insane. Insane to think of killing it.*

The gray cat, quite suddenly, opens its eyes to stare
at Fred Baxter. Unblinking. Evil.

He shudders, moves quickly on.

The cat continues to stare.

Foul thing knows what I'd like to do to it.

The hill, sloping steeply, is tinted with cool moonlight. Fred walks down this hill, filled with an angry
sense of frustration: he would very much have
enjoyed killing the gray cat in the drugstore window.

Hard against chest wall, his heart judders. Once,
twice, three times. Thud thud thud. He slows,
removes a tissue-wrapped capsule from an inside
pocket. Swallows the capsule. Continues to walk.

Fred reaches the bottom of the hill, crosses over.

Trees now. Big fat-trunked oaks and maples, fan-
ning their leaves softly over the concrete sidewalk.

Much darker. Thick tree-shadow midnight dark, broken by three street lamps down the long block. Lamps haloed by green night insects.

Deeper.

Into the summer dark.

When Fred Baxter was seven he wrote: "Today a kitty cat bit me at school and it hurt a lot. The kitty was bad, so I kilt it with a stick."

When he was ten, and living in St. Louis, a boy two houses up told Fred his parents wanted to get rid of a litter. "I'll take care of it," Fred assured him—and the next afternoon, in Miller Lake, he drowned all six of the kittens.

At fifteen, in high school, Fred trapped the janitor's Tabby in the gymnasium locker room, choked it to death, and carried it downstairs to the furnace. He was severely scratched in the process.

As a college freshman, Fred distributed several pieces of poisoned fish over the Rockhurst campus. The grotesquely twisted bodies of seven cats were found the next morning.

Working in the sales department of Hall Brothers, Fred was invited to visit his supervisor at home one Saturday—and was seen in the yard playing with Frances, a pet Siamese. She was later found crushed to death, and it was assumed a car had run over the animal. Fred quit his job ten days later because his supervisor had cat hands.

Fred married Louise Ferber when he was thirty, and she wanted to have children right away. Fred said no, that babies were small and furry in their blankets, and disturbed him. Louise bought herself a small kitten for company while Fred was on the road. He didn't object—but a week after the purchase, he took a meat knife from the kitchen and dismembered the kitten, telling his wife that it had "wandered away." Then he bought her a green parakeet.

ZZZZZZZ Click
This is Frederick Baxter speaking and I . . . wait, the sound level is wrong and I'll—There, it's all right now. I can't tell anyone about this—but today I found an old Tom in an alley downtown, and I got hold of the stinking, wretched animal and I—
ZZZZZZZ Click

The heart trouble started when Fred was thirty-five.

"You have an unusual condition," the doctor told him. "Your chest houses a quivering-muscled heart—fibrillation. This condition *can* prove fatal. Preventive measures must be taken. No severe exercise, no overeating, plenty of rest."

Fred obeyed the man's order—although he did not really trust a doctor whose cat eyes reflected the moon.

ZZZZZZZ Click

. . . awful time with the heart. Really awful. The use of digitalis drives me to alcohol, which sends my heart into massive flutters. Then the alcohol forces me into a need for more digitalis. It is a deadly circle and I . . .

I have black dreams. A nap at noon and I dream of smothering. This comes from the heart condition. And because of the cats. They all fear me now, avoid me on the street. They've *told* one another about me. This is fact. Killing them is becoming quite difficult . . . but I caught a big, evil one in the garden last Thursday and buried it. Alive. As I am buried alive in these black dreams of mine. I got excited, burying the cat—and this is bad for me. I must go on killing them, but I must *not* get excited, I must stay calm and not—here comes Louise so I'd better . . .

ZZZZZZZ Click

* * *

"What's wrong, Fred?"

It was 2 a.m. and she had awakened to find him standing at the window.

"Something in the yard," he said.

The moon was flushing the grass with pale gold—and a dark shape scuttled over the lawn, breaking the pattern. A cat shape.

"Go to sleep," said his wife, settling into her pillow.

Fred Baxter stared at the cat, who stared back at him from the damp yard, its head raised, the yellow of the night moon now brimming the creature's eyes. The cat's mouth opened.

"It's sucking up the moonlight," Fred whispered.

Then he went back to bed.

But he did not sleep.

Later, thinking about this, Fred recalled what his mother had often said about cats. "They perch on the chest of a baby," she'd said, "place their red jaws over the soft mouth of the baby, and draw all the life from its body. I won't have one of these disgusting things in the house."

Alone in the summer night, walking down Gillham Avenue, Fred passes a parked car, bulking black and silent in its gravel driveway. The closed car windows gleam deep yellow from the eyes inside.

Eyes?

Fred stops, looks back at the car.

It is packed with cats.

How many? Ten . . . a dozen. More . . . twenty, maybe. All inside the car, staring out at me. Dozens of foul, slitted yellow eyes.

Fred can do nothing. He checks all four doors of the silent automobile, finds them locked. The cats stare at him.

Filthy creatures!

He moves on.

The street is oddly silent. Fred realizes why: the crickets have stopped. No breeze stirs the trees; they hang over him, heavy and motionless in the summer dark.

The houses along Gillham are shuttered, lightless, closed against the night. Yet, on a porch, Fred detects movement.

Yellow eyes spark from porch blackness. A big, dark-furred cat is curled into a wooden swing. It regards Fred Baxter.

Kill it!

He moves with purposeful stealth, leans to grasp a stout tree limb that has fallen into the yard. He mounts the porch steps.

The dark-furred cat has not stirred.

Fred raises the heavy limb. The cat hisses, claws

extended, fangs balefully revealed. It cries out like a wounded child and vanishes off the porch into the deep shadow between houses.

Missed. Missed the rotten thing.

Fred moves down the steps, crosses the yard towards the walk. His head is lowered in anger. When he looks up, the walk is thick with cats. He runs into them, kicking, flailing the tree club. They scatter, melting away from him like butter from a heated blade.

Thud thud thud. Fred drops the club. His heart is rapping, fisting his chest. He leans against a tree, sobbing for breath. The yellow-eyed cats watch him from the street, from bushes, from steps and porches and the tops of cars.

Didn't get a one of them. Not a damn one . . .

The fireflies have disappeared. The street lamps have dimmed to smoked circles above the heavy, cloaking trees. The clean summer sky is shut away from him—and Fred Baxter finds the air clogged with the sharp, suffocating smell of cat fur.

He walks on down the block.

The cats follow him.

He thinks of what fire could do to them—long blades of yellow crisping flame to flake them away into dark ash. But he cannot burn them; burning them would be impossible. There are *hundreds*. That many at least.

They fill driveways, cover porches, blanket yards, pad in lion-like silence along the street. The yellow moon is in their eyes, sucked from the sky: Fred, his terror rising, raises his head to look upward.

The trees are alive with them!

His throat closes. He cannot swallow. Cat fur cloaks his mouth. Fred begins to run down the concrete sidewalk, stumbling, weaving, his chest filled with a terrible winged beating.

A sound.

The scream of the cats.

Fred claps both hands to his head to muffle the stab and thrust of sound.

The house . . . must reach the house.

Fred staggers forward. The cat masses surge in behind him as he runs up the stone walk to his house.

A cat lands on his neck. Mutely, he flings it loose—plunges up the wooden porch steps.

Key. Find your key and unlock the door. Get inside!

Too late.

Eyes blazing, the cats flow up and over him, a dark, furry, stifling weight. As he pulls back the screen, claws and needle teeth rip at his back, arms, face, legs . . . shred his clothing and skin. He twists wildly, beating at them. Blood runs into his eyes . . .

The door is open. He falls forward, through the opening. The cats swarm after him in hot waves, covering his chest, sucking the breath from his body. His thin scream is lost in the sharp, rising, all-engulfing cry of the cats.

Louise found him two days later, lying face down on the living-room floor. His clothes were wrinkled, but untorn.

A cat was licking the cold, white, unmarked skin of Frederick Baxter's cheek.

"Starblood" was selected for The Best Science Fiction of 1972 and I think the honor was justified. Certainly, even among the most experimental of my tales, this story is unique. Three of the six sections were originally written as opening chapters of aborted science fiction novels. I liked what I had in each instance, but saw no way to move forward. Which is when I got the idea of using all three in a six-section short story, framed by an alien "invasion."

This one's not about a space war. It's all about love and rejection.

Unique.

Starblood

(Written: December 1971)

Is the orbit stabilized ▌
Yes.
How much longer to penetration ▌
Soon now.
You first. Then I'll follow.
Do you think . . . I mean, is it possible, with this planet,
that we'll be able to succeed ▌
We'll try. That's all we can do. I have no answers.

-1-
Bobby

Bobby was still crying, his tiny face red, fists clenched, ignoring the roboMother who rocked and crooned to him.

Dennison walked over, switched off the machine, and picked up his son. He carried the squalling infant to the patio where his wife was playing Magneball with an android instructor.

"Bobby's been crying all afternoon," Dennison said. "Do something with him. See if you can't shut him up."

Mrs. Dennison glared at her husband. "Let Mother handle him."

"I switched her off," said Dennison. "She wasn't doing any good. Take him for a ride in the copter. He likes that. It'll shut him up."

"You do it," said Alice Dennison. "I'm perfecting my back thrust. I play tournament next week, you know."

"You don't give a damn about your son, do you?"

She nodded to the android, ignoring the question. "Ready," she said. A magnetic disc leaped from the instructor's hand and the woman expertly repelled it with a thrusting left glove.

"Well done, Mrs. Dennison," said the android.

In a silent rage, Dennison advanced on the android and beheaded the machine with a chair leg.

"I hope you're satisfied," said the wife. "They cost fifteen thousand dollars. I'll just have to buy another."

"You do that," said Dennison. "But first you take Bobby up in the copter. I can't stand any more of his squalling."

She scooped up the baby, who continued to howl, and took a riser to the roofpad. Activating the family flier, she placed Bobby inside and lifted off in a whir of gleaming blades.

Five miles above New Chicago, Mrs. Dennison switched the copter to autoflight, unlatched the main exit panel and held her baby son straight out into the blast of air.

She smiled at him—and released her grip.

Still crying, Bobby Dennison fell twisting and tumbling toward the cold earth below.

-2-
Tris

In Greater New York, under warm summer sun, the walkways sang. Heat from the sky stirred delicate filaments within the moving bands and a thin silver rain of music drifted up to the walk-riders, soothing them, easing away some small bit of city hive pressure.

For Tris, an ex-Saint at sixteen, the pressures were mounting and the song of the walkways did not ease her; she was close to an emotional breakpoint. When a Saint is cast out by the Gods she has nowhere to go. Society shuns the outcast. Her only chance lies in reinstating herself. If she cannot achieve this, she ceases to function as a viable entity and self-extinction is her only recourse.

Tris was beautiful and free-spirited, with a body built for Sainthood. Surely, she told herself, she would find her way back into Divine Favor.

"The Reader will see you now," said the wallspeak. "Inside and just to the left."

Tris moved ahead past the sliding wall and turned left.

Reader Sterning was ready for her, a tall man in flowsilks. His smile was warmly professional. They touched palms and Tris sat down.

"Well, well," said Sterning. "I can surface why you're here, and believe me when I tell you that I sympathize."

"Thank you, Reader," said the girl softly.

"How long were you a Saint?"

Tris knitted her fingers in her lap, twisting her hands nervously. She'd never been deeped before and it was a little frightening. "Could you turn off the wall?" she asked.

"Of course," smiled Sterning, and killed the hypnowall. The swirl of colors faded to black. "I really don't need it in your case. I want you to be as comfortable as possible. Now . . ." He tented his hands. "How long were you a Saint?"

She blinked rapidly. "For almost a year. One of the Gods selected me in Omaha. They were there to flare and I offered . . ."

"You offered your Eternal Self?"

"Yes, that's right. And they accepted me. One of them did, I mean."

"The one called Denbo, am I correct?"

She nodded, flushing. "He took me. He sainted me."

Sterning bowed his head. "A rare sexual honor. A beautiful selection. And you are. Quite."

Tris blinked again. "Quite?"

"Quite beautiful. Thighs . . . hips . . . breasts. You are ideally qualified for Sainthood." He sighed. "Your situation is most unfortunate. But let's get to it."

He moved around the desk, sat down close to her on the flow-couch, his dark eyes probing. "Lean back and relax. I'm going to deep you now. Close your eyes."

Tris shuddered; she knew there would be no pain, but the nakedness of it all! Her inner mind laid bare to another!

"You needn't be concerned about opening to me," Sterning said. "It's all quite normal. Deeping is a natural process for those of us who read. You have nothing to be afraid of."

"I know that," said Tris. "But . . . it isn't easy for me."

"Relax . . . just relax."

She settled back into the chair, her mind opening to his.

Sterning shifted to a below-surface level, sighed.

"Ah, sadness and guilt." He began reading. "You were a truly passionate Saint and the Gods were pleased. And you got on well with all the other Saints, sharing their life and dedication until . . ."

He hesitated, probing deeper. "Until you made a mistake which cost you Divine Favor."

"Yes," murmured Tris. Her down-closed lashes quivered against her white cheek. "A mistake. I should never have—"

"—criticized." Sterning finished the thought. "You criticized a God and they banished you. Your comments were cruel, caustic."

"I was angry," said Tris. "With Denbo."

"Because he was sexually favoring other Saints."

"Yes."

"But you had no right to be angry. A God may bestow his sexual favors where he will. That is his Divine right, is it not?"

"I know, I know," said the girl. "But I thought Denbo—"

"—would consider your feelings. But of course no God need consider a Saint's feelings. That is your mortal flaw. You cannot accept nor abide by Divine rule."

"I tried to obey, to accept." The girl was beginning to cry, her eyes still closed. Tears ran down her cheeks.

Sterning continued to probe, unmoved by emotion. "You failed out of sheer stubborn self-pride.

You felt . . ." He moved to a deeper level. "You felt equal to Denbo, equal to a God. You desired more than Sainthood."

"Yes." Softly.

"And what do you want from me?"

"An answer. Surely, within my brain, somewhere within it, you can read a way back."

The Reader stood up, breaking contact. He walked to his desk, sat down heavily. "Your self-will is too strong. There is no way back. Sainthood is behind you."

"Then I'll die," she said flatly, opening her eyes. "Will you aid me?"

"I dislike this kind of thing. I don't usually—"

"Please."

He sighed. "All right."

"Thank you, Reader Sterning."

And he killed her.

-3-
Morgan

The laser sliced into the right front wheelhousing of Morgan's landcar and he lost control. Another beam sizzled along the door as he rolled free of the car. It slewed into a ditch, overturned, flamed, and exploded. The heavy smoke screened him as Morgan worked his way along the ditch, a fuse pistol in his right hand. Not much good against beamguns, but his other weapons had been destroyed with the car.

The screening smoke worked both ways; he couldn't see them, verify their number. But maybe he could slip around them. It was quite possible they believed him dead in the explosion.

He was wrong about that.

A chopping blow numbed his left shoulder. Morgan hit ground, rolled, brought up the fuser, fired. His assailant fell back, grunting in pain. Morgan whipped up the pistol in a swift arc, catching a second enemy at chin-level, firing again. Which did the job.

Morgan rubbed circulation back into his numbed shoulder, his body pressed close in against the night-chilled gravel at the edge of the road. Behind him, in a flare of orange, the landcar continued to burn. He listened for further movement. Were there more of them out there, ready to attack him?

No sound. Nothing. No more of them. Only two, both dead now.

He took their beamers, checked the bodies. Both young, maybe fifteen to seventeen. Probably brothers, but Morgan couldn't tell for sure, since the face was mostly gone on the smaller one. At close range, a fuser is damned effective.

Morgan recharged the pistol and inspected the beamguns, breaking them down. They were fine. He could use them.

It was too late to find another car. Better to sleep by the lake and go on in the morning.

The lake would be good. It would cool him out, ease some of the tension that knotted his muscles. He'd grown up near lakes like this one, fishing and swimming with Jim Decker. Ole Jimbo. Poor unlucky bastard. The police got him in Detroit, lasered him down in a warehouse. Jimbo never believed he could die. Well, thought Morgan, we *all* die—sooner or later.

Lake Lotawana lay just ahead, less than a mile through the trees. Morgan threaded the woods, slid down the leaf-cloaked banking to the edge of the water. The lake flickered like a soft flame, alive with moonlight. Morgan bent to wash his face and hands; the water rippled and stirred as he cupped it, cold and crystalline.

He drew the clean air of September into his lungs. Good autumn air, smelling of maple and oak. He savored the smells of Missouri earth, of autumn grass and trees. A night bird cried out across the dark lake water. Morgan hoped he would live long enough to reach Kansas City and do what he was sent to do. He could easily have been killed in the landcar explosion—or in Illinois, Ohio, Pennsylvania, or a few nights ago in Kansas. They'd been close on his tracks most of the way.

He prepared a bed of leaves, spreading dry twigs in a circle around it for several feet in each direction. The twigs would alert him to approaching enemies. Morgan lay down with a beamer at his elbow. Tomorrow, he would find another car and reach Kansas City. The girl and the money would be waiting there. He smiled and closed his eyes.

Morgan was sleeping deeply when they came down the bank, shadows among shadows, moving with professional stealth. They knelt beyond the circle of twigs and began scooping the branches away quietly. They planned to use blades, and that meant close body contact.

Morgan heard them at the last instant and rolled sideways, snatching up the beamer as he rolled. Too late. They were on him in a mass of unsheathed steel.

He broke free, stumbled, dropped the useless weapon, blood rushing to fill his open mouth. Morgan folded both hands across his stomach. "I . . ." He spoke to them as they watched him. "I'm a dead man."

And he fell backward as the dark waters of the lake, rippling, accepted his lifeless body.

- 4 -
David

"I *hate* bookstores," said David.

"You're still a child," his Guardian told him. "As an adult, you'll see the value in books."

David, who was eleven, allowed himself to be guided into the store. You don't get anywhere if you argue with a Guardian.

"May I be of service?" A tall old man smiled at them, dressed in the long gray robe of Learning.

"This is David," said the Guardian, "and he is here to rent a book."

The old man nodded. "And what is your choice, David?"

"I don't have one," said David. "Let Guardian decide."

"Very well, then . . ." The Bookman smiled again. "Might I suggest some titles?"

"Please do," said the Guardian.

The old man pursed his lips. "Ah . . . what about *Moby Dick?* Splendid seafaring adventure, laced with symbolic philosophy."

"I hate whales," said David. "Sea things are disgusting."

"Hmmm. Then I shall bypass Mr. Melville and Mr.

Verne. Let us move along to Dylan Thomas and his spirited *Under Milk Wood*."

"Let's hear part of it," said David.

The old man pressed a button on the wall and a door opened. A rumpled figure stepped into the room. His nose was red and bulbous; his hair was wild. He walked toward them, voice booming. He spoke of a small town by night, starless and bible-black, and of a wood "limping invisible down to the sloeblack, slow, black, crowblack, fishingboatbobbing sea."

"I don't like it," said David flatly. "Send him back."

"That will be all, Mr. Thomas," said the Bookman.

The rumpled figure turned and vanished behind the door.

"I want a hunting story of olden times," said David. "Do you have any?"

"Naturally. We have many. What about *Big Woods*?"

"Who wrote that?" asked David.

"Mr. Faulkner. You'll like him, I'm sure."

David shrugged, and the Bookman pressed another button. A tall man with sad eyes and a bristled mustache stepped into view. He spoke, with a drawl, of woods and rivers and loamed earth, and of "the rich deep black alluvial soil which would grow cotton taller than the head of a man on a horse."

"We'll take him," said David.

"Indeed we will," said the Guardian.

"Splendid," said the Bookman.

William Faulkner waited quietly while the rental sheet was signed, then walked out with them.

"There is a story in my book," he said to David, "which I have titled 'The Bear.' Do you wish to hear it?"

"Sure. I want to hear the whole book if it's all about hunting."

"The boy has a strange fascination with death," the Guardian said to Mr. Faulkner.

"Then I shall begin with page one," drawled the tall man as they were crossing a gridway.

David, looking up into the sad eyes of William Faulkner, did not see the gridcar jetting toward him. The Guardian screamed and clawed at the boy's coat to pull him back, but was not successful. The car struck David, killing him instantly.

"Am I to be returned?" asked Mr. Faulkner.

-5-
Bax

They were having shrimp curry at the Top of the Mark in San Francisco when the sharks began to bother the girl.

"They're so *close*," she said. "Why are they so close?"

Bax snapped his fingers. A waiter appeared at their table. "Do something about those damn things," Bax demanded.

"I'm very sorry, sir, but our repel shielding has temporarily failed."

"Can you fix it?"

"Oh, of course, sir. That's being attended to now. We have the situation under control. At any moment the shielding should be fully operational."

Bax waved him away. "Are you satisfied?" he asked the girl.

She picked at her food, head lowered. "I just won't look at them," she said.

The sharks continued to bump the transparent outer shell, while a huge Manta Ray rippled through the jeweled waters. Far below, streaks of rainbow fish swarmed in and around the quake-tumbled ruins of office buildings, and the lichen-covered trucks and cable cars. An occasional divecab sliced past the restaurant, crowded with tourists.

Bax leaned across the table to take the girl's hand; his eyes softened. "I thought you'd enjoy it here. This place is an exact duplicate of the original. You get a fantastic view of the city."

"I feel trapped," she admitted. "I'm a surface girl, Bax, I don't like being here."

Bax grinned. "To tell you the truth, I don't like it

much myself. But, at the moment, we really don't have any choice."

"I know." She gave his hand a squeeze. "And it's all right. It's just that I—"

"Look," Bax cut in. "They've fixed it."

The nuzzling sharks thrashed back abruptly as the energized shielding was reactivated. The outer dome now pulsed radiantly, silvering the sea. The sharks retreated deeper into the green-black Pacific.

"It's something about their teeth," the girl said to Bax. "Like thousands of upthrust knives . . ."

"Well, they're gone now. Forget them. Eat your curry."

"When is the contact meeting us?" she asked.

"He's overdue. Should be here any minute."

"You don't think anything's wrong, do you?"

Bax shook his head. "What *could* be wrong?" He patted the inside of his coat. "I have the stuff. They pay us for it and we leave San Fran for the islands. Take a long vacation. Enjoy what we've earned."

"What about a crossup?" Her voice was intense. "What if they hired another agent to take the stuff and dispose of you?"

He laughed. "You mean dispose of us, don't you?"

The girl stared at him coldly. "No. I mean you, Bax."

Bax dropped his half-empty wine glass. "You lousy

bitch," he said softly, slumping forward across the table.

The girl darted her hand into his coat, withdrew a small packet, and placed it inside her evening bag as a waiter rushed toward them.

"I think my husband has just had a heart seizure," she said. "I'll go for a doctor."

And she calmly left the bar.

Outside, beyond the silvered fringe of light, the knife-toothed sharks circled the dome.

- 6 -
Lynda

The wind was demented; it whiplashed the falling snow into Lynda's eyes, into her half-open mouth as she stood, head raised to the storm, taking it in, allowing it to engulf her. The collar of her stormcoat was open and the cold snow needled her skin.

Then the wall glowed. Someone wanted her.

Annoyed, she killed the blizzard. The wind ceased. The snow melted instantly. The ceiling-sky was, once again, blue and serene above her head. She stepped from the Weatherchamber, peeling her stormcoat and boots.

Her father was there, looking his usual dour self.

"Sorry to break into your weather, Lynda, but I must talk to you."

She walked to the barwall, pressed an oak panel, and an iced Scotch glided into her hand. "Drink?" she offered.

"You know I never drink on the job."

She sipped at the Scotch. "I see. You're in town on a contract."

"That's right."

"I think it's revolting." She shook her head. "Why don't you get out of this business? You're too old to go on killing. You'll make a mistake and one of your contracts will end up doing you in. It happens all the time."

"Not to me it won't," said Lynda's father. "I know my job."

"It's sickening."

The older man grunted. "It's provided you with everything you've ever wanted."

"And I guess I should be humbly grateful. As the pampered daughter of a high-level professional assassin, I'm very rich and very spoiled. I'm, in fact, a totally worthless addition to society, thanks to you."

"Then you shouldn't mind leaving it," he said.

"What is that supposed to mean?"

"It means, dearest daughter, that my contract this trip is on you."

And the beamgun he held beneath his coat took off Lynda's head.

The pattern is fixed. It's hopeless.
You don't want to try again ▌
To what purpose ▌ *Each time one of us penetrates, we are rejected.*
This planet does not want us. We'll have to move beyond the system.
Would the host bodies have survived without us ▌
Everyone on Earth dies eventually. But we trigger quick, violent death.
It's their way of rejecting us. We must accept the pattern.
I liked the girl in New York . . . Tris. And the little boy, David. We could have flowered in them.
The universe is immense. We'll find a host planet that's benign.
Where we'll be welcome.
We're leaving Earth's orbit now.
The stars are waiting for us. A billion billion suns!
I love you!

I call this my vampire novel in miniature. There's enough in this brief little vignette for a 500-page Anne Rice saga. As a writer, a source of particular pleasure is seeing just how much large material I can fit into a very small space. The "less is more" principle. Never have I practiced this approach more stringently than here, in "Vympyre."

And I wouldn't want to add another word.

Vympyre

(Written: February 1991)

Blood. My own. Sweet Christ, my own! Seeping along my chest, soaking my white pullover, a spreading patch of dark red. So this is how it finally ends? With the stake being driven in another inch, each blow of the hammer like a thunderclap . . . closing my eyes in Paris with blood everywhere on the tumultuous streets, tasting it on my cool lips, with the guillotine hissing down, severed heads thumping wicker baskets . . . King Richard there (was it the Third Crusade?), his battle axe cleaving through the enemy's shoulder, sundering down through muscle, bone, and gristle, and watching the stricken rider topple from the tall back of the sweating gray horse . . . in Germany's Black Forest, barefoot, my flesh lacerated by thorn and stone, pursued by the shouting villagers, the flames of their torches wavering, flickering through the trees, a strange, surreal glow . . . gulls above the sunswept English Channel as I lower my head toward the child's white, delicately tender throat, with the warm sweet wine of her blood on my tongue. (So many myths about us. They call us creatures of the night, but many of us do not fear the bright sun. In truth, it cannot harm us, although we often hunt at night . . . so many myths) . . . on the high seat of the carriage, pitching and plunging through moonlit Edinburgh, wheels in thunderous clatter over the narrow, cobbled streets, hatless, my cape blown wild behind me as I lash at the straining team . . . the impossibly pink sands of the beach, with a stout sea wind rattling the palm fronds, the waves blood-colored, sunset staining the edge of horizon sky and the young woman's drugged, open, waiting flesh, and my lips drawn back, the needled penetration, and the lost cry of release . . . the limo driver's rasping voice above the surging current of Fifth Avenue traffic, recounting the intensity of the police hunt, and my quiet smile there with my back against the cool leather, invincible, the girl's corpse where no one can ever find it, with the puncture marks raw and stark on her skin . . . the stifling, musky darkness of the cave, the rough grained face of the club against my cupped fingers, the fetid tangle of beard cloaking my face, my lips thick and swollen, the hot roar of the saber-tooth still echo-sharp in my mind, and thinking not of the dead, drained female beside me but of the brute eyes of the beast . . . the stench of war, of cannon-split corpses, the blue-clad regiment sprawled along the slope, the crackling musket fire in the cool air of Virginia, the stone wall ahead of me in the rushing smoke . . . the plush gilt of the Vienna opera house, the music rising in a brassy tide and the tall woman beside me in blood-red velvet as I watch the faint heartbeat in the hollow of her arching throat, flushed ivory from the glow of stage lamps . . . the bitter-smoked train pulling into crowded Istanbul station, the towers of ancient Byzantium rising around me, the heavy leather suitcase bumping my leg, the thick wool suit pressing against my skin, the assignation ahead with the dark-haired little fool who trusts me . . . the bone-shuddering shock along my right arm as my sword sparks against the upthrust shield, the gaunt Christian falling back under the fury of my attack, the orgasmic scream of the Roman crowd awaiting another death . . . the long, baked sweep of sun-blazed prairie, suddenly quiet now after the vast drumming of herded buffalo, the young, pinto-mounted Indian girl riding easily beside me, with the flushed red darkness of her skin inviting me, challenging me . . . standing with Rameses II among the fallen Hittites, with the battle-thirst raging through me like a fever, the sharp odor of spilled blood everywhere, soaking deep into parched Egyptian sands . . . the reeking London alehouse along the Thames, the almond-eyed whore in my lap, giggling, her breath foul with drink, her blood-rich neck gleaming in the smoky light . . . the slave girl in Athens, kneeling in the dirt at my booted feet, begging me to spare her wretched life as the pointed tip of my sword elicits a single drop of crimson from her fear-taut throat . . . at the castle feast, soups spiced with sage and sweet basil, the steaming venison on platters of chased silver, the hearty wines of Auvergne aglow in jeweled flagons, with the Queen facing me across the great table, my eyes on the pale blue tracery of veins above the ruffled lace at her neck . . . and, at last, here— with all the long centuries behind me, their kaleidoscopic images flickering across my mind—hunted and found, trapped like an animal under a fog-shrouded sun along the soft Pacific shore, in this fateful year of one thousand nine-hundred ninety-two, as the ultimate anvil-ringing stroke of the hammer sends the stake deep into my rioting heart . . . to a sudden, unending darkness.

The final blood is mine.

In this story I explore the private world of a sniper. Years ago, why did a young man climb to a tower on a Texas university campus and begin firing randomly at his fellow humans? How does a sniper justify his actions—or does he? What kind of individual prowls urban cities in search of living targets?

Such questions challenged my imagination. Could I map the terrain of this bizarre mental landscape? Could I bring such a twisted man to life? In September of 1979 I sat down to try. My fictional experiment was validated when "A Real Nice Guy" won a place in Best Detective Stories of the Year.

Meet the Master of Whispering Death.

A Real Nice Guy

(Written: September 1979)

Warm sun.

A summer afternoon.

The sniper emerged from the roof door, walking easily, carrying a custom-leather guncase.

Opened the case.

Assembled the weapon.

Loaded it.

Sighted the street below.

Adjusted the focus.

Waited.

There was no hurry.

No hurry at all.

He was famous, yet no one knew his name. There were portraits of him printed in dozens of newspapers and magazines; he'd even made the cover of *Time*. But no one had really seen his face. The portraits were composites, drawn by frustrated police artists, based on the few misleading descriptions given by witnesses who claimed to have seen him leaving a building or jumping from a roof, or driving from the target area in a stolen automobile. But no two descriptions matched.

One witness described a chunky man of average height with a dark beard and cap. Another described a thin, extremely tall man with a bushy head of hair and a thick mustache. A third description pegged him as balding, paunchy and wearing heavy horn-rims. On *Time's* cover, a large blood-soaked question mark replaced his features—above the words WHO IS HE?

Reporters had given him many names: "The Phantom Sniper" . . . "The Deadly Ghost" . . . "The Silent Slayer" . . . and his personal favorite, "The Master of Whispering Death." This was often shortened to "Deathmaster," but he liked the full title; it was fresh and poetic—and *accurate*.

He *was* a master. He never missed a target, never wasted a shot. He was cool and nerveless and smooth, and totally without conscience. And death indeed whispered from his silenced weapon: a dry snap of the trigger, a muffled pop, and the target dropped as though struck down by the fist of God.

They were *always* targets, never people. Men, women, children. Young, middle-aged, old. Strong ones. Weak ones. Healthy or crippled. Black or white. Rich or poor. Targets—all of them.

He considered himself a successful sharpshooter, demonstrating his unique skill in a world teeming with moving targets placed there for his amusement. Day and night, city by city, state by state, they were always there, ready for his gun, for the sudden whispering death from its barrel. An endless supply just for him.

Each city street was his personal shooting gallery.

But he was careful. Very careful. He never killed twice in the same city. He switched weapons. He never used a car more than once. He never wore the same clothes twice on a shoot. Even the shoes would be discarded; he wore a fresh pair for each target run. And, usually, he was never seen at all.

He thought of it as a sport.

A game.

A run.

A vocation.

A skill.

But never murder.

His name was Jimmie Prescott and he was thirty-one years of age. Five foot ten. Slight build. Platform shoes could add three inches and body pillows up to fifty pounds. He had thinning brown hair framing a bland, unmemorable face. He shaved twice daily—but the case of wigs, beards and mustaches he always carried easily disguised the shape of his mouth, chin and skull. Sometimes he would wear a skin-colored fleshcap for baldness, or use heavy glasses—though his sight was perfect. Once, for a lark, he had worn a black eye patch. He would walk in a crouch; or stride with a sailor's swagger, or assume a limp. Each disguise amused him, helped make life more challenging. Each was a small work of art, flawlessly executed.

Jimmie was a perfectionist.

And he was clean: no police record. Never arrested. No set of his prints on file, no dossier.

He had a great deal of money (inherited) with no need or inclination to earn more. He had spent his lifetime honing his considerable skills; he was an expert on weaponry, car theft, body-combat, police procedures; he made it a strict rule to memorize the street system of each city he entered before embarking on a shoot. And once his target was down he knew exactly how to leave the area. The proper escape route was essential.

Jimmie was a knowledgeable historian in his field: he had made a thorough study of snipers, and held them all in cold contempt. Not a worthwhile one in the lot. They *deserved* to be caught; they were fools and idiots and blunderers, often acting out of neurotic impulse or psychotic emotion. Even the hired professionals drew Jimmie's ire—since these were men who espoused political causes or who worked for government money. Jimmie had no cause, nor would he ever allow himself to be bought like a pig on the market.

He considered himself quite sane. Lacking moral conscience, he did not suffer from a guilt complex. Nor did he operate from a basic hatred of humankind, as did so many of the warped criminals he had studied.

Basically, Jimmie liked people, got along fine with them on a casual basis. He hated no one. (Except his parents, but they were long dead and something he did not think about anymore.) He was incapable of love or friendship, but felt no need for either. Jimmie depended only on himself; he had learned to do that from childhood. He was, therefore, a loner by choice, and made it a rule (Jimmie had many rules) never to date the same female twice, no matter how sexually appealing she might be. Man-woman relationships were a weakness, a form of dangerous self-indulgence he carefully avoided.

In sum, Jimmie Prescott didn't need anyone. He

had himself, his skills, his weapons and his targets. More than enough for a full, rich life. He did not drink or smoke. (Oh, a bit of vintage wine in a good restaurant was always welcome, but he had never been drunk in his life.) He jogged each day, morning and evening, and worked out twice a week in the local gym in whatever city he was visiting. A trim, healthy body was an absolute necessity in his specialized career. Jimmie left nothing to chance. He was not a gambler and took no joy in risk.

A few times things had been close: a roof door that had jammed shut in Detroit after a kill, forcing him to make a perilous between buildings leap . . . an engine that died during a police chase in Portland, causing him to abandon his car . . . an intense struggle with an off-duty patrolman in Indianapolis who'd witnessed a shot. The fellow had been tough, and dispatching him was physically difficult; Jimmie finally snapped his neck—but it had been close.

He kept a neat, handwritten record of each shoot in his tooled-leather notebook: state, city, name of street, weather, time of day, sex, age and skin color of target. Under "Comments," he would add pertinent facts, including the make and year of the stolen car he had driven, and the type of disguise he had utilized. Each item of clothing worn was listed. And if he experienced any problem in exiting the target area this would also be noted. Thus, each shoot was critically analyzed upon completion—as a football coach might dissect a game after it had been played.

The only random factor was the target. Preselection spoiled the freshness, the *purity* of the act. Jimmie liked to surprise himself. Which shall it be: that young girl in red, laughing up at her boyfriend? The old newsman on the corner? The school kid skipping homeward with books under his arm? Or, perhaps, the beefy, bored truckdriver, sitting idly in his cab, waiting for the light to change?

Selection was always a big part of the challenge.

And *this* time . . .

A male. Strong looking. Well dressed. Businessman with a briefcase, in his late forties. Hair beginning to silver at the temples. He'd just left the drugstore, probably stopped there to pick up something for his wife. Maybe she'd called to remind him at lunch.

Moving toward the corner. Walking briskly.

Yes, *this* one. By all means, this one.

Range: three hundred yards.

Adjust sight focus.

Rifle stock tight against right shoulder.

Finger inside guard, poised at trigger.

Cheek firm against wooden gunstock; eye to rubber scopepiece.

Line crosshairs on target.

Steady breathing.

Tighten trigger finger slowly.

Fire!

The man dropped forward to the walk like a clubbed animal, dead before he struck the pavement. Someone screamed. A child began to cry. A man shouted.

Pleasant, familiar sounds to Jimmie Prescott.

Calmly, he took apart his weapon, cased it, then carefully dusted his trousers. (Rooftops were often grimy, and although he would soon discard the trousers he liked to present a neat, well-tailored appearance—but only when the disguise called for it. What a marvelous, ill-smelling bum he had become in New Orleans; he smiled thinly, thinking about how truly offensive he was on that occasion.)

He walked through the roof exit to the elevator.

Within ten minutes he had cleared central Baltimore—and booked the next flight to the West Coast.

Aboard the jet, he relaxed. In the soft, warm, humming interior of the airliner, he grew drowsy . . . closed his eyes.

And had The Dream again.

The Dream was the only disturbing element in

Jimmie Prescott's life. He invariably thought of it that way: The Dream. Never as a dream. Always about a large metropolitan city where chaos reigned—with buses running over babies in the street, and people falling down sewer holes and through plate glass store windows. Violent and disturbing. He was never threatened in The Dream, never personally involved in the chaos around him. Merely a mute witness to it.

He would tell himself, this was only *fantasy,* a thing deep inside his sleeping mind; it would go away once he awakened and then he could ignore it, put it out of his thoughts, bury it as he had buried the hatred for his father and mother.

Perhaps he had *other* dreams. Surely he did. But The Dream was the one he woke to, again and again, emerging from the chaos of the city with sweat on his cheeks and forehead, his breath tight and shallow in his chest, his heart thudding wildly.

"Are you all right?" a passenger across the aisle was asking him. "Shall I call somebody?"

"I'm fine," said Jimmie, sitting up straight. "No problem."

"You look kinda shaky."

"No, I'm fine. But thank you for your concern."

And he put The Dream away once again, as a gun is put away in its case.

*   *   *

In Los Angeles, having studied the city quite thoroughly, Jimmie took a cab directly into Hollywood. The fare was steep, but money was never an issue in Jimmie's life; he paid well for services rendered, with no regrets.

He got off at Highland, on Hollywood Boulevard, and walked toward the Chinese Theater.

He wanted two things: food and sexual satisfaction.

First, he would select an attractive female, take her to dinner and then to his motel room (he'd booked one from the airport) where he would have sex. Jimmie never called it lovemaking, a *silly* word. It was always just sex, plain and simple and quickly over. He was capable of arousing a woman if he chose to do so, of bringing her to full passion and release, but he seldom bothered. His performance was always an act; the ritual bored him. Only the result counted.

He disliked prostitutes and seldom selected one. Too jaded. Too worldly. And never to be trusted. Given time, and his natural charm, he was usually able to pick up an out-of-town girl, impress her with an excellent and very expensive meal at a posh restaurant, and guide her firmly into bed.

This night, in Hollywood, the seduction was easily accomplished.

Jimmie spotted a supple, soft-faced girl in the fore-court of the Chinese. She was wandering from one celebrity footprint to another, leaning to examine a particular signature in the cement.

As she bent forward, her breasts flowed full, press-ing against the soft linen dress she wore—and Jimmie told himself, she's the one for tonight. A young, awestruck out-of-towner. Perfect.

He moved toward her.

"I just *love* European food," said Janet.

"That's good," said Jimmie Prescott. "I rather fancy it myself."

She smiled at him across the table, a glowing all-American girl from Ohio named Janet Louise Lakeley. They were sitting in a small, very chic French restau-rant off La Cienega, with soft lighting and open-country decor.

"I can't read a word of this," Janet said when the menu was handed to her. "I thought they always had the food listed in English, too, like movie subtitles."

"Some places don't," said Jimmie quietly. "I'll order for us both. You'll be pleased. The sole is excellent here."

"Oh, I love fish," she said. "I could eat a ton of fish."

He pressed her hand. "That's nice."

"My head is swimming. I shouldn't have had that Scotch on an empty stomach," she said. "Are we having wine with dinner?"

"Of course," said Jimmie.

"I don't know anything about wine," she told him, "but I love champagne. That's wine, isn't it?"

He smiled with a faint upcurve of his thin lips.

"Trust me," he said. "You'll enjoy what I select."

"I'm sure I will."

The food was ordered and served—and Jimmie was pleased to see that his tastes had, once again, proven sound. The meal was superb, the wine was bracing and the girl was sexually stimulating. Essentially brainless, but that didn't really matter to Jimmie. She was what he wanted.

Then she began to talk about the sniper killings.

"Forty people in just a year and two months," she said. "And all gunned down by the same madman. Aren't they *ever* going to catch him?"

"The actual target total is forty-one," he corrected her. "And what makes you so sure the sniper is a male? Could be a woman."

She shook her head. "Whoever heard of a woman sniper?"

"There have been many," said Jimmie. "In Russia today there are several hundred trained female snipers. Some European governments have traditionally utilized females in this capacity."

"I don't mean women *soldiers*," she said. "I mean your nutso shoot-'em-in-the-street sniper. Always guys. Every time. Like that kid in Texas that shot all the people from the tower."

"Apparently you've never heard of Francine Stearn."

"Nope. Who was she?"

"Probably the most famous female sniper. Killed a dozen school-children in Pittsburgh one weekend in late July, 1970. One shot each. To the head. She was a very accurate shootist."

"Never heard of her."

"After she was captured, *Esquire* did a rather probing psychological profile on her."

"Well, I really don't read a lot," she admitted. "Except Gothic romances. I just can't get *enough* of those." She giggled. "Guess you could say I'm addicted."

"I'm not familiar with the genre."

"Anyway," she continued, "I know this sniper is a guy."

"*How* do you know?"

"Female intuition. I trust it. It never fails me. And it tells me that the Phantom Sniper is a man."

He was amused. "What else does it tell you?"

"That he's probably messed up in the head. Maybe beaten as a kid. Something like that. He's *got* to be a nutcase."

"You could be wrong there, too," Jimmie told her. "Not all lawbreakers are mentally unbalanced."

"This 'Deathmaster' guy is, and I'm convinced of it."

"You're a strongly opinionated young woman."

"Mom always said that." She sipped her wine, nodded. "Yeah, I guess I am." She frowned, turning the glass slowly in her long-fingered hand.

"Do you think they'll ever catch him?"

"I somehow doubt it," Jimmie declared. "No one seems to have a clear description of him. And he always manages to elude the police. Leaves no clues. Apparently selects his subjects at random. No motive to tie him to. No consistent M.O."

"What's that?"

"Method of operation. Most criminals tend to repeat the same basic pattern in their crimes. But not this fellow. He keeps surprising people. Never know where he'll pop up next, or who his target will be. Difficult to catch a man like that."

"You call them 'subjects' and 'targets'—but they're *people!* Innocent men and women and children. You make them sound like . . . like cut-outs in a shooting gallery!"

"Perhaps I do," he admitted, smiling. "It's simply that we have different modes of expression."

"I say they'll get him eventually. He can't go on just butchering innocent people forever."

"No one goes on forever," said Jimmie Prescott.

She put down her wineglass, leaned toward him. "Know what bothers me most about the sniper?"

"What."

"The fact that his kind of act attracts copycats. Other sickos with a screw loose who read about him and want to imitate him. Arson is like that. One big fire in the papers and suddenly all the other wacko firebugs start their *own* fires. It gets 'em going. The sniper is like that."

"If some mentally disturbed individual is motivated to kill stupidly and without thought or preparation by something he or she reads in the newspaper then the sniper himself cannot be blamed for such abnormal behavior."

"You call what *he* does normal?"

"I . . . uh . . . didn't say that. I was simply refuting your theory."

She frowned. "Then who is to blame? I think that guy should be caught and—"

"And what?" Jimmie fixed his cool gray eyes on her. "What would you do if you suddenly discovered who he was . . . where to find him?"

"Call the police, naturally. Like anybody."

"Wouldn't you be curious about him, about the kind of person he is? Wouldn't you *question* him first, try to understand him?"

"You don't question an animal who kills! Which is what he is. I'd like to see him gassed or hanged. . . . You don't *talk* to a twisted creep like that!"

She had made him angry. His lips tightened. He was no longer amused with this conversation; the word game had turned sour. This girl was gross and stupid and insensitive. Take her to bed and be done with it. Use her body—but no words. No more words. He'd had quite enough of those from her.

"Check, please," he said to the waiter.

It was at his motel, after sex, that Jimmie decided to kill her. Her insulting tirade echoed and reechoed in his mind. She must be punished for it.

In this special case he felt justified in breaking one of his rules: never pre-select a target. She told him that she worked the afternoon shift at a clothing store on Vine. And he knew where she lived, a few blocks from work. She walked to the store each afternoon.

He would take her home and return the next day. When she left her apartment building he would dispatch her from a roof across the street. Once this plan had settled into place in the mind of Jimmie Prescott he relaxed, allowing the tension of the evening to drain away.

By tomorrow night he'd be in Tucson, and Janet Lakeley would be dead.

Warm sun.

A summer afternoon.

The sniper emerged from the roof door, walking easily, carrying a custom-leather guncase.

Opened the case.

Assembled the weapon.

Loaded it.

Sighted the street below.

Adjusted the focus.

Waited.

Target now exiting.

Walking along street toward corner.

Adjust sight focus.

Finger on trigger.

Cheek against stock.

Eye to scope.

Crosshairs direct on target.

Fire!

* * *

Jimmie felt something like a fist strike his stomach. A sudden, shocking blow. Winded, he looked down in amazement at the blood pulsing steadily from his shirtfront.

I'm hit! Someone has actually—

Another blow—but this one stopped all thought, taking his head apart. No more shock. No more amazement.

No more Jimmie.

She put away the weapon, annoyed at herself. *Two* shots! The Phantom Sniper, whoever he was, never fired more than once. But *he* was exceptional. She got goosebumps, just thinking about him.

Well, maybe next time she could drop her target in one. Anybody can miscalculate a shot. Nobody's perfect.

She left the roof area, walking calmly, took the elevator down to the garage, stowed her guncase in the truck of the stolen Mustang and drove away from the motel.

Poor Jimmie, she thought. It was just his bad luck to meet *me*. But that's the way it goes.

Janet Lakeley had a rule, and she never broke it: when you bed down a guy in a new town you always target him the next day. She sighed. Usually it didn't bother her. Most of them were bastards. But not Jimmie. She'd enjoyed talking to him, playing her word games with him . . . bedding him. She was sorry he had to go.

He seemed like a real nice guy.

DARK UNIVERSE
WILLIAM F. NOLAN

Welcome to William F. Nolan's *Dark Universe*, a universe of horror, suspense and mystery. For the past fifty years William F. Nolan has been writing in each of these worlds—and compiling a legendary body of work that is unsurpassed in quality, style . . . and the sheer ability to send chills down the spines of readers. At long last, this volume collects many of Nolan's finest stories, selected from his entire career. These are unforgettable tales guaranteed to frighten, surprise, delight and even shock readers who like to explore the shadows and who aren't afraid of the dark.

FEARS
UNNAMED
TIM LEBBON

Tim Lebbon has burst upon the scene and established himself as one of the best horror writers at work today. He is the winner of numerous awards, including a Bram Stoker Award, critics have raved about his work, and fans have eagerly embraced him as a contemporary master of the macabre.

Perhaps nowhere are the reasons for his popularity more evident than in this collection of four of his most chilling novellas. Two of these dark gems received British Fantasy Awards, and another was written specifically for this book and has never previously been published. These terrifying tales form a window into a world of horrors that, once experienced, can never be forgotten.
